D1479238

BRITAIN'S CIVIL WARS

BRITAIN'S CIVIL WARS

Counterinsurgency in the
twentieth century

Charles Townshend

faber and faber

LONDON · BOSTON

First published in 1986
by Faber and Faber Limited
3 Queen Square London WC1N 3AU

Typeset by Goodfellow & Egan, Cambridge
Printed in Great Britain by
Butler & Tanner Ltd, Frome, Somerset
All rights reserved

British Library Cataloguing in Publication Data

Townshend, Charles
Britain's civil wars.
1. Great Britain——Military policy
I. Title
355'.0335'41   UA 647
ISBN 0-571-13802-0

Library of Congress Cataloging-in-Publication Data
Townshend, Charles.
Britain's civil wars.
Bibliography: p.
1. Counterinsurgency—Great Britain.
2. Great Britain—Colonies—Defenses.
3. Military history, Modern—20th century.
I. Title.
U241.T68   1986   355'.02184'0941   85-29371
ISBN 0-571-13802-0

For Leo and Max

Contents

List of Maps

Preface

I have set out in this book to construct a wide-angle view of the British experience of rebellion in the present century. The sheer range of this experience across a world empire was unequalled by any other country. The 'civil wars' of the title have been variously labelled civil disturbances, emergencies, internal security operations, revolts, insurrections and rebellions. Yet the welter of crises had a common core, the endeavour to apply British ideas of law and order, and that core gives the book its inner unity.

There have of course been able analyses of many of the individual struggles which are studied here, and I have relied heavily on the work of previous writers. There have been a few pioneering efforts at comparative treatment, such as Julian Paget's *Counter-Insurgency Campaigning*, published nearly twenty years ago by Faber, and one or two uniquely valuable participants' accounts, most notably Frank Kitson's *Bunch of Five*, also published by Faber, ten years later. I have tried to complement these existing works by drawing together a wider range of events, and using a variety of original source material to illuminate them and the fundamental problems they raised.

Whilst providing a wide-angle view, my aim has been to keep in tight focus the most baffling of these problems. The introductory chapter sets out the central framework within which governments take action against rebels, the public law. The difficulty of finding an appropriate legal response to internal emergency has been recurrent and acute for Britain, with its liberal-democratic political self-image and its common law tradition. This difficulty has appeared not only within the United Kingdom itself, which is the subject of Chapter II, but also in colonial and mandated territories. Chapters III, IV and V survey these on a regional basis, in order to assess the extent

9

to which common problems were created by geography or culture. At the same time I have tried within each of these regional chapters to assemble a self-contained general narrative which conveys some of the drama and pressure of critical events within an empire under strain. There is, I hope, a story as well as a lesson in this history.

The heart of the problem in each of these crises is the extent to which violence can be used to counter violent or semi-violent challenges, and to preserve or restore the kind of order on which the informal British constitutional system rests. I hope that the sense of immediacy which the original records can recreate will help to make this dilemma comprehensible to everyone with an interest in these fundamental issues. In researching these records I have been greatly aided by the generosity of my own institution, Keele University, and the untiring helpfulness of its Inter-Library Loan staff, and I also owe a debt of gratitude to other institutions, most notably the Middle East Centre at St Antony's College, Oxford, and the Public Record Office, London. Transcripts of Crown Copyright records appear by permission of the Controller of HM Stationery Office.

Abbreviations Used in the Text and Notes

AC: records in the Air Ministry, London
ACM: Air Chief Marshal
AIR: Air records in the Public Record Office
AOC: Air Officer Commanding
c; cD; cmd; cmnd: Parliamentary Papers, Command series
CAB: Cabinet (records in the Public Record Office)
CAS: Chief of the Air Staff
CID: Committee of Imperial Defence
CIGS: Chief of the Imperial General Staff
CO: Colonial Office (records in the Public Record Office)
DC: District Commissioner
DCAS: Deputy Chief of the Air Staff
DDOI: Deputy Director of Operations and Intelligence
DMO: Director of Military Operations
FARELF: Far East Land Forces
FO: Foreign Office (records in the Public Record Office)
GOC(-in-c): General Officer Commanding(-in-Chief)
HC: High Commissioner
HO: Home Office (records in the Public Record Office)
IOR: India Office records, London
MEC: Middle East Centre, St Antony's College, Oxford
MED: Middle East Department, Colonial Office
MELF: Middle East Land Forces
MFC: Microfilm copies in Royal Air Force Museum, Hendon
NWFP: North-West Frontier Province, India
OAG: Officer Administering the Government (in lieu of HC)
P/TJ: Palestine and Transjordan
PRO: Public Record Office, London
RUSI: Royal United Services Institute
TJFF: Trans-Jordan Frontier Force
VCIGS: Vice-Chief of the Imperial General Staff
WO: War Office (records in the Public Record Office)

I

Introduction:
The Complex of Counterinsurgency

1 Recognizing insurgency

The British constitution, so far as it exists at all, does not recognize insurgency. That is to say, British public law makes no provision for a form of internal political crisis which has become increasingly familiar in the twentieth century, when rebellious groups wage a campaign of violence less intense than open war, but nonetheless systematic and coherent. British law recognizes war, and recognizes peace. Both are fairly approximate concepts, but their common sense is well enough understood. War involves the open clash of armed forces, and creates a state of absolute insecurity in which only force counts. Peace is a state of individual and public security. It may be ultimately guaranteed by force, but it works from day to day through general consent.

Rebellion may create a state of war. At the time when the dominant ideas of British public law were being shaped, rebellions (such as Monmouth's and Bonnie Prince Charlie's) usually did. Indeed, until well into the nineteenth century the normal mode of rebellion – mostly unsuccessful – was open insurrection. Most radical revolutionaries were insurrectionists, believing in the seizure of state power by a single, sudden knockdown blow, the classic *coup*.[1] But the end of the nineteenth century brought a new approach. The resistance of the French in the Franco-German war of 1870–71, and of the Boers in the long-drawn-out South African war, showed that untrained citizens could fight by methods which vastly increased their chances of survival and success against even the most sophisticated regular armies. The guerrilla concept revolutionized the revolution, creating a new threat to governments everywhere – domestic as well as colonial.

The essence of modern insurgency lies in diffusion in space and time. In place of the conventional military strategic priorities of concentration and speed, it puts the avoidance of decisive battles and the acceptance of an indefinitely protracted timescale. In conventional war, time is expensive to governments; in irregular war it is cheap to their opponents. Delays incur few costs; the achievement of surprise remains vital, but it can result from the ability of guerrilla forces to appear and disappear with ease, rather than from rapid strategic movements. Provided that the insurgents can demonstrate regularly that they are still in business, a time lapse is likely to favour them, in that time is needed to build up political support. For the really decisive battle is for public opinion. The insurgency is not an outright clash of physical force, but an attempt to convince the people that the government will be beaten in the long run. Anything that weakens the government's credibility is militarily valid. Thus insurgents can use a wide repertoire of operations, ranging from recognizably conventional military actions like ambushes or small attacks on government posts, through sabotage, hijacking, bank robbery, to assassination, kidnap and intimidation. All can be carried out by quite weak forces linked by rudimentary organizational structures.

If the violent acts of insurgency are less intense than those of war – the phrase 'low intensity operations' has played a distinctive part in modern counterinsurgency thinking – they are obviously more systematic and formidable than the occasional eruptions of violence known to English law as 'breaches of the peace'. Their binding thread is their aim of expelling or overthrowing the government, of changing the political order. Like open war they are an extension of politics by 'other means'.[2] By their nature they face governments with inescapable problems; but the natural inclination of British governments has been to try to escape them.

The reason for this is a mixture of political culture and strict legal tradition. The natural leaning of liberal democracy towards reasonableness, negotiation and compromise has been linked with a common-law-based set of restrictions on executive power, which assume the existence of a self-regulating 'normal' civil society. This law recognized breaches of the peace like 'riot' and 'commotion', but assumed them to be transient, aberrant happenings. The idea of a special legal framework to deal with a sustained challenge to the state – a challenge which, in modern times, usually involves the undermining of the legal system itself – was more or less consciously excluded. Thus no 'state of emergency' was envisaged. (As will be seen, even after the passage of a series of Emergency Powers Acts since 1920, the emergencies provided for are economic rather than political.) The 'state of siege' familiar on the continent was conspicuous by its absence. Britain had not experienced great sieges on the continental scale, and the possible relevance of the siege model to a diffuse civil war had no chance of being recognized – except, perhaps, in Ulster.

The absence of a legal 'third way' between peace and war reinforced a natural governmental reluctance to admit the breakdown of normality and the failure of consensus, and hence, to some extent, of legitimacy.[3] Any government, elected or otherwise, can fall victim to a tendency to minimize the seriousness of internal threats: often this is seen as vital to the maintenance of public morale or international credit. It can, however, often lead to self-delusion. For liberal-democratic governments the admission of political bankruptcy implicit in a resort to force is especially unattractive. Britain, in particular, has been uniquely sensitive to the threat of military rule; an abhorrence of martial law is rooted in the experience of the seventeenth century, the impact of Stuart absolutism and Cromwellian military administration. The conflicts studied in this book will show that there are good reasons for refusing to sanction military control. But these were not usually the reasons that weighed with politicians. Very often it seemed that the illusion of civil control was to be preserved at almost any cost, even if this meant worsening a crisis.

2 The framework of counterinsurgency

It may be suggested that any coherent counterinsurgency effort starts from a recognition that an insurgency exists. Coherence may not guarantee success, but incoherence may well be fatal. The recognition that a state of affairs must be dealt with as an insurgency is by no means straightforward. A batch of ill-defined or undefined terms – public order, law and order, public security – indicate, like bobbing marker buoys, the existence of an underlying concept of normal or desirable order. This ideal concept may be labelled 'peace'. In English legal history the 'King's Peace' has quite a clear meaning, but as an operational guide it is surprisingly unhandy. One small but clear signpost of change in the twentieth century has been the growing use of the word 'peacekeeping' in place of 'pacification'. The change implied not only that the process of pacifying turbulent and uncivilized peoples had been brought to a successful end, but also that the old dynamic self-confidence had given way to a more tentative attitude.

As a result, the already imprecise understanding of basic concepts like 'order' became still looser, as did newer terms describing threats to order – the most elastic being 'subversion'. The subtitle of the most influential modern work on counter-insurgency, Frank Kitson's *Low Intensity Operations*, is *Subversion, Insurgency and Peacekeeping*.[4] The general message is that the enormous complexity of political movements in modern societies calls for a corresponding sophistication in defence of the legitimate order. It is worth noting that the problem was recognized a generation earlier by another lucid military writer, Major-General Sir Charles Gwynn, in his study *Imperial Policing*.

> Subversive movements take many forms and are of varying intensity; but even when armed rebellion occurs, it presents a very different military problem from that of a deliberate small-war campaign. There is an absence of a definite objective, and conditions are those of guerrilla warfare, in which elusive rebel bands must be hunted down, and protective measures are required to deprive them of opportunities.
>
> Excessive severity may antagonize the neutral or loyal element, add to the number of rebels, and leave a lasting feeling of resentment and bitterness. On the other hand, the power and resolution of the Government forces must be displayed. Anything which can be interpreted as weakness encourages those who are sitting on the fence to keep on good terms with the rebels.[5]

Gwynn was aware of the difficulties in judging fine gradations of 'intensity', but his main concern was with relatively straightforward insurgent movements. Kitson has extended the definition of both subversion and insurgency so that they become parts of a continuum: major insurgencies grow from minor subversion. The resulting emphasis on 'nipping subversion in the bud' seems, to radical critics at least, a sinister development. The tendency to identify legitimate dissent as subversion could erode basic civil liberties such as freedom of speech and the right of peaceful protest.[6]

Kitson's approach is certainly rooted in what is, at best, a misleading oversimplification of liberal democracy. His assumption is that a government which has won an election is legitimate, and that any pressure exerted on it except through the constitutional system is subversive. But liberal-democratic constitutions, whether written or unwritten, are never as definite as soldiers would like. Rather than forming the letter of the public law, they express the spirit of a plural polity. In Britain, recurrent crises over the definition of 'political' or 'unconstitutional' industrial action have shown most dramatically the difficulty of giving precise shape to this spirit, though fuzzy areas can also be found in nearly every aspect of governmental legitimacy.

What Kitson's work demonstrates is the need, long felt by executive officers, for an operational clarity which British law does not provide.[7] If it were possible to establish that every instance of civil disobedience was the start of a linear process leading, like a form of drug addiction, to major disaffection and finally armed insurgency, the task of the intelligence services would be enormously simplified. (One might say, would become feasible instead of impossible.) Unfortunately this characterization is a grotesque distortion of the real nature of disobedience in a liberal society. If the legitimate order in such a society is to be defended, the security forces must preserve something which is cruelly elusive.

The elusiveness is inherent in the terminology used, at the heart of which lies 'public security'. What is public security? How, if at all, can it be measured? At what point can it be judged to be under threat, and at what point to have 'broken down' (the 'breakdown of public security' being a widely used though rarely defined phrase)? It appears to be a compound of individual security and the safety of the state. Attacks on individuals may or may not be seen as damaging public security – even widespread violent crime, such as 'mugging', for instance, is not taken to be a threat to public security. The public, in this context, is not the people at large but the people in the abstract, the *res publica*, the political expression of the society. The distinction is unnervingly difficult to draw. The pioneering effort of the French Revolution to distinguish between *sûreté générale* and *salut publique* boiled down in effect to dividing areas of responsibility between external defence (handled by the Committee of General Security) and internal security (under the Committee of Public Safety). In Britain the term 'public safety' has been little used – probably because of its historical overtones – though references sometimes appear to the 'safety of the state' or even, for good measure, the 'public safety of the state'.[8]

Direct challenges to the state are usually easier to identify than the indirect approach taken by insurgencies, where what is attacked is not so much the machinery of the state as its legitimizing qualities, its monopoly of the use of force and its capacity to protect its citizens. Here the two senses of public security come closest together. The operability of the legal system can be broken down or paralysed by attacks on individual witnesses or jurors. The credibility of the state itself may be damaged, even destroyed, by failure to guarantee the safety of individuals. Hence the mere existence of a small terrorist group may seem a greater threat to public security than may a large criminal organization. Equally it may not. The essence of the issue is political perception.

A good example of the perceptual problem can be found in the Secretary of State for India's response to Bengali terrorism in the early twentieth century:

> Although these acts of lawlessness may not be a serious menace to the state, they do seem to me a very real danger to society, and the worst of it is that the longer they continue the less will be your chance of securing the active cooperation of the population in the detection and conviction of the criminals. I am quite ready to admit with John Bright, at whose feet I sat as a boy, that 'force is no remedy for a just discontent', but Bright himself never pretended that this was a reason for allowing free play to the forces of disorder.[9]

The delicacy of the calculations involved has made the

characteristic British mode of response to public security challenges, one which may well be labelled the 'British way', a pragmatic, limited application of traditional legal doctrines. These doctrines, whether common or statute law, have been marked by an aim of containing rather than extirpating resistance to law, through the use of minimal rather than exemplary force.

The archetypal public order statute, the Riot Act, which imbedded itself so deeply in the general consciousness that its impress endured long after the Act had fallen into disuse, displayed this tendency. With its insistence on warning and time-lapse before the use of force, its effect (if not its original intention) was to end disorders with the minimum damage to life and property, rather than to deter future disturbance. It exemplified a general spirit of dealing with problems on an *ad hoc* basis, and of reluctance to create models, rules, or even guidelines.[10]

The dominant minimalist doctrine, underlying the responses which appear throughout this book, is the common law principle of 'necessary force'. In common law the executive has the right and the duty to 'repel force with force', but the degree of force used must be no more and no less than is absolutely necessary to restore the peace. The executive may set aside the ordinary legal system, but the necessity for illegal action must afterwards be demonstrable in the ordinary courts. The agents of the state, armed or unarmed, have the same powers and duties as ordinary citizens. Soldiers, though armed with lethal weapons and controlled by military law, are merely a collection of private individuals in the eyes of the common law.[11] Each must use his individual judgment to decide the exact degree of force needed.

As a formula for practical action this doctrine was transparently unworkable by the eighteenth century. The idea that every forcible act to restore order would be justiciable once order had been restored was not merely impractical; it assumed that decisions taken in conditions of instability and uncertainty could be fairly judged after the event, which is rarely the case. The fear of unfair judgment inevitably haunted officers of the law, and created a reluctance to act that could be as dangerous as excessive zeal. Consequently, Acts of Indemnity were passed as a matter of practice to ensure that actions taken in good faith to restore order would be shielded from subsequent judicial inquiry. But even this tampering with the common law could not blunt the other horn of the peace officer's dilemma – the requirement that the degree of force used should be no *less* than is necessary. A chilling reminder of this requirement came after the Bristol riots of 1831, when the Mayor of Bristol and the responsible military commander were both found guilty of using inadequate force: the military officer was cashiered, and committed suicide.

Thus at the beginning of the twentieth century the legal basis for preserving or restoring order remained as it had been for many generations. In 1837 General Napier had put the hapless officer's dilemma with black humour: confronted by a mob his thoughts 'dwell upon the (to him) most interesting question, shall I be *shot* for my forbearance by a court martial, or *hanged* for over zeal by a jury?' The eminent jurist and future Lord Chancellor R.B. Haldane pithily confirmed in 1908 that 'the judges have laid down, over and over again, that a man is on the verge of two precipices, and he has to get along' – adding encouragingly, 'and he does get along'. When a doubtful House of Commons committee asked whether regulations could be drawn up to 'save the officer from falling over these precipices', Haldane replied, 'If you do, you will make the law go over the precipices.'[12]

The necessity principle governed the whole spectrum of internal security action, from military aid to the civil power through to martial law. The intention behind the insistence on individual responsibility was to protect civil liberty. But the result, inevitably, was a high degree of confusion in the minds of those responsible for making the judgments. The difficulty of using legal doctrine as a formula for action can be illustrated by the ruling of the Home Secretary in 1867 on the position of the military when acting in aid of the civil power: 'The military are entirely subordinate to the civil power, but the Military Officer in charge of a Party is in sole command over his own force and disposes of it according to his military orders or to the best of his judgement.'[13]

In spite of the inescapable ambiguities of the law, a workable custom governing the use of armed forces to suppress breaches of the peace was well established by 1900. But more extensive military involvement raised questions to which there were no answers. The long banishment of martial law from respectable legal discourse meant that when in the last resort it became necessary – as it did not only in the colonies but also in the United Kingdom – it was generally misunderstood. Legally, martial law was simply a state of affairs which occurred when the legal system became inoperative:

> When it is impossible for Courts of Law to sit or to enforce their Judgments, then it becomes necessary to find some rude substitute for them, and to employ for that purpose the Military, which is the only remaining Force in the Community.[14]

Thus Sir James Mackintosh put the matter in 1824. It followed that, as the Crown Law Officers pointed out in 1838, martial law 'cannot be said in strictness to *supersede* the ordinary tribunals, inasmuch as it only exists by reason of those tribunals having been already practically superseded'. Hence martial law did not have to be 'proclaimed'; proclamation did not create an altered legal state but merely gave notice that the courts could not function.[15] Unfortunately for the clarity of the doctrine, some lawyers by this time believed that the power to apply martial law derived from the Royal Prerogative, not the common law, a belief which seems to have been fostered by the habitual use of Acts of Indemnity. This view put much more emphasis on a proclamation as a legal instrument, so that instead of the seamless process implicit in the common law, there appeared a sharp disjunction at the moment of proclamation.

This moment naturally looked to statesmen like a point of political crisis. Together with the necessity (by then assumed) of passing an Act of Indemnity later, it raised the already unattractive profile of martial law. Yet the twentieth century brought a remorselessly growing crop of violent movements which could not be contained by the civil power using the ordinary law. The new style of insurgency could paralyse the legal system without producing the traditional symptoms of a 'state of war'. The obvious necessity was for a hybrid legal state, a 'third way' between peace and war, in which military force could be applied whilst preserving the essence of civil authority. This was profoundly difficult to achieve in the British political context, for both legal and organizational reasons. In addition, remarkably little energy was put into achieving it. It certainly took a long time, and even now no viable framework has been established within the United Kingdom, although several models were developed for colonial use. The situation in Northern Ireland remains as confused and ambiguous as any to be found in this book.

A trenchant critic of British efforts to curb insurgency, writing in the 1930s, observed that in Palestine

> The point of importance was, and still [in 1938] is, the extraordinary delay in deciding what form emergency rule was to take. The delay arose because the problem of emergency rule has never been tackled as a problem . . .

and he added that there was 'no reason whatever to suppose that we have made any progress in the last sixteen years' (since the Anglo-Irish war) 'in ability to deal with well-organized rebellion on modern lines'.[16] The unstable framework in Palestine, not only in the 1930s but a decade later as well, bore testimony to the recalcitrant issues involved. Eventually, Palestine saw the new hybrid emerge blinking into the sunlight under the label 'statutory martial law', soon replaced by the euphemism 'controlled areas'. By this time some form of emergency powers had become quite a normal response to political challenges throughout the Empire. The parentage of the hybrid was easily identifiable. The suspension of *habeas corpus* was a step that had been taken several times, even in Britain, in the nineteenth century. Then it had been denounced as the 'abrogation of the constitution', since the guarantee against arbitrary imprisonment was taken to be the most fundamental civil right. But detention, or internment without trial, was to become the keystone of almost every set of emergency powers, just because the ordinary processes of the law, so dependent on the co-operation of vulnerable individuals, could easily be paralysed by insurgent action.

Changing terminology is perhaps indicative of changing attitudes. Until the 1920s, internees were often referred to as *détenus*, echoing the professed English aversion to the sort of police state associated with Fouché and France. By the 1950s they had become 'detainees'. The whole process had grown regrettably familiar. Not so much in Britain itself, though even there two sets of special powers grew up, one to meet the exigencies of the world wars (Defence of the Realm Acts 1914 and 1915, Emergency Powers Acts 1939 and 1940), the other to cope with industrial disruption (Emergency Powers Acts 1920 and 1964). Neither were framed to counter insurgency, but they played a part in softening up the old standards. The result was visible in the sweeping powers taken, with astonishingly little public protest, under the Prevention of Terrorism Act, 1974. The legal framework is still not as flexible as counterinsurgency theorists like Sir Robert Thompson or Brian Crozier seem to require, but a lot of its stubborn backbone has been chipped away.[17]

3 The level of intervention

Modern counterinsurgency theorists lay stress on the need to maintain the legality of all the actions of the security forces. They sometimes stray perilously close to the point of merely rewriting the laws to cover any required action. Their insistence that extraordinary laws must be seen to be temporary is not quite enough to guard against the dangers of this line.[18] The real issue is not the fine print of legislation, but the social tolerances which make laws operable. These tolerances also govern the level of armed force that can be used to impose order without generating counterproductive effects. In Britain these sorts of limits have been strict.

Following the sharp distinction between peace and war, Britain developed a peace force that was the polar opposite of the army – unarmed and decentralized. The remarkable (and still not altogether explicable) success of the police forces in the nineteenth century made the unarmed constabulary, the 'bobby on the beat', the ideal image of British normality. But the sharp contrast between the operating modes of the police and of the army caused problems on the occasions when internal disorder got beyond police control. The most serious of these occasions after the establishment of the county constabulary was the 'massacre' of rioting miners at Featherstone in Yorkshire in 1893. This clash highlighted the shock effect of the sudden transition from unarmed crowd control action to the use of deadly weapons. The resulting political crisis led to a painful but ineffectual reappraisal of the rules governing the use of force, and in particular an effort to find some intermediate way between these distinct forms of action.

Attention was concentrated primarily on technicalities: whether troops called out to aid the civil power could be armed with non-lethal weapons, or have non-lethal ammunition (blank cartridge, or possibly buckshot), or at least fire over the heads of a rioting crowd as a warning. Other forms of warning, like bugle calls or drumbeats, were also discussed. The army took the view that fancy warnings were likely to be misunderstood, and that the sight of armed soldiers should be ample warning in itself. It argued against tinkering with their weapons, holding that if troops were called for they must act as troops and not as auxiliary police. The rule that if fire had to be opened it must be 'with effect' was the result of bitter experience with superficially more humane alternatives.[19]

The question whether deadly weapons were as likely to provoke as to overawe remained, and was never satisfactorily resolved. In the 1920s it was still felt by some military authorities that the successful use of troops during the General Strike was due only to 'the sound common sense of the average citizen and the absence of bitterness, rather than the correct application of the use of force'. The technical issue at this time verged on farce, when the proposal to arm soldiers with non-lethal weapons turned out to involve chair legs. Great changes subsequently took place, and there is no doubt that recent technical developments, such as high-pressure hoses and rubber bullets (whose police intent is piously conveyed in the official description 'baton rounds') are an improvement on resorts like buckshot, clubbed rifles or bayonets. But technology is not a substitute for doctrine, and it is doubtful whether the sophistication of modern riot control gear has done much more than disguise temporarily the real problems of troops confronting people.[20]

A different line of solution lies in the creation of a militarized police. In fact, for all the strength of its image, the British unarmed police system was seldom exported, and certainly not to territories that were hard to control. Instead an alternative model, the armed and centralized Royal Irish Constabulary, dominated colonial policing. Armed police were obviously capable in theory of dealing with more serious disorder, or at least of postponing the moment at which troops were required. In practice their ability to do this was obviously related to their size, which was usually strictly limited by inadequate funding. Even where adequate force was provided, there remained an operational contradiction between civil policing and quasi-military action which could not be resolved simply by giving service weapons to the civil police. Many officers brought up to admire the English model believed that attitudes were crucial, and that these had to fall on one side or the other of the great divide. A police force that became 'too military' would be fatally distanced from the community.[21]

The deleterious effect of militarizing the police on the one hand, and of using soldiers as policemen on the other, naturally raised the question of creating a 'third force' which would be neither one nor the other. The obvious attractions of such a hybrid force, matching the hybrid legal state of 'emergency', produced repeated discussions and experiments. But practical achievements have seldom lived up to theoretical expectations. Raising a wholly new force, rather than adapting existing police or military forces, might be expected to resolve the crisis of role and identity. For this to happen, however, absolute clarity of purpose is essential. In practice compromise is more normal, and most of the new forces have been at root either military (as were many so-called *gendarmeries*: once again, the foreign terminology bespeaks uncertainty) or police, whether 'auxiliaries' or 'special mobile forces'. Operating methods have varied accordingly, and no uniform role has emerged.

Moreover, the creation of 'third forces' has been peculiarly difficult in the framework of the British tradition and institutional conservatism. Such novelties have inevitably been seen by many as dangerous precedents, symptomatic of foreign police states, and as signals of constitutional failure. Sometimes they have looked like a rather transparent ruse for concealing the reality of military rule behind the illusion of civil authority.

Whether the two can be combined in some genuine way, without deception, and whether such a combination might not pose the greatest of all threats to liberal democracy, are questions of fundamental importance. Preservation of civil responsibility, in spirit if not always in body, has always been the most consistent aim of British counterinsurgency action. Eventually this came to be expressed in the doctrine of 'the primacy of the police', but long before that it was clearly visible as a set of conscious priorities and unspoken assumptions. In this form it shaped a multiplicity of arrangements, though not necessarily with any clear or consistent effect. Indeed it could quite easily produce conflicting impulses in separate parts of the administrative machinery. In every emergency, the cry for more 'coordination' or 'cooperation' went up sooner or later: often it went unanswered. Growing recognition that coordination was vital to any counter-insurgency campaign vied with the glaring fact that the logic of coordination was at odds with the 'British way'. The old principle of 'separation of powers', although it was too mechanistic to provide a real understanding of the British constitution (it was after all the attempt of a French rationalist to come to terms with the organic English system), still expressed a sentimental resistance to the concentration of power. The most severe problems in every campaign arose at the top, over the question of command and the coordination of intelligence.

4 Command

Soldiers value martial law first and foremost because it resolves all uncertainties of command and responsibility. Dislike of such uncertainties is fundamental to their outlook and training. They have other, somewhat more mystical, reasons for believing in the efficacy of martial law, but the kernel of their beliefs is unity. It may well be that civilians dislike the idea of martial law in large part for the same reason. Statesmen embody, in a way that soldiers professionally cannot, the assumptions of a plural society. They may recognize the virtues of unity in principle, but they are reluctant to incorporate it in actual machinery of government. They would prefer harmony to emerge spontaneously, through some sort of self-regulating process akin to the model of the free society and the free economy.

Soldiers can demonstrate from universal experience, however, that if military operations are what are required, divided or uncertain control is likely to be fatal to their success. As always the problem lies at the level of political decision – the extent to which military operations are accepted as necessary, or, put another way, a state of war is accepted as existing. Usually military commanders have not been given all the powers they have thought necessary to conduct counterinsurgency operations – only occasionally have they been offered them and turned them down, as did Macready in Ireland in 1920. Their minimum demand has usually been for operational control of all security forces during an emergency. Sometimes this demand has been met indirectly, by the appointment of a separate 'Director of Operations'. Such a step highlights the administrative preference for keeping the police and military organizations distinct, for political reasons that often clash with military ideas of what is necessary. Military commanders frequently end up calling not only for operational control of the police, but also for disciplinary control, on the ground that the day-to-day behaviour of the security forces can have a greater cumulative effect on the outcome of a campaign than their formal operations. Such calls have usually fallen on deaf ears.

Perhaps surprisingly, British military commanders have usually been more aware than governments of the limits of military action in internal war. They have repeatedly advised that 'purely military' solutions cannot be reached in such circumstances. Counterinsurgency thinkers have gradually come to recognize that a total political-military strategy needs to be established from the outset. The fullest expression of such integration at the policy-making level is the appearance of a 'supremo' (once more the consciously exotic word) combining the functions of civil governor and military commander. Here the restraints of the British tradition have been most obvious. The surprising thing, in fact, is that on one occasion – in Malaya for two years of the Emergency – this step was actually taken. It was an unique occurrence. Although it was nominally repeated in Cyprus, Field-Marshal Harding did not have quite the same political responsibility as Templer. When General Erskine in Kenya asked for the same powers as Templer, he was refused. In most other places, even under martial law, a delicate balance and tension was maintained between High Commission and GHQ.

5 Intelligence

If unity of command is a precondition of military action, an efficient intelligence system is the basis of all viable operations. Modern theorists agree that intelligence is the key to guerrilla warfare in general, and counterinsurgency in particular. Governments and armies were both slow to learn the lesson. An effective intelligence system requires two things: first, the wholehearted application of resources, both quantitative and qualitative, and second, the central collection, evaluation and feedback of information. Obviously, certain special technical skills or aptitudes are needed in both of these, but they seem most likely to be found after energy and integration have been applied.

The obstacles to meeting the two requirements are that the first is expensive, in both money and time, while the second runs counter to the widely observable – if rationally inexplicable – tendency of governments to spawn multiple intelligence agencies. In Britain, military intelligence, naval intelligence, and the 'secret service' (SIS) have all existed alongside the various Special Branches of police forces in the United Kingdom and overseas. In Ireland in 1916, for instance, five intelligence services gathered information and sent it through separate channels, sometimes to the same and sometimes to different destinations; nowhere was it cross-checked or fed back. The problem was not tackled until an intelligence coordinator was appointed in 1920.[22] Then a degree of integration was achieved; but two serious difficulties remained, and were to recur throughout Britain's counterinsurgency experience.

The first was the divergence between the ordinary intelligence-gathering machinery – the security forces as a whole – and the specialized intelligence operatives, who combined information gathering with counter-intelligence activity. Genuine functional differences stood in the way of a truly integrated system (though in Ireland the army blamed the Director of Intelligence for his penchant for 'cloak and dagger' work). As a result much of the most important 'hot' information was still prevented from getting to where it might be most useful. The second difficulty lay in the unbridgeable gulf between police and military approaches. Even with the best will in the world, the two systems remained differently designed, constructed, and oriented.

The nominal answer which was found in the most successful counterinsurgency campaigns was to base the integrated intelligence system on the police special branch, and subordinate military intelligence to that. This certainly represented an improvement on the misunderstandings, jealousies, and outright conflicts which marred less successful campaigns, but it did not get to the root of the issue, of which the police and military stereotypes were only symbols. Different modes of operation need different types of information, and the sort of information that police forces habitually worked on was not appropriate for military action. The issue was most clearly formulated by Kitson in the 1950s, though it had always existed. He identified it as a problem of 'developing' 'background information' into 'contact information'.[23] Police information was background – on the organization and identity of insurgents; what troops on patrol needed to know was the exact whereabouts of insurgent groups. In the circumstances of insurgency they could not develop this sort of information by asking the general public, as would police pursuing of criminals in 'normal' times.

The process of development under these handicaps is extremely time consuming, and calls for a dedication which is all too hard to find in ordinary military units. It boils down to continuous alertness amongst the whole rank and file, and dogged thinking by the few who prove sufficiently keen and adept to become intelligence specialists. The difficulty of getting regimental soldiers to become intelligence-conscious was obvious during the Irish conflict, and the problem was compounded in under-strength battalions whose officers felt they had no time to spare for an activity which they did not instinctively associate with 'soldiering'.[24]

Since the 1950s, the association has undoubtedly become more instinctive; the fundamental priority of information has become obvious and the sophistication of intelligence techniques has increased out of all recognition. Yet the problems to be overcome will always remain formidable, if not insuperable. By definition a competent insurgent organization will be able to block the normal flow of information from the public to the security forces – if it cannot it will rapidly become insignificant. Attempts to unblock the flow by counter-terror have sometimes been made, either deliberately or, more often, in exasperation;

but such action spells political bankruptcy. The cooperation of the public has to be sought by other means, such as political and economic reforms, which are slow in taking effect. In the interim, and perhaps as a precondition of public support, the security forces have to substitute their own eyes and ears for those of the people. Otherwise the simplest military operations are reduced to a game of blind man's buff.

6 Operations

Military operations are, in analytical terms, usually the simplest aspect of war, though one must never forget Clausewitz' dictum that in war the simplest thing is difficult. Their logical simplicity stems from the direct clash of physical force. The measurement of conventional military 'victory' is straightforward enough: loss of ground, loss of force, loss of will, building to a sum which determines the loss of the war. Though psychological factors weigh heavily in any war, and though all war – as Clausewitz again stressed – is a political activity (so that to talk of 'purely military' planning is an absurdity), the balance of physical force is the primary determinant of the outcome. The form and sequence of military operations aim to maximize the application of force to overpower the enemy.

In counterinsurgency no such simple logic exists. The guerrilla principle of avoiding battle and refusing to defend fixed positions negates the principle on which regular armies are designed. In the light of this negation, much of the organizational and material paraphernalia of modern armies becomes a liability rather than an asset. More serious still, in internal conflict a force designed to maximize shock faces a situation in which minimum force may be necessary. On the face of it, this is the best reason for preferring to use police rather than troops. The problem is that once insurgency passes beyond the stage of episodic violence, which the police can deal with, it definitely becomes a form of warfare, fought by distinctly military techniques which it is neither easy nor, perhaps, desirable for the police to master. As a hybrid form of conflict it calls for a synthesis of police and military skills.

The first necessity is obviously for armies in such cases to adapt as quickly as possible, and develop a new repertoire of techniques suited to the complexity of the problem. It is, however, not always easy to see at the outset what skills will be useful; and vision can be further restricted by military conservatism. Soldiers may not want to develop new skills. Precisely because normal military logic is negated in counterinsurgency, soldiers have an intense dislike of internal security duties. When called to aid the civil power, they naturally try to preserve as large a sphere of autonomy, within which they can maintain their traditional priorities, as they possibly can. Thus at the beginning, and often throughout the course of each campaign, there has been a direct clash between civil and military logic.

The clash centres on the issue of concentration *versus* dispersion, or, put another way, offensive *versus* defensive action. Ideally, as both civilians and soldiers recognize, both should occur simultaneously. In reality, force is never sufficient, and priorities have to be decided. The civilian priority is protection and dispersion, the military aggression and concentration. Time after time the military authorities found themselves resisting civil demands for small detachments to support the police, or to guard buildings or even individuals. They were right to resist, insofar as a cardinal strength of guerrilla strategy lies in weakening the government forces by spreading them thin in just this way. But they were usually right for the wrong reasons.

They wanted to keep their forces concentrated because that was the conventional military wisdom; only thus could recognizable military operations be mounted. They rightly insisted on the need for offensive operations, but the sort of operations they envisaged were big 'sweeps' and harrassing or punitive marches by flying columns. The need to maintain a programme of training for 'real' war, which could so easily wither away when the troops were dispersed in small detachments, reinforced their ingrained predeliction for large-scale operations. These impulses were nonetheless misconceived. The army looked at its guerrilla opponents, ubiquitous yet intangible, emerging and vanishing at will (like a gas, as T.E. Lawrence described the Arab insurgents), and concluded that the answer lay in 'mobility'. Much of the history of British counterinsurgency is the history of repeated efforts to find this elusive quality, which would allow troops to speed forth from central garrisons to intercept rebel bands in the aftermath of an incident. To begin with, velocity itself seemed the key, and motor transport seemed a heaven-sent answer to the whole problem.[25] Yet it is obvious in retrospect that the real key lay not in mobility as such, but in the precision with which mobile forces could put their mobility to use. Without accurate intelligence their movements achieved nothing except, as was so often claimed *faute de mieux*, to 'show the flag' and hearten the law-abiding section of the public.

Intelligence was likewise the key to other large-scale operations such as sweeps, drives, and cordon searches aimed at 'clearing' or 'cleaning up' areas in which insurgents were active. Faulty information almost invariably rendered these time-consuming searches nugatory: mere handfuls of insurgents were picked up after day or week-long operations by thousands of troops and police. Keenness and skill on the part of the rank and file were certainly needed in the techniques of throwing cordons, mounting searches, and carrying out surprise raids, and in most cases it must be concluded that these ambitious offensive operations were unrealistic in their demands on inexpert personnel.[26]

After concentration for the wrong sort of operations, the army tended to revert reluctantly to the 'wrong' strategy – dispersion – and so arrive indirectly at the right sort of operations. Consistently it was forced to accept the need to subdivide insurgent areas into districts which could be closely controlled by local garrisons. Only thus could a proper intelligence infrastructure be built up, as units gained a gradual understanding of 'their' localities, much like a normal civil police, and so reduced or removed some of the operating advantage of the insurgents. Only thus, too, could areas be prevented from falling back under insurgent control after being 'swept' by mobile forces. This subdivision might or might not be marked by the construction of fortified posts and wired lines, and accompanied by the resettlement of the population in defended villages.

A tendency towards mutual imitation, on the part of both rebels and regimes, has been noticed by one of the most perceptive historians of war.[27] This mimesis is clearly as necessary as it is dangerous. Only by adopting successful techniques from the opponent can real mastery of the situation be hoped for. Intelligence based on local knowledge is the most important example, but direct imitation can go further. The term 'special operations' and 'special forces' has come to describe the most complete adaptation of style to insurgency (though 'special operations' can also, of course, include specialized action during conventional war), in which the security forces literally replicate the operating methods of the insurgents. Cautious moves in this direction began towards the end of the Anglo-Irish war in 1921, when small foot columns were used in place of motorized convoys, whose movements were too easily monitored by the rebels. The smaller forces could disappear into the countryside for several days in the manner of the IRA Active Service Units ('flying columns'). Later, in Palestine, the idea of the 'counter-gang' flourished under the charismatic leadership of Orde Wingate. It was to reach its most sophisticated form in Kitson's idea of the 'pseudo-gang'.[28]

This mimetic process held considerable moral and political dangers. Where the security forces saw the insurgents as 'criminal terrorists' they might use counter-gangs to create a counter terror. Even if the gangs did not commit atrocities – as their critics claimed they did in Kenya – in order to discredit the insurgents, their use exemplified an attitude that had no respect for the traditional boundaries and restraints of the British system.

7 Public opinion

The consistent aim of British counterinsurgency action has been the 'restoration of law and order'. Whilst soldiers sometimes take a rather formalistic view of order – as the mere absence of disturbance – civil administrators see it as the embodiment of the spirit of consensus, a positive endorsement of the political system. British statesmen often speak of 'constitutionalism' as meaning the pursuit of reasonable (as against extreme) political ends by means of peaceful persuasion (as against violence). In effect they seek to maintain the legitimacy of government and its associated political culture. Thus public opinion was central to their perceptions long before the 'battle for hearts and minds' entered into political discourse. Most of the debate over the use of force to restore order has concerned the obvious contradiction involved in maintaining by means of violence a system grounded on moderation. The persuasive idea that a 'short, sharp shock', an exemplary application of force, will permit a quicker return to normality, has vied with the fear of alienating the moderate majority who must provide the foundation for any eventual settlement. Exemplary force may cow the people or break the grip of terrorism, but it is likely to hurt the innocent as much as the guilty, and hence generate bitterness. (There may also be an unspoken fear that the whole governmental order could be perverted by reliance on force: as when a hawkish Liberal Home Secretary remarked during the Irish terrorist scares of the 1880s that coercion is like caviar – 'unpleasant at first to the palate, it becomes agreeable with use'.)[29]

British governmental attitudes to public opinion have varied according to circumstances. In the process of imposing law and order ('civilization') on undeveloped colonial territories, force was mandatory. But with development, force became less acceptable. At the beginning of the twentieth century, the British showed few qualms about crushing resistance in colonies by the most expeditious methods. This was not just because breaking native heads was less likely to cause a political crisis; there was also a frank recognition that a sound public opinion could only be established by resolute government. The King's Peace in England, the keystone of the whole ideology of order, had after all been externally imposed. This outlook was well expressed by an Indian administrator in 1919, writing on the subject of 'punitive police' (the transfer of extra police to disturbed districts at their own expense).

> The main value of a punitive force is that its cost falleth upon the just and upon the unjust, the result being that the just does his best to coerce the unjust into the paths of righteousness. A punitive force is the creator of a proper public opinion.[30]

In this confident spirit a repertoire of collective punishments, usually some form of fine, was widely used. The 1947 Internal Security manual listed 'punitive searches', 'raids of a disturbing and alarming nature, particularly by night', punitive police posts, collective fines, seizure of property, demolition of houses, taking hostages, and using forced labour. But it emphasized the political sensitivity of such coercive measures. 'The military object is to restore civil government, and no measures should be taken which would inflict needless indignities on the civil population, or lead to subsequent bitterness.'[31]

By that time, there was an air of uncertainty which had been less noticeable in 1919. For one thing, the easy assumption that the law-abiding majority could 'coerce' terrorists had fewer adherents. For another, world developments symbolized by the United Nations Covenant and Convention on Human Rights, followed by the European Convention, could not be ignored.[32] Britain, which saw itself as the pioneer of civil rights, sometimes found itself in the embarrassing position of being judged an infringer of them. Yet there was no change in the basic perception of the role of public opinion. In Ireland, Palestine, Malaya, and Kenya alike the authorities recognized that the elimination of terrorism was impossible except through active public co-operation. As the last High Commissioner of Palestine put it, terrorism was 'essentially a matter to be dealt with by the police. Their best weapon was the assistance of the civil population.'[33]

How could public cooperation be focused? Besides the important issue of providing information to the security forces, there was a concrete way of mobilizing the people against insurgency. Often it was conceded that to ask defenceless people to take sides against insurgents was asking too much where the government could not guarantee their security. Yet the precondition of such a guarantee was public participation. One way out of this vicious circle was the organization of 'home guards', local militias which could offer a realistic means of self-defence. The most decisive success of such a policy came in Kenya, where the Kikuyu Guard played a crucial role in eliminating Mau Mau. But this sort of success depended on public willingness to act; in other circumstances, repeated efforts were made to raise similar forces with very different results. It was all too easy to use compulsion to try and get the process started and overcome public fear or reluctance. The army was alleged to have done this in South Africa and Ireland as well as Malaya. Then the home guard could become yet another weapon in the insurgents' propaganda arsenal.

35

For propaganda seemed to be the ultimate key to legitimacy. Modern propaganda-consciousness dates from the First World War, though the value of armed action as propaganda had been argued by anarchists some time before that. Since the development of a full-scale 'psychological warfare executive' and apparatus in the Second World War, propaganda has become an obsession of media-saturated western societies. The belief that terrorism is fuelled by publicity has become an *idée fixe*, although it has no historical basis. This creates a severe dilemma for a liberal democracy, in which freedom of speech is a definitive civil right. Press censorship has often seemed the only way of countering insurgent propaganda, yet it is a course which is in some respects more dangerous than violence itself.[34] The imagined science of psychological warfare seemed to offer a way out of this baffling maze. French counterinsurgency theorists leapt on this to explain their military failure in Vietnam, and echoes of their vision of *la guerre révolutionnaire* spread far and wide. It seems, though, that British administrators were able to maintain a healthy scepticism about this miracle cure. When the Kenya Emergency authorities asked to be sent an expert, the Colonial Office remarked:

> Your object here is to enlist support from the Gikuyu tribe for the Government and at the same time to build up their ability and determination to resist terrorist pressure. We frankly cannot see how any outside 'expert' is going to help you in this nor do we believe that any new organization can provide a short cut or a substitute for the necessarily arduous and slow task of winning the people over, a task in which all Government departments should be made to realize that they have a part to play.[35]

This was perhaps as clear an expression of British counterinsurgency doctrine as any that could be found.

Notes to Chapter I:
The Complex of Counterinsurgency

1. W.J. Fishman, *The Insurrectionists*, London 1970.
2. Clausewitz, *On War*, bk 1, ch.1, sections 11, 24.
3. Peter Paret suggests that notwithstanding the evidence of history and Clausewitz' dictum, 'men generally find it difficult not to succumb to the temptation of drawing a rigid line between war and peace'. *Internal War and Pacification: The Vendée, 1789–1796*, Princeton Research Monograph No.12, 1961.
4. London 1971.
5. Sir C. Gwynn, *Imperial Policing*, London 1934, p.5.
6. P. Schlesinger, 'On the Shape and Scope of Counterinsurgency Thought', in G. Littlejohn et al. (eds), *Power and the State*, London 1978.
7. For a more practical example of this feeling, see R. Evelegh, *Peace Keeping in a Democratic Society: The Lessons of Northern Ireland*, London 1978.
8. T. Bowden, *The Breakdown of Public Security*, London 1977, offers no definition. Cf. usage in Colonial Office circular letter, 14 Dec. 1866. CO 323 287. 'Powers for Dealing with Subversive Activities', 11 Jan. 1950. CO 537 5381.
9. Austen Chamberlain to Lord Carmichael, 17 Dec.1915. Austen Chamberlain papers, 63/4/4.
10. On Riot Act, D. Williams, *Keeping the Peace: The Police and Public Order*, London 1967. The most recent set of guidelines is the 'Yellow Card'; earlier efforts were made to specify grounds for firing: 'Orders for Officers in Command of Troops Acting for the Assistance of the Civil Authorities', Somaliland Protectorate, 22 Mar.1920. CO 537 679, 883.
11. The classic statement of the doctrine is A.V. Dicey, *Introduction to the Study of the Law of the Constitution*, London 1885, ch.VIII.
12. Gen. Sir C. Napier, *Remarks on Military Law*, London 1837; *Report of the Select Committee on Employment of Military in Cases of Disturbances*, Parliamentary papers VII, 1908.
13. D. Richter, *Riotous Victorians*, Athens 1981. Hardy to Mayor of Salford, 6 Nov.1867. HO 41/21/57.
14. C. Townshend, 'Martial Law: Legal and Administrative Problems of Civil Emergency in Britain and the Empire, 1800–1940', *Historical Journal* 1982, p.172.
15. Opinion of Attorney General and Solicitor General, 16 Jan.1838. Jamaica rebellion file, WO 32 6235.
16. H.J. Simson, *British Rule, and Rebellion*, London 1938, pp.12, 257.

37

17. K. Jeffery and P. Hennessy, *States of Emergency*, London 1983. D. Bonner, 'Combating Terrorism in Great Britain: the Role of Exclusion Orders', *Public Law* 1982, pp.262–281. For a more alarmist view, C. Ackroyd et al., *The Technology of Political Control*, Harmondsworth 1977.

18. R. Thompson, *Defeating Communist Insurgency*, London 1966, ch.4. B. Crozier, *A Theory of Conflict*, London 1974, ch.5.

19. *Report of the Departmental Committee appointed to inquire into the disturbances at Featherstone*, Parliamentary Papers 1893–4, C.7234.

20. Memo. by Col. W.G.S. Dobbie, 28 Jan.1927. WO 32 3456. Cf. D. Barzilay, *The British Army in Ulster*, Vol.III, Belfast 1978, p.12.

21. S. Hutchinson, 'The Police Role in Counter-insurgency Operations', *RUSI Journal* CXIV, 1969, p.57.

22. C. Townshend, *The British Campaign in Ireland 1919–1921*, Oxford 1975, pp.125–8.

23. F. Kitson, *Low Intensity Operations*, London 1971, ch.6.

24. Townshend, *British Campaign*, pp.50–1.

25. C.E. Callwell, *Small Wars. Their Principles and Practice*, 3rd edn., HMSO 1906, ch.XI. T.H.C. Frankland, 'Notes on Guerrilla Warfare', *United Service Magazine* Vol.33, 1912. B.C. Dening, 'Modern Problems of Guerrilla Warfare', *Army Quarterly* Vol.13, 1927.

26. *Internal Security Duties* 1947, ch.8, pp.68–73. CO 537 1971.

27. Paret, *Internal War and Pacification*, p.72.

28. D.A. Charters, 'Special Operations in Counter-Insurgency: the Farran Case, Palestine 1947', *RUSI Journal* CXXIV, 1979.

29. C. Townshend, *Political Violence in Ireland*, Oxford 1983, p.165.

30. Chief Sec., Madras Govt., 26 Sep.1919. D. Arnold, 'The Armed Police and Colonial Rule in South India, 1914–1947', *Modern Asian Studies* Vol.II, 1977, p.121.

31. *Internal Security Duties* 1947, pp.75–7.

32. Colonial Office circular, 'Powers for dealing with subversive activities', 1950. CO 537 5381.

33. CO 537 1731.

34. Ordinances on Press Censorship, CO 537 5382.

35. CO letter [draft], 22 Aug.1953. WO 216 857.

Notes on Further Reading

As far as I know there is no general study of emergency powers and/or martial law in the twentieth century (apart from the present work). For the historical doctrine, two nineteenth-century writers, C.M. Clode, *Military and Martial Law* (John Murray, London 1872), and W.F. Finlason, *Martial Law* (Butterworth, London 1872), provide full guidance, and A.V. Dicey's *Introduction to the Study of the Law of the Constitution* (Macmillan, London 1885) created the classically simplified canon of the subject. I have started on an account for the twentieth century (see note 14 above), and hope eventually to enlarge it into a general study. All the constitutional law textbooks contain an analysis, sometimes rather sketchy, of martial law. The most substantial and interesting is in Keir and Lawson, *Cases in Constitutional Law* (various editions) Oxford University Press (5th edn. 1972). D. Williams, *Keeping the Peace* (Hutchinson, London 1967), is a thoughtful study of the police and public order. The major work of reference in this field is *Brownlie's Law of Public Order and National Security* (second edition, ed. M. Supperstone, Butterworth, London 1981).

General works on counterinsurgency are rarer on the British side of the Atlantic than on the other. The best are based on direct personal experience, like Frank Kitson's three books, *Gangs and Counter-Gangs* (Barrie and Rockliff, London 1960), *Low Intensity Operations* (Faber & Faber, London 1971), and *Bunch of Five* (Faber & Faber, London 1977). J. Paget's *Counter-Insurgency Campaigning* (Faber & Faber, London 1967) is a laudable attempt to build a general analytical framework out of a collection of cases. This pattern-building can, however, be taken too far towards superficial schematization, as in B. Crozier, *A Theory of Conflict* (Hamish Hamilton, London 1974). Britain's colonial experiences generated several useful works, outstanding amongst which is Sir Charles Gwynn, *Imperial Policing* (Macmillan, London 1934). H. Simson, *British Rule, and Rebellion* (Blackwood, London 1938), is a forceful, idiosyncratic view. J. Lunt, *Imperial Sunset* (Macdonald, London 1981), is an agreeable survey of a vast collection of colonial and semi-colonial armed forces.

The contemporary experience of terrorism has inevitably generated still more writing, much of it poorly conceived. An exception is G. Wardlaw, *Political Terrorism* (Cambridge University Press 1982). There is a collection of interesting essays in P. Wilkinson (ed.) *British Perspectives on Terrorism* (Allen & Unwin, London 1981), and an attempt to come to terms with the legal complexities facing the serving soldier in R. Evelegh, *Peace Keeping in a Democratic Society* (Hurst, London 1978). D. Hamill, *Pig in the Middle* (Methuen, London 1985) provides a lively account of the British Army's experience in Northern Ireland between 1969 and 1984.

II

The United Kingdom

---

1 Britain

Britain itself has, so far, been spared civil war in the twentieth century. The fabric of the state has been stressed by the pressures of modernization, but has remained substantially intact. Regional challenges to centralization have been insignificant. Ethnic minority movements have emerged but have hardly spilled over into violent conflict. Federalism has proved unexpectedly feeble as a political impulse. The social fabric has perhaps been less secure. The shifting centres of gravity of urban development, the degeneration of the inner cities, has been accompanied by real tension and unease. Occasional eruptions of collective violence indicate the existence of an as yet unmeasurable magma of discontent. But discontent alone does not cause revolutions. Frustration may produce aggression, but only organization can render a challenge effective.

Since the late nineteenth century the most likely focus of internal political conflict has lain, ostensibly, in the movement of organized labour. And whilst it may appear that the early hopes of the revolutionary left and the fears of the reactionary right alike were absurdly exaggerated, civil strife has never been closer during the last fifty years than in the struggle over industrial relations legislation in the early 1970s. (Especially the miners' strike of 1973, renewed in 1984 with different but equally serious confrontations.) At the beginning of the twentieth century, expectations of internal conflict were routine. The 'challenge of socialism' was widely believed to pose a threat to the state as the embodiment of bourgeois rule. The state itself was, as always, in line with its self-proclaimed duty, willing to use force in the last resort to counter such threats.

The anti-extremism of the 'British way' (which is extreme

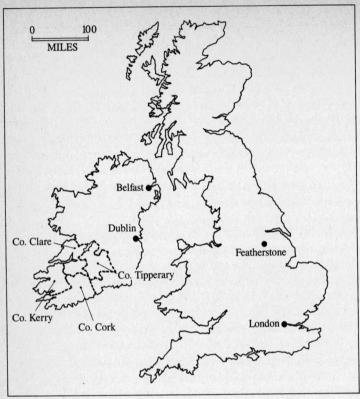

Britain and Ireland

only in its moderation) has always, in the event, relegated this eventuality to the realms of theory. The English preference for inaction in every sphere has extended, to general satisfaction, into the defence of the established order. Governments have been aware that a resort to force could be counterproductive, strengthening rather than removing opposition. Accordingly an event such as the small clash between troops and rioting workers at Featherstone in Yorkshire in 1893 was subjected to stifling scrutiny involving both an interdepartmental inquiry and an independent commission headed by the eminent judge Lord Bowen.[1] The result of these investigations was not to tighten up the rules governing the use of military force to preserve public order. Rather it was to stress that the very imprecision of the rules, so disturbing to soldiers, was part of the British way. Vagueness was a barrier against despotism.

This view was accepted by a further inquiry, held by a House of Commons select committee in 1908, after a violent clash between cavalry and rioters in Belfast. The leading expert witness was the lawyer R.B. Haldane, then Secretary of State for War in the Liberal government. Haldane restated almost brutally the classical common law doctrine (see Chapter I) of 'meeting force with force'. It was not up to the executive to produce hard-and-fast rules; it was up to individual soldiers to reach their own decisions about the necessary level of force in each specific crisis. In answer to the question whether it might not be more effective, or more humane, to shift the burden of decision and responsibility from the shoulders of individual military officers on to a joint civil-military committee, Haldane remarked with grim jocularity that it was 'much better to have one man whom you can hang, if necessary'.

So the 'British way' of dealing with the question of civil emergency was to shroud it in obscurity. If troops were called out to preserve or restore order, their officers went into action guided only by a forcible but indistinct sense of social constraint. In Britain itself, this obfuscatory method has, by and large, worked. A few hapless soldiers have made mistakes and suffered for them. But a few subtle officers have steered the precipitous path with distinction – and their rarity has enhanced their worth accordingly. Pre-eminent amongst them was General Sir Nevil Macready, whose unusual abilities were first revealed during the industrial troubles in South Wales in 1910. Here the threat of insurrection seemed, for a moment, real. The deployment of troops by the Home Secretary, Winston Churchill, appeared to his opponents to amount to a veiled declaration of martial law.[2] Indeed 'Tonypandy' stands in labour tradition as evidence of the state's readiness to respond violently to any worker challenge. In reality, though, Tonypandy demonstrated above all that the circumspect vagueness of the British system enabled the society to which it was tailored to muddle through without pushing conflict to violent extremes.

The same pattern was demonstrated in the postwar years when fears of industrial crisis reached another peak, especially in the mind of Sir Henry Wilson, the Chief of the Imperial General Staff, until the revolutionary threat finally fizzled out with the 'General Strike' in 1926. There was one significant legal development. The 1920 Emergency Powers Act sanctioned military action to preserve essential services endangered by strikes, even though strikes as such did not represent breaches of the peace. But this military intervention was in a non-military form – using soldiers to replace workers, not to coerce them – and the 'emergencies' envisaged did not resemble a state of siege on the continental model. The severest of them was the 'General Strike' of 1926, which the union leaders preferred to call a 'national strike' in order to deny any revolutionary syndicalist intent. A governmental machine, the Supply and Transport Organization (STO), was set up to manage the emergency; a citizen militia (Civil Constabulary Reserve) was established, and censorship erratically imposed. At the time these seemed dramatic departures from the 'British way', but in retrospect the strike seems most notable for the cautious incompetence shown by both sides. A small detail which captures the essence of the British way with crises is the fact that the Household Cavalry sentries outside the Horse Guards in Whitehall remained resplendent in their useless ceremonial dress and antique armament. To protect them, comrades in service dress, armed with rifles, hovered just out of public view. The CIGS thought this 'an absurdity', and insisted that in a future emergency all guards should be made effective: 'I do not believe that the General Public would view the matter in any other light than that the authorities meant business.' Yet it is surely the case that such a public gesture would have dramatic political significance as an advertisement of abnormality. 'Meaning business' as a British government in these circumstances is a complicated matter.[3]

Since 1926 the main issue over emergency powers has been the definition of the phrase 'essentials of life', which the 1920 Act and its 1964 successor exist to guarantee. It is obvious that the government has considerable latitude in defining essentials, and has increasingly come to place the working of 'the economy' as a whole, rather than specifics like bread and water, in this category. This is a significant trend whose outcome cannot yet be predicted. As one legal writer put it, 'to permit the Act to be used when an interruption in *any* supplies or services threatened serious economic injury would obviously expand enormously the definition of an emergency, and probably enable the executive to assume emergency powers on a permanent basis.'[4] UnBritish as this may seem, it is now a possibility in a way it would not have been at the beginning of the century.

2 The Irish difference

Despite alarms and occasional excursions, the severest strains of industrial society did not produce a crisis that could correctly be labelled a civil emergency. Military intervention never went beyond providing aid to the civil power, and only a handful of shots passed between soldiers and people. However, the system that worked so unobtrusively in Britain was more cruelly stretched in other contexts for which it had not been designed. Of these the nearest, in both the geographical and the cultural sense, was Ireland. Although sometimes called the 'sister island' (an interestingly meaningless term), the contrast between the two islands was marked. The struggle to govern Ireland may fairly be regarded as Britain's longest counterinsurgency campaign. 'The internal history of Ireland', in the words of Lord Salisbury, prime minister at the beginning of the twentieth century, 'has been a continuous tempest of agitation, broken by occasional flashes of insurrection.' The British state apparatus met there, on a day-to-day basis, stiffer resistance than it encountered in major crises in Britain. Open rebellions in 1848, 1867 and 1916 were followed by a guerrilla struggle in 1918–21 and, recently, by a long decade of 'suppressed civil war'.[5] In between there was less spectacular but often more widespread resistance to the legal and administrative system.

This was especially the case at the beginning of the twentieth century. In 1900 the United Kingdom of Great Britain and Ireland was 100 years old, and that century had been filled with various forms of diffused insurgency on the Irish side, countered by a steady stream of repressive legislation on the British side. 'Insurgency' may seem a strong term to use. Few of the actions in this day-to-day struggle were military ones, and few if any of the groups involved were overtly opposed to the state in political terms. However, the sense of general resistance to British law was often observed by outsiders to coalesce into a sort of 'rival government'. These shadowy entities took more concrete form when agrarian agitation reached periodic peaks of intensity, as in the 'Tithe War' of the 1830s, the 'Land War' of the 1880s, and its successor movement at the turn of the century. They still carried none of the administrative paraphernalia or verbal baggage of the government which occupied Dublin Castle. They merely enforced a simple set of ideas (the 'unwritten law' of the land) – for instance that tenants should not be evicted from their farms if they were unable, in hard times, to pay their rents. If another tenant took over a farm from which the previous occupant had been evicted, he would be punished.

Land occupancy was the central issue, and the demand for security of tenure was defended by violence and intimidation. In some desperate cases farms would be directly defended against eviction squads ('crowbar brigades' hired by landlords and escorted by Crown forces) by communal action which took the form of open battle. More commonly, however, violence was applied indirectly and covertly by small groups under *noms-de-guerre* such as Captain Thresher, Captain Rock, Molly Maguire, or Captain Moonlight. These groups were inevitably branded by the government as thugs, assassins, terrorists and murderers. No doubt there was a naturally turbulent element in the Irish rural population, but it seems more accurate to say that the enforcers of the 'unwritten law' were representatives, or in some sense agents, of the community. The state's mislabelling of rural resisters was important because it was not

merely a political propaganda exercise: it reflected a real misunderstanding of the situation. Irish 'disorder', as the government called it, was a manifestation of communal action through
the medium of secret societies. These societies formed the basic
organizational framework without which no action could have
been effective, and which enabled the government to perceive
communal violence as a threat not only to public order but also
to public security. Since the first Whiteboy movement in the
1760s the activities of these oathbound groups had remained
much the same. Although the white shirts which gave them
their original name were soon abandoned, secret societies continued to enforce the 'unwritten law' on fellow tenants – and
sometimes landlords or their agents – by the same violent
means: rick-burning, cattle-driving, cattle-maiming, assassination, beating, rape. 'Whiteboyism' was endemic in the Irish
countryside well into the nineteenth century. The illusion of a
wider 'association' amounting to a regional or national challenge
to the state was fostered by this natural similarity, and in
particular by the limited repertoire of titles, secret oaths, and
forms of intimidation available to these simple, low-level organizations.[6]

If it is true that there was a diffuse insurgency in Ireland, it
follows that the state was engaged in a protracted counterinsurgency campaign. Again, this may seem too strong a term.
Yet the enforcement of law and order in Ireland required efforts
of a wholly different order from those needed in Britain – and
even so was never fully achieved. These efforts were generically,
if not nominally, military. Nominally law enforcement was
in the hands of the police and under the aegis of the civil
government. But the Irish police were very different from
the English pattern, in two respects above all: they were under
central command, and they were armed. Only the Dublin
metropolitan force followed the English model. The Constabulary which policed the provinces was a *gendarmerie* which was,
in turn, to provide the model for many colonial police forces. It
was military in organization, training, appearance, and, for a
long time, attitude (even if its technical expertise in drill and
marksmanship did not always meet professional military standards). The rhetorical denunciations of the police by nationalists
as the 'army of occupation' were no doubt extravagant. The

rank and file were exclusively Irish in origin, and showed a strong tendency to forget their military training as soon as possible. But the rural population certainly saw the Constabulary as a military force, and this, coupled with its centralized regulation, formed a serious obstacle to the establishment of 'normal' relations between police and public. The fact that police stations were called barracks said little about their (usually puny) size and strength, but spoke eloquently of their function.[7]

That the government of Ireland was an unceasing struggle was attested not only by the nature of the executive arm, but also by the legal framework within which it operated. As part of the United Kingdom, Ireland was never declared to be in a 'state of emergency'. Such a concept could not be formally used, though many unofficial observers used the continental term 'state of siege' to characterize the general impact of repressive legislation in Ireland. A series of Insurrection Acts in the first half of the century provided Dublin Castle with powers akin to martial law. Indeed, the Union began with Ireland already under martial law in consequence of the 1798 rebellion, and martial law was maintained by statute for the first five years of the century. Habeas corpus, the fundamental guarantee of civil rights, was suspended several times in the second half of the century – in 1866, 1870, and 1881. A mass of Arms Acts, Party Processions Acts, Peace Preservation Acts, and so on, in the intervening years furnished a wide range of powers short of arbitrary arrest and detention without trial. Yet despite (some said because of) this legal stiffening, the enforcement of the ordinary law in Ireland remained weak. Such trivial processes as the serving of eviction writs were frequently impossible unless the sheriffs were escorted by dozens of police and troops. Local magistrates were themselves subject to intimidation or bribery, and had to be reinforced by a corps of Resident Magistrates whose loosely-defined powers could amount to those of special commissioners. They directed criminal investigations and had, at times, operational command of the police in their districts, whose own officers were increasingly paralysed by a mountain of administrative red tape.

The forces employed to combat disorder worked under the characteristic disadvantage of never being given a definition of order. Just what features of Irish criminal activity had to be removed or suppressed before it could be said that 'order' had been 'restored'? The only occasion on which the government showed an awareness of this problem was when Gladstone asked Earl Spencer, then Lord Lieutenant of Ireland, to compile statistics to show 'the minimum of Irish crime and its attendant circumstances which may have been thought to justify exceptional restraints, or the maximum of these which may have been allowed to subsist without them'. Even this request for a fairly crude indicator was not met, and the idea of defining a threshold of repression went no further.[8] The hesitancy sometimes shown by local law enforcement officers reflected an uncertainty permeating the system from the top downwards.

It was through the local magistracy that the army became routinely involved in the endemic crisis of order. The army's role was both extensive and limited. Extensive in that the local authorities made frequent demands for military assistance, and kept up heavy pressure to have troops stationed in small detachments across the countryside. Demands for such dispersion conflicted, of course, with military priorities: the need to keep forces concentrated and to pursue training programmes. But to a large extent they were met – in 1848 the army sent out no less than 2898 parties of troops to aid the civil power. At the height of the land agitation in 1882, when secret-society violence reached an intensity which almost lived up to the sensational title 'Land War' then coined, the number of military posts was doubled.[9]

But if the army was ubiquitous, its role remained limited. All its operations – patrolling, guarding buildings, enforcing the execution of writs, controlling riots, evicting tenants and escorting prisoners – were in aid of the civil power. Disorder never reached the point (undefined, as we have seen) at which the civil authorities felt obliged to hand over to the military. Once, in 1867, this seemed inevitable. The Fenian movement was indubitably political; it aimed at the achievement of absolute sovereign independence for Ireland, rather than economic or social change. It repudiated all 'constitutional' activity as corrupt, and insisted on the expulsion of British power by physical force.[10] When the Fenian rebellion was launched, military forces were concentrated to form mobile columns, whose commanders were given special legal powers (in effect being made magistrates). This experiment was given little chance to work, however. The rebellion proved insubstantial; coherent rebel bodies were few and far between, and were rapidly dispersed by the police. The army accused the police of opening fire prematurely and losing chances to surround and capture the rebels, but a question mark hung over the effectiveness of its own flying columns. Could they rely on the enemy obligingly forming themselves up to be crushed by military superiority? Could not troops be more effectively used against insurgency in other ways? These are of course perennial questions of counter-insurgency practice, the fundamental problem being to decide the proportion of available forces to be employed in local duties. The military preference for achieving 'mobility' by freeing as many troops as possible from static duties has always been marked, and is justified theoretically as the only way of regaining the initiative. But mobility as such is no guarantee of success against an enemy of 'unlike kind' with the capacity to disperse and disappear. And whilst subsequent experience has shown that offensive operations are vital for intelligence-gathering, such a task was not envisaged in 1867. Conflicting interpretations of the function of the flying columns – the Commander-in-Chief's idea of 'showing the flag' was repudiated two years later by Dublin Castle – suggest that it may have been primarily aesthetic.[11]

The legal powers of column commanders were no sooner extended than they were once again curtailed, causing considerable bewilderment. Yet the move showed a recognition of the need, at critical junctures, for unity of command. This need was to be met at the height of the Land War by the creation of Special Resident Magistrates with very wide-ranging authority, and later in the 1880s by the appointment of a Commissioner for the two most disturbed counties, Kerry and Clare. The first man to hold this post was a serving military officer, Major-General Sir Redvers Buller; and the fact that Buller moved on to head the civil administration as Under Secretary at Dublin Castle indicated that the government had come close to appointing a 'generalissimo'.[12] This was a measure of the dislocation caused by the Land War, though the important fact remains that the inbuilt restraints of the British system prevented such a concept from emerging.

3 Ireland: the first critical decade 1911–21

It may be said that at the beginning of the twentieth century a degree of confusion in the legal doctrine of counter-insurgency was matched by confusion in military doctrine. Surprisingly little of the army's experience in South Africa (see Chapter V) seems to have fed back into domestic thinking. Colonial circumstances were not seen as comparable with those in the United Kingdom. In any case, these experiences had failed to eradicate such deepset confusion as was to be illustrated during the succession of crises in Ireland between the drafting of the third Home Rule Bill in 1911 and the conclusion of the Anglo-Irish Treaty in 1921.

Three distinct, though interlocking, crises developed during this decade. The first was potentially the most dramatic from a military point of view. The renewed threat of Home Rule, now more real than ever since the veto power of the House of Lords had been removed, triggered a counter-threat in the Protestant north-east. The Ulster Volunteer Force, 100,000 strong, was formed to resist Dublin rule. The Unionist leaders hoped that the threat of force would be enough, and because no open military action materialized it is again difficult to describe the ensuing crisis as insurgency. Yet the UVF's meticulous military preparations eventually compelled the government to make military plans for preserving control. It was clear that if the UVF were to attempt to establish an Ulster Provisional Government by a *coup* the police would have no hope of preventing them. Battered by repeated failures to control sectarian rioting in Northern cities, the RIC – whose own position and indeed existence was threatened by Home Rule – had an unhealthy respect for its political opponents. The UVF enjoyed both numerical and moral ascendancy and planned to exploit these to the full.[13]

The government's military counter-planning was beset by political problems. Unionist resistance to Home Rule was unprecedentedly passionate, even hysterical, and the army was fundamentally conservative in attitude. More specifically, many of its members were Protestant Ulstermen. The government tried to spare the Ulster officers a conflict of loyalties by

offering them the chance to 'disappear' during military operations in Ulster.[14] But the mechanics of this unprecedented
concept were never worked out; the ambiguity of the operations
envisaged led to a fatal confusion in the handling of the offer,
and the resulting 'Curragh mutiny' in March 1914 raised the first
serious question in modern times of the political subordination
of the army. In fact the recalcitrant officers secured from the
Secretary of State for War a written limitation of the government's power to use the army, though the document was
repudiated by the Cabinet and the minister resigned. In May
1914 the UVF carried out a spectacular gun-running, and in
July a shooting affray between soldiers and civilians in Dublin
marked the spread of the crisis into the nationalist south, which
had so far backed the government against the Loyalist 'rebels'.
General Macready was given a dormant commission as Military
Governor of Belfast and stood ready to cross to Ireland at a
moment's notice. He later denied that there were any plans to
impose martial law, but it is hard to see what alternative would
have been left to the government.[15] Many contemporaries
believed that only the greater crisis in Europe averted a descent
into civil war in Ireland.

The second crisis followed generically from the first, since the
creation of the UVF had called forth an opposing nationalist
force. The Irish Volunteers were initially intended to put indirect rather than direct pressure on the government – they
were trying not to resist it but to keep it up to the mark in
carrying through the home rule policy. The Great War, however, transformed this situation as it transformed so many others.
Under the party truce at the beginning of the war, the government pushed home rule through into law. Immediately the
constitutional nationalists, who dominated the Irish Volunteers,
backed the British war effort. But the Fenian minority split
away, refusing to allow that Ireland could join in the war except
as an independent state. Mocking the hypocrisy of the British
claim to be fighting for 'the rights of small nations', they
planned to exploit England's own involvement in war.

Amongst them were a number of advocates of a new style of
insurgency, which they called 'defensive warfare'. Based on the
precepts of self-reliance preached by *Sinn Féin* ('ourselves alone'),
this idea distinctly foreshadowed the 'protracted war' which was

52

to be elaborated in the 1930s in China and later in Vietnam. It proposed a truly modern insurgency which would derive its strength from the gradual accretion of popular support. Its advocates recognized that the people would not automatically support a policy of physical force, and that it would be necessary to wait for the government to take aggressive action before violent resistance would be widely endorsed. They believed that the Great War would force Britain into such action because it would require the use of military conscription. When the government tried to enforce this in Ireland it would provoke tremendous opposition and guarantee the ultimate success of organized resistance.[16]

This was a powerful analysis whose main drawback, from the point of view of republican activists, was that it involved an indefinite postponement of action. The traditional Fenian prescription – 'England's difficulty is Ireland's opportunity' – was more immediately attractive. These activists launched an insurrection in the hope that the people would rally to the cause, and the certainty that even if they did not an heroic gesture would have been made to affirm the continuity of the Irish national claim. At Easter 1916 the Irish Republic was declared in Dublin, and a week of open fighting followed, as about 1500 Volunteers seized and defended major buildings in the city centre.[17]

For a moment the British army became the British state. Its reflex action in mounting an assault on the rebel positions was, in the military sense, a considerable achievement. Preparations had been kept, for political reasons, to a minimum, and many of the reinforcements hastily despatched from Britain were raw recruits with less training than the amateur militia which faced them. But unpreparedness had heavy political costs. Beleaguered in the Viceregal Lodge the Lord Lieutenant, with no small sense of personal drama, proclaimed martial law. This had not been done in the United Kingdom for over a century, but in the circumstances of executive paralysis it was justified by the common-law criterion of necessity. Less justifiably the Cabinet went on to give martial law parliamentary sanction, extending it across the whole of Ireland – most of which had remained completely peaceful – and keeping it in force after open conflict had ceased.[18]

Having thus acquired a great deal of opprobrium, the government went on to ensure that martial law powers were never actually used, so denying itself any possible practical benefits from the measure. The suppression of the rising was carried out under the Defence of the Realm Acts (DORA) in force throughout the whole UK since the beginning of the war. The rebel leaders were tried and executed by courts martial under DORA, not by military tribunals under martial law – though naturally the distinction was lost on the majority of the public who assumed they were under a military regime. When General Sir John Maxwell arrived in Dublin after four days of rebellion as – or so he thought – Military Governor of Ireland, he found his powers disturbingly undefined. Three months later he wrote in a puzzled way to one of the Cabinet's Irish specialists, Walter Long, 'apparently you and other Cabinet Ministers think that I have some definite powers'. Misunderstanding could hardly have gone further.[19]

To begin with he was left entirely without political supervision or advice. In accordance with the established wartime practice of Asquith's government, military planning for the recapture of Dublin was left in the hands of the army. Yet, as Clausewitz held, there can really be no such thing as a 'purely military plan', and the rough-and-ready military methods used in Dublin had inescapable political consequences. Politicians were slow to see this. Caught off balance by the rising, disoriented by the greater European war, and in any case never at their best in Irish matters, they made no effort to lay down policy. Only after a fortnight had elapsed, during which there had been several highly-publicized clashes between nervy soldiers and noncombatants, and Maxwell had shot a dozen rebel leaders, did Asquith suddenly intervene. But the image of military rule could not be erased.

The government's mismanagement validated the action of the insurrectionists. But in another sense it also bore out the argument of the advocates of 'defensive warfare' that it was possible to rely on British blunders to change Irish public opinion. This view was finally confirmed in 1918 when the conscription issue at last erupted. British public opinion impelled the government to declare its intention to enforce military service in Ireland. Like martial law, conscription remained a threat rather than a reality, but the threat was enough to generate public outrage, expressed powerfully by the Roman Catholic church, and to give Sinn Féin undisputed leadership of the Irish national movement. During 1918 and 1919 the re-formed Irish Volunteers, adopting the title Irish Republican Army, began small operations to acquire weapons. By 1920 they were waging a guerrilla war which was paralyzing the British administration. The last and most serious of the three crises had broken.

Once again, as in the nineteenth century, the 'breakdown of law and order' became the central problem of the state as the government tried to implement two distinct, and possibly con-tradictory policies. Its constitutional objective remained con-stant throughout the decade: home rule, devolution within the framework of the United Kingdom. But this policy was pro-gressively stymied by resistance not merely from Unionists but also, and increasingly, from radical nationalists. Their opposition was expressed unconstitutionally (for instance Sinn Féin's re-fusal to send MPs to Westminster) even when it was not openly violent. The government demanded a 'return to constitutionalism' as a precondition for discussing constitutional revision. Trans-lated into executive terms, this meant the familiar business of restoring law and order.

But what was the order that was to be restored? Had it indeed ever existed? Was it not perhaps the case that the imposition of British law in Ireland actually provoked disorder? These questions were not asked, much less answered, by the government before it returned to the use of force to suppress the Republican movement. Restoration of order was a con-venient interim policy backed by Liberals and Conservatives alike, and that was enough. Similarly, the government showed no desire for precise analysis of the challenge it faced. It was, ironically, slower to identify the reality of this insurgency than its predecessors had been to overreact to less formidable – sometimes imaginary – movements. The haphazard evolution of the legal framework was, accordingly, allowed to continue. The special powers provided by DORA gradually lapsed as the war ended, though they had been extensively relied on in 1918 to allow close control of disturbed districts (Special Military Areas). Critically, too, the 'unBritish' system of travel permits, to control movement between Britain and Ireland, which had been established in 1918 was immediately abandoned as inappropriate to peacetime conditions.[20] Subsequent calls for its restoration were to prove unavailing.

In 1920 the insurgent challenge was far more severe. By the spring, outlying police stations had been abandoned, larger barracks fortified and several of the latter attacked. The legal system was indisputably paralysed, and perhaps in chronic breakdown. Not a single rebel had yet been convicted of a violent act, because witnesses would not come forward and jurors would not bring guilty verdicts. Indeed few had been arrested for the commission of outrages (as distinct from membership of proscribed organizations, for which several hundred had been interned without trial) as the police were unable to pursue investigations effectively. Since mid-1918 the RIC had been the target of a general boycott organized by Sinn Féin, and in 1919 the political section of the Dublin Metropolitan Police (G Division of the Crime Special Branch) had been subjected to frequent attack by the IRA. By 1920 the police intelligence system, rather clumsy at the best of times despite its reputation as the 'eyes and ears of Dublin Castle', was in a state of disintegration.

Not until after the humiliating failure of the 1920 summer assizes, however, did the government screw itself up to bringing in special legislation. In July the circuit judges everywhere, even in the areas of greatest violence, were presented with the 'white gloves' signifying that there were no cases to be tried. The criminal law had become inoperable; the civil law had been hijacked by the republicans through the Dail Eireann 'arbitration courts', which began within the British law but soon claimed original jurisdiction and the power to impose penalties. Even now the government acted with marked hesitation, seeing it as 'a decision of the gravest moment to utilize machinery intended for time of war in time of peace', and expressing 'considerable anxiety . . . at thus handing over the whole administration of the law to soldiers'.[21] The Restoration of Order in Ireland Act was finally rushed through parliament in seven days at the beginning of August, enlarging the jurisdiction of military courts and the army's powers of search and arrest, but falling some way short of the kind of 'statutory martial law' seen later in, for instance, Palestine. The C-in-C was not given control over the police forces. Politically, it was important to insist that the situation was one of peace: the government was well aware of the Republic's claim to belligerent status under international law. When the Lord Lieutenant, Field-Marshal French, asked the government to take warlike measures against the Volunteers – meaning an end to uncertainty and half measures – Lloyd George retorted 'you do not declare war on rebels'. This constricted idea of war seems to have prevented statesmen from recognizing the nature of insurgency.

The main symbol of 'peace' as against 'war' was of course the primacy of the police force in the effort to restore order. Accordingly military intervention was veiled, even after it was evident that unless the law was administered by soldiers it would not be administered at all. The primacy of the police was an important principle, but its value depended on the capacity of the police to survive and to preserve some sort of 'normal' civil role. The general weakness and demoralization of the RIC made this doubtful. Nonetheless, the government assumed that the force should be shored up rather than that military involvement should be increased. In 1920 the RIC was expanded, mechanized, and increasingly militarized in armament (rifles and Lewis guns replacing its old carbines). Its expansion was achieved by altering the base of its recruitment and importing ex-servicemen from Britain. In this process the whole nature of the force was transformed.

The 'Black and Tans' were a new phenomenon, in a sense a 'third force' between police and troops.[22] But they were not a hybrid force, except insofar as the war veterans never managed to adapt completely to a police outlook. The first proposal, for eight special 'garrison battalions' (perhaps resembling the later Ulster Defence Regiment, or the Kenya Regiment) under War Office control and military law, gave way to a police auxiliary force, in line with political preferences. The original hope that these non-Irish recruits would merge unobtrusively into the regular RIC was quickly dashed. In fact the Inspector General of the RIC had predicted from the outset that the combat experience of the new recruits, added to their unfamiliarity with Ireland, would make them useless or even dangerous as policemen. The old RIC disciplinary code would just not be strong

57

enough to control them. In the event, the obtrusiveness of the newcomers was heightened by an administrative bungle, the shortage of uniforms which put them into an odd mixture of regular RIC dark green and military khaki.

As soon as this ill-timed error was rectified, the 'Black and Tan' label was given a new lease of life by the decision to create a separate force in July 1920. The RIC Auxiliary Division (ADRIC), recruited almost exclusively from ex-officers, was the nearest approach to a specialist counterinsurgency force so far, organized in mobile independent companies of about a hundred. They received minimal police training, and for the most part made little attempt to act as police. Plunged into the boredom of rainswept rural Ireland, and frustrated by the harrassing operations of a near-invisible opponent, too many of them took refuge in drink. As the former Inspector General had predicted, RIC discipline proved unable to restrain them from taking violent revenge on the population for its tacit support of the rebels. Auxiliary reprisals grew more and more destructive during the autumn of 1920. All this might have been acceptable to the government if the ADRIC had succeeded in crushing the IRA. But counterinsurgency doctrine was too primitive to give them much chance of doing this.

The real weakness manifested in the deployment of the ADRIC stemmed from misinterpretation of the insurgency. The government became trapped by its own political propaganda – its contention that the Republicans were a tiny, unrepresentative minority who dominated the moderate majority by naked terrorism. There was, of course, a modicum of truth in this analysis. But that modicum, reinforced by wishful thinking, pushed the government into serious self-deception. The conclusion which followed was that order could be restored, and a moderate constitutional settlement (home rule) accepted, if the terrorization of the community could be ended.[23] The 'murder gang' had to be eliminated.

But how could the vicious circle of terror – whereby the community, unprotected from the IRA, refused to risk giving the information which would permit the IRA to be eliminated – be broken? In the light of the Irish experience it became clear that the security forces could not expect to secure significant public cooperation until they had displayed an ability to strike with effect. This required them to build up their own intelligence service so that it could work without public assistance. Such a process requires perception, skill, patience, and time. These things, especially the last, seemed to be in short supply. The Auxiliaries were sent in to rupture the vicious circle in a crude way – by out-terrorizing the terrorists. In the words of a disillusioned southern Irish Unionist, 'the Irish rapparee was to be beaten by the British rapparee'.[24]

In a sense this was no more than an implementation of the legal rule of meeting force with force. But if the nature of the challenging 'force' is misunderstood, then the counter-application of force is likely to be wrong. The IRA were branded as thugs and murderers by the government; the Black and Tans in turn were given the same label by the insurgents. In each case the label was partly justified, but it was infinitely more damaging when fixed on the upholders of law and order. Admittedly the most extreme allegations against the Black and Tans – that they had been specially released from British gaols with an unwritten licence to shoot first and ask questions afterwards – were wild exaggerations. But the documented behaviour of the new RIC was quite bad enough to give solid colour to the assiduously-spread republican propaganda. Even 'spontaneous' reprisals, defended by the responsible minister as the natural reaction of men who had been goaded beyond endurance, were not in a legal sense the meeting of force with force. The lapse of time, and still more the shift of place, between rebel blow and police counterstroke were too obvious. (Though the minister, himself a lawyer, never admitted this even in private.) Obvious, too, were the endemic inadequacy of police discipline and the occasional descent into outright criminality.[25]

Amongst the severest critics of RIC indiscipline were the military authorities. The army was very slow to adjust itself to the novel demands of guerrilla warfare. Its tardy reorientation was to some extent to blame for the inadequacy of ADRIC training, since there was little in the way of counterinsurgency theory to teach them. But the army was always opposed to the creation of a special 'gendarmerie', holding that to employ war veterans in an armed force outside the control of military law was an unacceptable risk. In this there was, inevitably, an element of organizational egocentrism, which played a part in

aggravating friction between the police and the army throughout the conflict. Nonetheless, the army's prejudices proved on
balance to be more correct than those of the politicians. As the
actual practitioners of force, soldiers may generally be expected
to have valid ideas of its possibilities and its limitations. If they
sometimes unthinkingly exaggerate the former, their thoughts
return surprisingly often to the latter.

Regrettably it was the inadequacy of the police which compelled the army to develop a clearer counterinsurgency doctrine.
This was especially the case in the crucial spheres of command
and intelligence. Month after month of poor coordination drove
the military authorities to enunciate the principle of unity of
command as the *sine qua non* of effective operational planning
and action. Ironically, the army had once had this in its grasp,
and refused it. When the indispensable General Macready returned, reluctantly, to Ireland as Commander-in-Chief in
March 1920, he was offered conjoint command of the RIC. His
ostensible reason for refusing it was his belief that setting the
RIC straight would be a full-time job in itself. This was no
doubt true, though it missed the point that the direction in
which the RIC was set would vitally affect relations between it
and the army, and would depend on the character of the man
who took on the job. In the event, Macready did not get on with
the officer appointed. Major-General Hugh Tudor was Macready's junior in military rank, and in fact had none of Macready's
remarkable experience in police affairs (Macready's most
recent post had been as Commissioner of the London Metropolitan Police), but he showed no inclination to defer to the
Commander-in-Chief. He saw his political task as to maintain
the independence and power of the RIC, and he accomplished
it by expanding, militarizing, and in every possible way 'backing
up' the force. In this he was encouraged by senior ministers,
especially the Secretary of State for War, Winston Churchill.

As a result, the army was never given another chance to
rectify Macready's mistake. The primacy of the police meant
that the army was kept in low profile through the spring and
summer of 1920. Special legal powers (of search and arrest) had
been given to battalion commanders after the attempted
assassination of Lord French in December 1919, but were
withdrawn again. By the time of the Restoration of Order in

Ireland Act in August 1920, when the military profile was raised on a long-term basis, the police had been so extensively bolstered that there was no question of direct military control. By the late autumn of 1920 Macready was being driven, against his judgement, to press for martial law. He doubted whether it would be effective in crushing the IRA, because public opinion would revolt against any full-scale use of it ('I do not for one instant think that the British public would stand for martial law, as I understand it, for a week over here').[26] It might even worsen the political situation. But he saw it as the only way left to achieve proper control over the police, who, if left to themselves much longer, would make the situation impossible.

In December, after months of hesitation, the government finally responded to the escalation of IRA activity by proclaiming martial law in four (later eight) south-western counties. The army's jubilation was shortlived. The geographical limitation of martial law, from which the government would not budge, signalized other equally significant restrictions on military rule. Not only was the army unable to secure the unequivocal supersession of the civil legal system by military tribunals, but it failed in its primary object of attaining unity of command in the martial law area. The independence of the police was almost undented. In vain did Macready seek to cut the links between Tudor and his political backers. The essence of the matter was that the policymakers had concluded that the police might be able to overpower the IRA, but the army could not. In Lloyd George's words, the 'Irish job' was 'a policeman's job supported by the military and not *vice versa*. So long as it becomes a military job only it will fail'.[27] Unfortunately the Prime Minister did not make this unequivocally clear until June 1921, only a month before the Government decided to end the conflict.

This lack of political confidence was to some extent instinctive, and obviously correct, in a liberal democracy. Beyond that, however, it reflected the inconclusive performance of the army in extended operations over a period of eighteen months. Not all of this could be blamed on divided command. Military efforts to build up an intelligence system had for too long been erratic and halfhearted, since their necessity was not recognized. In 1918 and 1919 practically nothing was done in this direction. When the first intensive programme of searches and arrests was set on foot at the beginning of 1920 the impossibility of relying on the police to supply usable information became obvious. But, even so, regiments were not easily shaken out of ingrained attitudes. Intelligence remained a low priority, and the lone intelligence officer in many battalions was not relieved of his other duties. The need for constant alertness and activity by all ranks in gathering front-line intelligence was rarely appreciated. There was, as there will no doubt usually be, some lack of enthusiasm, but the root cause was failure to recognize intelligence as an integral aspect of operations.[28]

Formal operations were correspondingly hampered. The first round of large-scale arrests was not successful; nearly all those arrested were quickly released. When extensive administrative reforms were made in Dublin Castle between March and May 1920, the intelligence system received new leadership, in common with most other departments. The appointment of Brigaddier Ormonde Winter as director of police intelligence was really the first of its kind since that of Colonel Brackenbury in 1882, and certainly indicated recognition of the problem. But while Winter had a good deal of 'star quality' ('a most amazing original' in the view of one Castle official) he lacked Brackenbury's weight in the military establishment. He was, one suspects, just too exotic. He made improvements in the central filing and distribution of information, but his real *penchant* was for secret service and counter-espionage work.[29] The army recognized the importance of cloak-and-dagger activity, but became convinced that the overriding necessity was for operational intelligence. It found Winter's organization unpredictable in this sphere, and gradually reached the unpalatable conclusion that it would have to do the job itself.

The decisive moment was 'Bloody Sunday'. The shooting of a dozen British officers – several of them secret intelligence men – by Michael Collins' 'Squad' in the early hours of Sunday 21 November led to a sudden concentration of the military mind. In the excited burst of activity which followed, the ADRIC characteristically became involved in a shoot-out on Sunday afternoon at Croke Park football stadium, in which several innocent spectators were killed. The army managed to avoid the appearance of taking reprisals, but its intensive raiding operations were not particularly successful. (It did manage to seize the Sinn Féin leader Arthur Griffith – a political not a military figure – but was promptly ordered to release him.) Despite its now extensive experience of these tasks, its technique remained somewhat slapdash.

Gradually, however, these methods delivered results. 'Raid and search' was the dominant military activity in 1920, especially in Dublin, and as these tiresome minor operations rolled ceaselessly on they became increasingly directed towards intelligence-gathering – partly because they gathered so little else. Suspects remained elusive; arms were hard to find. As the Dublin divisional command put it, a 'bow wave' of suspicion preceded 'any but the most rapidly moving force'.[30] Hence patrols in daylight had practically no chance of encountering rebels – except by being ambushed. Raids were mounted at night, under curfew, by motor transport, but still were up against formidable obstacles. Troops lacked the special skills required to search out well-concealed *caches*; suspects even when taken could often not be identified. These weaknesses were particularly noticeable when large-scale cordon and search operations were attempted, as in the aptly-named Operation 'Optimist' in central Dublin in January 1921.

The same structural problems afflicted military action outside Dublin. This tended to take the form of patrols rather than raids, especially after the IRA started to organize Active Service Units ('flying columns') in the late autumn. Like raids, patrols had a dual nature. They were both offensive and defensive; their utility depended on accurate intelligence, but they could themselves assemble much of the information they needed. In practice, unfortunately, they worked in the dark as often as not. The impetus to work on the collation of intelligence was missing. Military commands displayed a noticeable preference for larger-scale operations bearing a closer resemblance to conventional military action. This was a rational prejudice insofar as such operations helped to provide the basic training which was alarmingly attenuated by constant guard and patrol duties. But big operations were subject to a law of diminishing returns in strict counterinsurgency terms. Major cordon and sweep manoeuvres consumed much time and energy, and were ineffectual in netting rebels. No IRA flying column was ever trapped by such a manoeuvre.[31] There were some close shaves, but in such situations a miss is as good as a mile.

63

Confronted by the challenge of a new form of warfare, the first military response was to seek mobility. The guerrilla insurgents created the impression of mobility through their capacity to appear and disappear at will. Coupled with their dispersed, decentralized organization, this enabled them to achieve what a modern writer calls 'ubiquity combined with intangibility'.[32] This was not mobility in the ordinary sense, however, and military attempts to match it by increasing the provision of motor transport was never more than a partial answer. Motorized patrols with armoured vehicles certainly raised the stakes for the IRA flying columns, and in some areas such as open flatlands drove them back to small-scale operations. Here the IRA's 'offensive against communications' – which involved widespread blocking of roads with trenches and felled trees – had an air of defensive desperation about it, and never looked to have more than nuisance value. But in the more dangerous areas of the south-west, the mechanical limitations of slow, noisy vehicles were a serious handicap. Only the Rolls-Royce armoured car had the technical capacity to surprise rebels in the hills of Tipperary, Cork and Kerry. The weapon which offered the prospect of almost unlimited mobility was, of course, the aircraft, and great faith was initially reposed in it. However, inadequate technology together with inexperience in ground-air cooperation (not assisted by the RAF's urge to develop its independent identity as a service), conspired to restrict the effect of air operations. More significant for the future perhaps were the inherent limitations of air reconnaissance in locating and identifying guerrilla forces, and the problems of using airborne weapons to strike at them. A very interesting joint exercise mounted in May 1921 revealed that aircrew could not spot small groups on the ground except when they were moving; primitive communications technology – sign boards and message-dropping rather than radio – hampered coordination; and political restrictions on the use of airborne weapons left them impotent.[33]

The declaration of martial law was expected to provide definite advantages in the intelligence and operational spheres. Critically, the army sought a means of reversing the information flow which had so far shielded the rebels from effective pursuit.

Macready recognized that reprisals had an observable impact in this direction. He could not, however, accept the disciplinary implications of casual reprisals, and he looked for a way of achieving the same effect on public consciousness through controlled action. 'Official punishments' were his solution: not so much the collective fines which were to become familiar in other countries, as the formal destruction of buildings from which shots were fired at Crown Forces (with or without the occupants' consent), or from which the preparations for an IRA ambush could have been seen and should have been reported to the authorities. In addition the army tried to set up 'Civic Guards', which in theory were local self-defence forces. In practice they were usually little more than compulsory working parties engaged in refilling, under the guns of the troops, the trenches which the IRA (or possibly the 'Civic Guards' themselves) had earlier dug. Such methods of putting pressure on the ordinary population to get off the fence and commit themselves to assisting in the restoration of order were seen as eminently reasonable by the military authorities. As General Strickland, Military Governor of the Martial Law Area, announced, an 'attitude of neutrality' was 'inconsistent with loyalty'.[34] The struggle between the Crown Forces and the rebels was not a sideshow in which the public were mere spectators.

The army was taken aback by the political repercussions of its martial law regime. 'Official reprisals', as everyone else called them, were denounced by the liberal press in Britain, which was moving towards the view that even the violence of the IRA could not negate the validity of the Irish national cause. They were also frowned on by the Cabinet, which was showing signs of alarm at the drift of public opinion away from support for the campaign to restore order. Tragi-comic scenes as tenants and chattels were bundled out of their houses before each laborious act of military arson provided if anything worse publicity than the random, unavowed violence of the Black and Tans. Most seriously, the actual financial damage was largely sustained by loyalist landlords, who owned most of the houses burned in official punishments, and whose own 'big houses' were burned on a large scale in the counter-reprisals of the IRA. In this, as in other matters, the overall effect of martial law was modest.

Muffled by political constraints, the army was unable to generate the atmosphere of general apprehension which it thought to
be the essence of martial law.[35] Fearsome in concept, military
rule was tamed by the traditions of British society.

In the end, the significant advances in the intelligence sphere
were made via technical improvements. As the system became
more elaborate, a sort of 'critical mass' of information was
reached which began to generate results. This accumulation was
aided, unintentionally, by the slow rotation of units serving in
Ireland. For instance, the Essex battalion in southern Cork
stayed in the same area throughout the two-year campaign.
(Admittedly its area was too large for a single battalion which
was usually under strength, and this weakness was common to
the whole Martial Law Area.) In Dublin the improved gathering and handling of operational intelligence led to a noticeable
change in the spring of 1921. Instead of narrowly missing arms
caches or raiding recently-vacated republican headquarters, the
Crown Forces made consistent damaging finds. In the rural
south-west, a new operational style made some headway against
military conservatism. The use of small infantry columns imitat-
ing IRA methods, operating away from roads and from their
base for several days, carrying out observation and sometimes
counter-ambushes, adumbrated a true counter-guerrilla strategy. For the first time it put pressure on the IRA in the 'safe'
areas which had been effectively under its control since the
winter of 1919–20. Here was a realistic, adaptive response to
insurgency which conventional motorized mobility had not provided.

It was, however, too little and too late. Despite the successes
of spring 1921, the counterinsurgency failed. Ireland was not
pacified. The government succeeded neither in restoring order
nor in implementing the constitutional policy enshrined in the
Government of Ireland Act. Failure can be accurately monitored in the field of publicity and propaganda. The government
was slower than the insurgents to create a publicity organization,
and the one they created was weaker in performance.[36] In point
of fact the overall situation in 1921 was not altogether unfavour-
able to the government: the IRA's military position was increasingly insecure. Its arms holdings were being eroded, as was
its ascendancy in the intelligence sphere. Its capacity to mount

66

difficult operations had been reduced – attacks on police barracks had for instance largely given way to the 'offensive against
communications', more widespread but less demanding – and
its regional variations were being mercilessly exposed. Large
parts of the nation had ceased to play any visible part in the
national struggle. Yet the IRA sustained its credibility, while
that of the government was in continuous decline.

The legitimacy of the state in Ireland had never been undisputed since the Union. The events of 1916 underlined its
marginality: the rebellion was initially greeted with the same
hostility by the middle class in Dublin as in Britain, but military
repression reversed the direction of Irish hostility with dramatic
swiftness. By the time of the unilateral declaration of independence in Dáil Eireann at the beginning of 1919 it is unlikely, to
say the least, that the moderate majority favoured British
policy, even though outright republicans may have been few
and far between. By autumn 1920, the mainstream nationalist
newspaper, the *Irish Independent*, had reached the point of
declaring that 'nobody in Ireland accepts as truthful any statement made by the British Government'.[37]

Such journalistic sedition was beyond the state's power to
control. Attacks on the 'liberty of the press', as when the
Dublin Castle administration prosecuted and imprisoned the
owner and editor of the other major nationalist paper, the
Freeman's Journal, for publishing false reports, were followed
by hasty retreats under bombardment from Fleet Street. The
government's Irish policy proved unconvincing to British public
opinion – both liberal and unionist – and its methods progressively more unattractive. Scepticism also echoed from around
the world, where the republican case, as tirelessly expounded in
the ostensibly factual *Irish Bulletin*, frequently outweighed
British explanations. In 1919 British opinion, remembering the
stab in the back of 1916 and the 'German plot' of 1918, was
still hostile to the pretensions of the Irish republicans as well as
to the violence of their methods. Two years of covert warfare,
however, generated what may be called the 'dirty war syndrome'.
The sordid Irish melée was morally, if not financially, too
expensive to prolong. The IRA had demonstrated its capacity
to survive long enough to sap the will of its opponents.

4 The Northern Ireland crisis

The weaknesses of the counterinsurgency campaign which ended in the severance of twenty-six counties from the UK in 1922 were inherent in the British system. It is not therefore surprising that similar features have emerged in the protracted crisis in the other six counties. There is, however, a danger in drawing easy parallels. The present problem in Northern Ireland is quite different from any that have preceded it, including the 'Ulster crisis' of 1911–14. The shift in geographical centre of gravity from south-west to north-east involves a shift of substance. While it is evident that an insurgency has developed since 1969, its potential scope is subject to two critical limitations. The first is that the existence of a separate six-county unit generates political ambiguity. Roman Catholics (who have always been labelled 'nationalists' by their advocates and opponents alike – with or without their consent) have in fact a choice of political strategies. They may aim at incorporation in the Irish Republic, or they may seek improvement of their political and economic status within Northern Ireland. The second strategy was tacitly rejected for a generation after 1922, but since the civil rights movement of the late 1960s many 'realists' would argue that it is now the only practical one.

The other, more immutable, limitation upon the insurgency is ethnic geography – the concentration in the north-east of a million diehard Protestant Unionists. As long as the Irish Republic maintains its studied neutrality – 'stands idly by' in the words of one of its leaders – the potential popular support for the insurgents in the six counties can never reach even a bare, let alone an overwhelming, majority. The insurgency thus resembles tribal war more than revolution: modern Irish rebels are engaged, first and foremost, in the defence of communities and localities. Their main political threat consists in their capacity to render some areas ungovernable, not in their capacity to overwhelm the state. It is this weakness that has repeatedly led them into the use of terrorism, the only way of striking outside their territorial limits. The substitution of terrorist for guerrilla action is always – however alarming it may appear – a symptom of weakness rather than strength.

Far from simplifying the problems facing the security forces, however, these limitations have tended to complicate them. In the first place, the complexity of the Ulster imbroglio has made the British government's political objectives even more indefinite than in the past. Positive decisions have been made: the commitment of troops in 1969 and the resumption of direct rule in 1972. Subsequently, though, inability to pursue a policy which would close other options – either full integration of the six counties into the UK, or negotiations for Irish unity – and the failure of novel constitutional compromises such as power-sharing, have revealed the familiar pattern of drift. As before, constitutional paralysis has thrown day-to-day emphasis on the restoration of order, a makeshift policy which other political parties cannot decently oppose, whether it facilitates or interferes with political settlement.

The evident limitations of the republican constituency have naturally encouraged the government's reluctance to identify the struggle as an insurgency. The political usefulness of denouncing all republican armed action as 'terrorism' has proved too great for the temptation ever to be resisted, even when the action is patently military, such as ambushes of security forces or attacks on barracks, or self-directed violence such as hunger-striking. (The implication that it is possible to terrorize the armed forces in the same way as ordinary civilians is surely not accepted by those forces themselves; and the extent to which suicide can be properly described as a terrorist act is dubious.) No state of emergency has been declared, except indirectly *via* Britain's derogation from Article 5 of the European Convention on Human Rights, on the grounds of an 'emergency threatening the life of the nation'.[38] At the same time, sweeping changes in the legal system have been effected. The 1973 Northern Ireland [Emergency Provisions] Act effectively put the much-criticized 1922 Northern Ireland Civil Authorities [Special Powers] Act on the British statute book. The 1974 Prevention of Terrorism [Temporary Provisions] Act has drifted on into apparent permanence ten years later. Internment without trial was enforced during the first half of the decade; and when Habeas Corpus was eventually restored, jury trial was suspended. The result is an unprecedented legal framework whose oddity makes it hard to place in the British tradition.

One expert military commentator, writing in 1974, suggested

that the government had 'provided a great deal of the substance of martial law in Northern Ireland while avoiding its form'.[39] Insofar as this is true, it follows a practice worked out in other colonial contexts, which will be seen developing elsewhere in this book. But in Ireland the intention may be doubted. A species of military rule, including a degree of visible presence which is foreign to the 'British way', has evidently been unavoidable. Yet great efforts have been made to preserve the control of the civil power, even though the Secretary of State wields powers quite unlike those of any other minister of the Crown, and to preserve the primacy of the police, even though the Royal Ulster Constabulary's role has had to be reversed more than once.

The RUC has indeed been, in many ways, the epicentre of the crisis. Its markedly Protestant composition makes it easy to denounce as a sectarian force. Its disciplinary failure in 1969 was the direct cause of British military intervention. The subsequent attempt to 'normalize' it by disarming it came far too late to have any chance of immediate success.[40] Its seemingly inevitable rearmament then followed the pattern of increasing sophistication established by General Tudor in 1920. An analogous, but still more significant, process has transformed the exclusively Protestant part-time constabulary reserve (the 'B' Specials) into the Ulster Defence Regiment. Officially there was no continuity between the two organizations, and the new one looks on the face of it like a 'third force'. But its undoubted vigilante origins and extreme ethnic divisiveness throw grave doubts on its social effectiveness. Some critics would hold that the UDR's main function is to give the state some degree of control over groups who would otherwise be far more dangerously employed. This is not, however, an argument which looks very well to outsiders.

Appearances notwithstanding, the level of military intervention has been confined to aiding the civil power. The preservation of the semi-military police force has been matched by the preservation of traditional command structures. Neither of these things has generated operational weaknesses to quite the same extent as in 1920–21, largely because an advanced intelligence system was developed fairly rapidly. At the outset, colonial experience in this sphere threatened to be something of a liability. The direct importation of interrogation methods from Aden and elsewhere into a vastly more sensitive and exposed environment led to Britain's indictment by the European Commission on Human Rights for the use of torture.[41] The 'five techniques' as used on the first big batch of detainees swept up in Operation Demetrius were also pronounced illegal in domestic law by a commission under Lord Gardiner.[42] However, modern methods have been more successfully applied in building up computerized information banks at the centre of an integrated intelligence system. Covert intelligence operations also appear to have been more successful than in the past.

The crux of counterinsurgency, however, lies in the concurrent effectiveness of military and police operations. These have been successful, within their political limits, in containing the impact of the insurgency. A professional army may naturally be expected to possess, to a greater extent than a conscript force, the technical skills needed for internal security work. There has never been any question but that when the army has been required, for political reasons, to take major action – as when 'no-go' areas were opened up by Operation Motorman in 1973 – it can achieve its objectives. But technology can be double-edged. It has transformed the power of the portable weapons usable by insurgents, and made possible urban guerrilla operations by very small groups (or cells) with the capacity for very destructive military action. The absolute neutralization of such groups is not, in the political circumstances, feasible. At the same time, modern riot control equipment, whilst highly effective in a technical sense, may reduce the army's social effectiveness.[43]

The deployment of forces has at times been open to criticism. It would be rash at this juncture to hazard an opinion on the value of the SAS; but at the day-to-day level the employment of self-conscious elite units such as paratroops in urban policing has had disastrous results. A single new 'Bloody Sunday' is, in martyrogenic terms, quite enough for a whole generation. The rapid rotation of battalions is militarily preferable to the poorly-planned system of 1919–21, which in fact reduced the Commander-in-Chief to presenting an ultimatum to the Cabinet in May 1921 stating that unless the war had been won by October 'steps must be taken to relieve practically the whole of the troops together with the great majority of the commanders and their staffs'. (The realization that resources were insufficient for this played a major part in the British climbdown.)[44] But short tours of duty are less than ideal for building up public relations and local familiarity.

In the end, it must be repeated that the effectiveness of counterinsurgency is determined by government. Security forces cannot control the political and legal framework within which they act, though their actions may well indirectly alter it. Their success can only be measured by the role assigned to them. In the army's case, its original task of holding apart two communities on the brink of civil war was for a time fulfilled. But prolonged exposure on the streets made that task manifestly impossible. The emergence of 'paramilitary' organizations in both communities altered the context and further isolated the army. It may be thought that the continued employment of troops then became unjustifiable, unless they were seen as the 'only remaining force' to uphold the state. Yet if that were so, the situation would be in a legal sense one of martial law, and the army should operate according to purely military criteria. It has not been permitted to do so, and the resulting situation is a contradictory one. The capacity of the civil courts to function has only been preserved by radically altering their nature. The divisive police forces are further than ever from the English model. Is it true that, given such circumstances, the remedy would be worse than the problem?[45] As it stands, the problem has powerful elements of self-perpetuation, and governmental efforts to hold a line of equilibrium are likely to heighten rather than cure the 'general malaise' which, in the view of the Hennessy inquiry, underlay the dramatic security failure at the Maze gaol in September 1983.[46] Fears of a 'bloodbath' or total societal collapse may be exaggerated, yet the civil war as it is is as bad as any with which Britain has been afflicted. Ireland still seems to be at once too metropolitan to permit the colonial-style departures from the 'British way' which might allow some sort of forcible pacification, and too colonial to compel absolute adhesion to British standards. Disguised military rule may still be better than overt military rule, but there is great force in Colonel Evelegh's contention that the maintenance of the present system involves serious self-deception.[47]

Notes to Chapter II:
The United Kingdom

1. Report of the Interdepartmental Committee on Riots appointed by the Home Secretary, May 1894. Parliamentary Papers XXXV, C.7650.
2. K.O. Fox, 'The Tonypandy Riots', *Army Quarterly* Vol.104 No.1, Oct. 1973.
3. On the history of the STO, K. Jeffery and P. Hennessy, *States of Emergency: British Governments and Strikebreaking since 1919*, London 1983. London District Report, WO 32 3455.
4. Gillian S. Morris, 'The Emergency Powers Act 1920', *Public Law* 1979, p.322.
5. The phrase employed by *The Times*, 8 Feb. 1984.
6. The analysis by G. Cornewall Lewis, *Local Disturbances in Ireland*, London 1836, remains valid. G. Broeker, *Rural Disorder and Police Reform in Ireland 1812–36*, London 1979; S. Clark, *Social Origins of the Irish Land War*, Princeton 1979; M.R. Beames, *Peasants and Power: The Whiteboy Movements and their Control in Pre-famine Ireland*, Brighton 1983.
7. There is no full-scale history of the Irish Constabulary. Cf. C. Townshend, *Political Violence in Ireland. Government and Resistance since 1848*, Oxford 1983, pp.67–84; T. Bowden, *Beyond the Limits of the Law. A Comparative Study of the Police in Crisis Politics*, Harmondsworth 1978, pp.163–70.
8. Gladstone to Spencer, 28 Dec. 1869. BL Add.MS 44306. Townshend, *op.cit.*, p.61.
9. R. Hawkins [ed], 'An Army on Police Work, 1881–2: Ross of Bladensburg's Memorandum', *Irish Sword* Vol.XI, 1973.
10. T.W. Moody (ed), *The Fenian Movement*, Cork 1968. This collection has an extensive bibliography; there is as yet no single major study of Fenianism, but see R.V. Comerford, *The Fenians in Context: Irish Politics and Society 1848–82*, Dublin 1985.
11. Townshend, *Political Violence*, pp.88–99.
12. Ibid., pp.202–3.
13. A.T.Q. Stewart, *The Ulster Crisis*, London 1967.
14. Sir J. Fergusson, *The Curragh Incident*, London 1964; E.R. Holmes, *The Little Field-Marshal: Sir John French*, London 1981.
15. General Sir Nevil Macready, *Annals of an Active Life*, Vol.I, London 1924, p.188.
16. B. Hobson, *Defensive Warfare*, Belfast 1909.
17. Although the Easter Rising has been widely written about, there is

no definitive account. Cf. F.X. Martin [ed], *Leaders and Men of the Easter Rising: Dublin 1916*, London 1967.

18. Townshend, *Political Violence*, pp.310–11.
19. Memorandum by Walter Long, 21 July 1916. Bonar Law papers 63/C/29.
20. Home Office letter, 20 Nov. 1918. CO 904 169. C. Townshend, *The British Campaign in Ireland 1919–1921*, Oxford 1975, p.13.
21. Cabinet Conference, 26 July 1920. PRO CAB.23 22, C.51(20)App.IV.
22. There is a lively account in R. Bennett, *The Black and Tans*, London 1959; for a more recent examination, see Townshend, *The British Campaign in Ireland*.
23. Townshend, *op.cit.*, *passim*.
24. Sir James O'Connor, *A History of Ireland 1798–1924*, London 1925, Vol.2, p.317.
25. Townshend, *op.cit.*, pp.95–7.
26. Commander-in-Chief to Chief Secretary for Ireland, 17 July 1920. Lloyd George papers, F/19/2/12.
27. Cabinet minutes, 2 June 1921. T. Jones, *Whitehall Diary*, London 1971, Vol.3, p.73.
28. Townshend, *British Campaign*, pp.125–8.
29. His own account is in O. de L'E. Winter, *Winter's Tale*, London 1955.
30. Dublin District, Instructions for 26th [Provisional] Brigade. WO 35 93[1]/4.
31. IRA flying column experience is analysed in C. Townshend, 'The Irish Republican Army and the development of guerrilla warfare, 1916–1921', *English Historical Review* XCIV, 1979.
32. B.H. Liddell Hart, foreword to Mao Tse-tung and Che Guevara, *Guerrilla Warfare*, London 1962, p.xiv.
33. Report of exercise, 27 May 1921. AIR 5 776 [Operations of 6th Division in Ireland].
34. *Irish Times*, 3 Jan. 1921.
35. Macready, *op.cit.*, p.590.
36. The best general study of public opinion is D.G. Boyce, *Englishmen and Irish Troubles. British Public Opinion and the Making of Irish Policy 1918–22*, London 1972; but see Townshend, *British Campaign*, p.117.
37. *Irish Independent*, 30 Oct. 1920.
38. European Court of Human Rights, *Ireland v. United Kingdom*, 1978.
39. K.O. Fox, 'Public Order: the Law and the Military', *Army Quarterly*, Vol.104, 1974, p.305.

40. D. G. Boyce, '"Normal Policing": Public Order in Northern Ireland since Partition'. *Eire-Ireland* XIV, 1979.
41. C. Townshend, 'Human Rights in Northern Ireland', in J. Vincent (ed.), *Human Rights and Foreign Policy*, London 1986.
42. Cmnd.5847, 1975.
43. See ch.I above.
44. Memorandum 'B' by Commander-in-Chief Ireland, 23 May 1921. CAB 24 123, CP 2965.
45. Fox, *op.cit.*, p.307.
46. See *The Times*, 8 Feb. 1984.
47. R. Evelegh, *Peace-Keeping in a Democratic Society. The Lessons of Northern Ireland*, London 1978, pp.1–5.

Notes on Further Reading

There are few general histories covering the United Kingdom throughout the twentieth century. Most end or begin in 1914 or 1945. This is true of the most compulsively readable of all, A.J.P. Taylor's *English History 1914–1945* (Clarendon Press, Oxford 1965). The most recent, R. Blake, *The Decline of Power 1915–1964* (Paladin, London 1985), is unconventional in this respect. A. Marwick, *Britain in the Century of Total War* (Bodley Head, London 1968), does provide a synoptic view of the century. A pioneering path has been beaten by K. Jeffery and P. Hennessy in *States of Emergency: British Governments and Strike-breaking since 1919* (Routledge & Kegan Paul, London 1983), though the result is a bit laboured.

The imperial dimension has of course been well worked over. (Though the same periodizations tend to appear.) C. Cross, *The Fall of the British Empire* (Hodder & Stoughton, London 1968), was an early and lucid post-mortem on the whole show. B. Porter, *The Lion's Share: A Short History of British Imperialism* (London 1976, 1984), is widely regarded as the most stimulating single view.

Ireland has been even more fertile. There is a fine general history in F.S.L. Lyons, *Ireland Since the Famine* (Weidenfeld & Nicolson, London 1971), and a history of Irish nationalism in R. Kee, *The Green Flag* (Weidenfeld & Nicolson, London 1972). A challenging recent view is T. Garvin, *The Evolution of Irish Nationalist Politics* (Holmes & Meier, New York 1981). In my book *Political Violence in Ireland* (Oxford University Press 1983) I have tried to provide a survey of the clash between governments and resisters since 1848. On Fenianism, the best work is that of R.V. Comerford, whose most recent book is *The Fenians in Context* (Wolfhound Press, Dublin 1985). His *Charles J. Kickham* (Wolfhound Press, Dublin 1979) is required reading for any study of Irish republicanism, as is Ruth Dudley Edwards' brilliant biography *Patrick Pearse: The Triumph of Failure* (Gollancz, London 1977). There is as yet no full-scale scholarly study of the 1916 rebellion, and in some ways the best general account of the Anglo-Irish struggle is still E. Holt, *Protest in Arms* (Putnam, London 1960). There are plenty of good memoirs, amongst which Tom Barry, *Guerilla Days in Ireland* (Anvil Books, Tralee 1949), and General Sir Nevil Macready, *Annals of an Active Life* (2 vols., Hutchinson, London 1924) are especially important. The high decision-making process is uniquely exposed in Tom Jones' *Whitehall Diary*, edited by K. Middlemas (vol.III, Oxford University Press, London 1971).

The Ulster problem has been deluged with words from all sides, and it is supremely difficult to find any middle ground. Yet it would be hard to think of a better historical work on any subject than A.T.Q.

Stewart's *The Ulster Crisis* (Faber & Faber, London 1967), unless it is his very different but equally illuminating *The Narrow Ground* (Faber & Faber, London 1977). Notwithstanding the author's Unionist sympathies these are models of detachment which have seldom been approached on the other side. An important aspect of the recent troubles has been carefully investigated by P. Taylor in *Beating the Terrorists?* (Penguin Books, Harmondsworth 1980). The changed legal system is ably criticized in K. Boyle, *Law and State: The Case of Northern Ireland* (Martin Robertson, Oxford 1975).

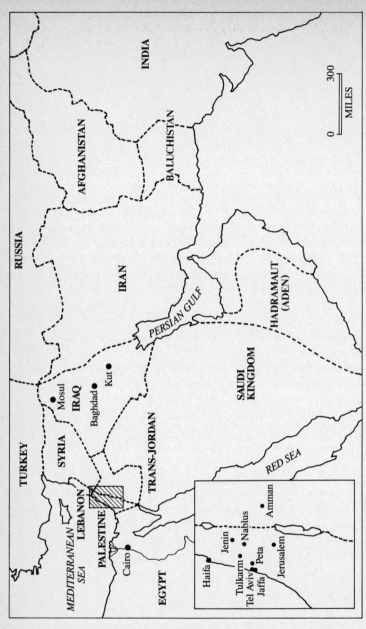

The Middle East 1920 – 48

III

The Middle East

1 The British presence

In the Middle East Britain was confronted with internal problems in a more acute form than anywhere else outside the United Kingdom. The intractability of these problems was partly due to the widespread tradition of resistance to governmental authority, and partly created by British policy itself. Above all, the policy of establishing a Jewish 'national home' in Palestine generated irreconcilable communal antagonisms and a spiral of violence.

The difficulties of the situation manifested themselves at several levels. The most fundamental was the nature of British authority itself. The enormous expansion of British-controlled territory during and after the First World War did not follow the familiar colonial pattern. Before the war, British presence was limited to the periphery of the region rather vaguely labelled the 'Middle East'; Cyprus, Egypt, Aden, Persia, the North-West Frontier of India and Afghanistan. In Egypt Britain created a curious dual-power structure which found its most outlandish expression in the Anglo-Egyptian 'condominium' in the Sudan. Inevitably, given the imbalance of power and pride, this duality was in the last analysis illusory. But it was evidence of a well-founded hesitation to impose straightforward colonial authority. In Afghanistan and Persia also, where the idea of the 'sphere of influence' developed, Britain showed a reluctance – rooted in military and financial weakness – to take direct control. Even before the war, Britain had reached the effective limit of its power.

The sudden and dramatic enlargement of the British presence was triggered by Turkey's entry into the war on the side of the Central Powers. The British reflex action of protecting com-

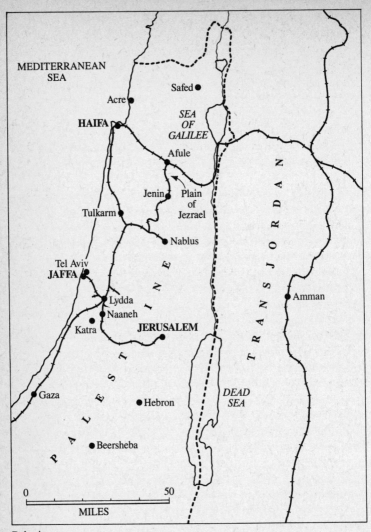

MEDITERRANEAN
SEA

Acre

HAIFA

*SEA
OF
GALILEE*

Safed

Afule

Jenin

Plain
of
Jezrael

Tulkarm

Nablus

Tel Aviv
JAFFA

Lydda
Naaneh

Katra

JERUSALEM

T R A N S J O R D A N

Amman

P
A
L
E
S
T
I
N
E

Gaza

Hebron

*DEAD
SEA*

Beersheba

0   50

MILES

Palestine

munications with India, combined with the restless search for alternative avenues of attack against Germany, produced a series of military offensives in the Middle East. From India a campaign was mounted in Mesopotamia, which in 1915 promised brilliant achievements and brought jarring humiliation. A small, inadequately-supplied army proved operationally superior to the much larger Turkish garrison, but was drawn on by its success and the Napoleonic pretensions of its commander, Sir Charles Townshend, into a strategically hazardous attempt to seize the capital, Baghdad. Townshend was forced to break off his final attack when the Turks called his bluff by standing firm, and his retreat to Kut was followed by an agonizingly long siege. His surrender in April 1916 was a blow to British prestige only partly avenged by the creation of a major base at Basra and the build-up of an army capable of steamrollering the Turkish defenders and finally capturing Baghdad in March 1917.

The British triumph in Palestine was more resounding. The forces from Egypt under Allenby took Jerusalem in December 1917, and on the 11th Allenby made his entry into the city on foot. This pious action displayed an awareness of the historic responsibilities which Britain was taking up, though it is doubtful whether Allenby could foresee their eventual scale. His onward advance into Syria automatically created an administrative vacuum. To fill it, a temporary military government was set up, so that Britain at first exercised control by old-fashioned right of conquest. This fact was to be used more than once in the future to curb the pretensions of both Zionists and Arab nationalists. But there could be no question of this simple relationship persisting: the question was, what sort of relationship should replace it? When British control of Palestine and Mesopotamia (but not Syria, of which Palestine had usually been regarded as the southern part) was regularized in the postwar settlement, it was put on a novel basis. Instead of outright colonial rule, or even a more veiled form of control such as a 'protectorate', authority was conferred by Mandate of the League of Nations. Power was explicitly coupled with responsibility. The idea of gradual progress towards self-government, which was vaguely promised in the rest of the Empire, was subject here to international scrutiny and definite timetabling.

In the case of Palestine, Britain's responsibilities were specified with particular exactness. The specification was in fact laid out initially by Britain itself, in the form of the Balfour Declaration of 1917. The motives underlying the Declaration have been widely debated. Altruism and the exigencies of war both played a part, but the important thing for the future was that the terms of the undertaking formed the grounds of both government and resistance. Britain promised to facilitate 'the establishment in Palestine of a national home for the Jewish people', with the proviso that this development should not 'prejudice the civil and religious rights of existing non-Jewish communities'. The League of Nations Mandate substantially repeated this tall order. The fact that it did not look impossibly tall at the time attests to certain tacit assumptions which were crucial to the exercise of British rule in the Middle East.

The first assumption was that the Arabs would not, or at least ought not to, object to the growth of the Jewish community. There was, after all, a vast expanse of territory (all pretty much of a muchness from the Western standpoint), liberated from Ottoman oppression by British arms, nearly all of which was to be handed over – one way or another – to the Arabs. There was no idea that a specifically Palestinian as well as a more generalized Arab nationalism would have to be considered. It was assumed, moreover, that Palestine was a semi-derelict country which would be restored to prosperity by Jewish enterprise (the view energetically propounded by the Zionist Organization). Nothing would actually be taken away from the Arab population, in an economic sense at least. At the political level, it has sometimes been suggested that the British government did not originally entertain the idea of a Jewish national *state* as such, and that it was unprepared for the aggressive ambitions of the Zionists. The studied vagueness of the phrase 'national home . . . in Palestine' appears, on the face of it, to support this suggestion, as does the awful irony of a later High Commissioner's observation (in October 1941) that the Zionist movement 'cannot be cleared of the charge that it has been misdirected to the creation of a national-socialist state rather than a national home'.[1] It is quite clear, however, that the leading British policymakers – Lloyd George, Bonar Law, Churchill – had no doubt from the start that they were talking about an eventual Jewish state. What is equally clear is that they assumed that the eventuality would be far – perhaps centuries – distant. This assumption was implicit in the notion of the 'economic absorbtive capacity' of Palestine which was to govern the rate of Jewish immigration. The political viability of the concept depended on Jewish immigration remaining a mere trickle. The general belief was that few Jews would take up or stick out the challenge of Palestine.

Only thus could the Balfour declaration be squared with the promises simultaneously made to encourage the Arab national revolt against Turkey. These promises were given their most resonant form in the Anglo-French declaration of 8 November 1918 that 'the goal envisaged . . . in prosecuting in the East the war set in train by German ambition' was the 'complete and final liberation of the peoples who have for so long been oppressed by the Turks, and the setting up of national governments' deriving their authority from popular choice. By one of those errors that regularly vitiate the credibility of governments, the British intention of excluding Palestine from this promise was not communicated to the authorities in Jerusalem in time to prevent the declaration from being published there.[2]

The assumption of a protracted timescale also underlay British strategic thinking about Palestine. Here the Balfour Declaration and the Mandate unquestionably masked a powerful impulse of self-interest. When the Committee of Imperial Defence examined the strategic importance of Palestine in 1923, it accepted that 'to lose Palestine is to lose Arabia'. The security of Egypt depended on 'isolation from both physical and moral attack'; and since the security of Egypt was the guarantee of secure communications with India, it is clear that Palestine was first and foremost a bulwark of Indian defence. Despite the Montagu-Chelmsford reforms by which 'dyarchy' was established, full self-government for India remained a distant, and to many an unthinkable prospect. (In this sense there is an element of logic in the fact that the two were eventually abandoned at roughly the same time.) Palestine was also to become an important link in the chain of oil movement.[3] Without accepting the extreme view propounded by, amongst others, Menachem Begin, that Britain pursued a calculated 'divide and rule' strategy, it is obvious that the protracted task envisaged in Palestine justified a long-term British strategic presence. Merely to assist Arab states towards self-government would not provide this: the British mandate in Iraq was to be terminated in 1927, the French mandate in Syria in 1936.

As a novel basis of authority, the mandates raised novel problems of governmental form. It is significant that the British administration was vested in the Colonial Office, via a special section, the Middle East Department [MED]. The Foreign Office at first assumed that it would oversee the region, but it was outmanoeuvred by the determination and agility of Winston Churchill. To a great extent the shape of the modern Middle East is Churchill's work. As Secretary of State for War and Air in 1919–20 he fostered the concept of air control, which was to be of central importance in the machinery of British rule; and as Colonial Secretary from January 1921 he established the outline (separating Transjordan from Palestine, to the dismay of the Zionists) and the political structure of the Arab states (forwarding the adoption of the Sherifian princes as rulers of Transjordan and Iraq). The lines of his policy were laid out at the Cairo Conference in March 1921, a highly Churchillian event facetiously labelled a 'durbar' by one commentator.[4] The dominant political imperative was made crystal clear when the Colonial Secretary, in the same writer's words, 'harangued the assembled consuls and pro-consuls' on 'the hardships, the suffering and the misery, of the poverty and unemployment in Great Britain', and urged the 'paramount necessity of relieving the British taxpayer'. The motif of financial retrenchment was to run henceforth through all British imperial history. (Some wondered, only half in jest, 'whether England today can afford such a luxury as a foreign policy, with or without mandates'.)[5] The new Middle Eastern territories were to be administered on the cheap, and the extent to which security could be risked in the interest of economy was to remain uncertain. The resulting balancing act by the local administrations was of critical importance in determining the events of the next decade.

2 The Palestine problem 1917–27

Few Imperial posts possessed the cultural echoes of 'the seat of Pilate'. 'There is no promotion after Jerusalem,' wrote the first military governor of the city, Ronald Storrs. The army officers who staffed the Occupied Enemy Territory Administration [OETA] in Palestine set to work with a certain sense of mission. Bringing what they saw as all that was best in British traditions of overseas administration to a neglected land, they made rapid and impressive strides in raising standards of public health and education. But for all its efficiency and impartiality, OETA lacked a sense of long-term purpose. It was, in a way, an illustration of the bankruptcy of pure efficiency. Its political brief was narrow and rigid: following Chapter 14, Articles 353 et seq. of the *Manual of Military Law*, it aimed at preserving the status quo. No doubt this was an admirable improvement on the earlier practice of conquerors. As the *Manual* observed, it was 'no longer considered permissible' for a military administrator to 'work his will unhindered, altering the existing form of government, upsetting the constitution and domestic laws and ignoring the rights of the inhabitants'.

The initial assumption, of course, was that OETA would be short-lived – a matter of months rather than years. In the event, this holding operation went on for nearly three years, from late 1917 until mid-1920. This was a long time to try to hold to an immobilist policy, especially in the wake of the Balfour Declaration. The millenarian hopes inevitably excited amongst Jews ensured that the administration would be subjected to tremendous Zionist pressure. The methods and aims of this Zionist activity are well enough known; here it is necessary to concentrate on the powers and the duties of the administration. Zionists repeatedly charged it with pro-Arab (or anti-Semitic) bias. OETA responded, justly according to its lights, that in the circumstances a duty to uphold the status quo was bound to appear, in the eyes of a Zionist enthusiast, to favour the Arabs. Like it or not, Arabs were the vast majority of the population. What is perhaps most remarkable about this three-year period is that the British Government saw no need to instruct the Palestine administration to modify this immobile policy in the light of the Balfour Declaration.[6] There seems to have been no sense of any need for rapid action.

The resulting drift had important, possibly disastrous consequences for the whole British position in Palestine. From the
outset the British showed their characteristic knack of getting
the worst of both worlds, by seeming pro-Zionist at the level of
Westminster policy-making and anti-Zionist at the level of local
implementation. Thus important elements amongst the leadership groups (if not yet the majority) of both sides were antagonized. There was a long way to go before either would directly or
violently challenge British rule, but the violence of the Jerusalem
riots in Easter week 1920 – which marked the beginning of the
end for OETA – was ominous. The riots were not an insurrection, but they were a warning of the way in which the explosive
fusion of communal and religious antagonisms could undermine
Britain's capacity to maintain order.

In particular the powerful combination of secular Arab
nationalism (embracing both Moslem and Christian Arabs)
with the religious enthusiasm (or, as the British persistently
called it, fanaticism) of the Moslem majority, instantly de-
molished the tacit premise of the Balfour Declaration that there
would be no significant Arab resistance to the establishment of
a Jewish national home. In Jerusalem the Nabi Musa pilgrimage
began on Friday 2 April in traditional manner, with the gathering of pilgrims from villages all over Palestine around their local
banners. The religious processions which made up the pilgrimage
had military undertones which had traditionally been simultaneously stressed and controlled by the Turkish government's
practice of supplying some three or four thousand troops as a
ceremonial escort which both honoured the procession and
inhibited its turbulence. Such extravagant use of manpower was
unthinkable to the British authorities for both military and
political reasons. The Chief Military Administrator in 1920
refused to allow any use of troops for ceremonial purposes, and
refused at first to furnish even the military band which the
British army, following Turkish practice, had since 1917 provided. Here he followed Allenby's direct orders as C-in-C
Middle East, reflecting Zionist – and perhaps also Christian –
protests against any appearance of official participation in
Moslem rites.

In the event, Storrs secured a military band on the Friday,
but no military forces were on the streets to assist the weak city

police force in controlling the processions on the following days. On the morning of Sunday 4 April, with the arrival of a column of pilgrims from Hebron, a grim drama commenced. A quite new 'tradition', which seems to have been started in 1919, caused the procession to halt at frequent intervals to hear speeches. The police realized that the speeches this year were openly political – supporting the Sherifian claim that Faisal's kingdom of Syria (including Palestine) should be immediately recognized – but had neither orders nor inclination to intervene. Their sole contribution was to reroute the procession once it became clear that the speechmaking had resulted in a long delay. (Zionists were to allege that the rerouting by the Jaffa Gate, past the Jewish quarter, showed that the authorities were instigating a pogrom.)

Storrs has recorded his horror when an orderly brought him the ominous news, 'there has been an outbreak at the Jaffa Gate, and a man has been wounded to death'.[7] Worse was to follow, and Storrs' actions to stifle the outbreak were not altogether effectual. As Arabs attacked the Jewish quarter armed with sticks, stones and knives, the available troops turned out. One British (1st Yorks) and elements of two Indian battalions (20th Punjabis and 51st Sikhs) brought the city centre under control, forming an outer cordon to isolate the inner city, with close picquets to regulate movement within it. But by an inexplicable decision the outer cordon was withdrawn overnight, and the inner picquets were concentrated in the old Turkish barracks by the Jaffa Gate. A military committee of inquiry was later unable to do more than record conflicting evidence over this 'very serious error of judgment', but it indicated little inclination to accept Storrs' contention that he only envisaged the withdrawal of the outer cordon to permit the normal flow of food supplies to the city.

With the military presence removed, violence broke out again in full force on Monday, and martial law was eventually proclaimed at 3 p.m. Even after this, as the military inquiry disapprovingly recorded, looting continued for nearly twenty-four hours, the disturbances gradually petering out by the evening of Tuesday 6 April. The total recorded casualties were 251, of whom 216 were Jews. Five of these were killed (two by troops) and eighteen dangerously wounded (nearly all by knives, stones and sticks), as against four Moslems killed (all by gun-shot) and one dangerously wounded.[8]

This riot, or communal war, has been looked at in some detail here because its sudden eruption starkly foreshadowed the recurrent problem faced by the British Mandate. The regular repetition of ritual gatherings – on a scale which dwarfed the processional challenges of Northern Ireland – provided a permanent mechanism for triggering and shaping violent conflict. In this case the Chief Military Administrator actually approved the procession on the grounds that it acted as a safety valve for popular emotion. But even had he not done so, the administration was in no position to prohibit it. The maintenance of order required machinery of control.

The military committee of inquiry fell foul of Storrs (whose mockery appeared in print, while the committee's report remained, for political reasons, unpublished), and has been criticized by a recent scholar.[9] Yet it produced some important conclusions. It may have exceeded its brief in trying to analyse the long-term causes of communal tension in Palestine, but it was surely right to insist that in spite of ample evidence of the involvement of political activists in the Nabi Musa procession on 4 April, the riots could not be dismissed as 'manufactured'. They represented deep-seated popular forces which would certainly manifest themselves again in the future. The only prospect of control lay in the broad sphere of policy, and to a more limited extent in the narrower sphere of policing. In the political sphere, immigration was identified as the key issue on which both sides would judge the attitude and intentions of the British government. The critical defect in the administration's capacity to cope with the outbreak was the weak and poorly trained police force, a mere 8 officers and 183 other ranks as against an estimated minimum requirement of 14 and 370. The estimate had been made by the OETA Assistant Administrator of Public Security as early as June 1919, but financial restrictions had prohibited recruitment. (Here the committee struck a note that was to echo down the years.) It drew attention, also, to the 'curious defects in the intelligence system', which had led, amongst other things, to the administration being in ignorance of the creation of an armed Jewish defence force (*Haganah*) by Vladimir Jabotinsky.[10]

Perhaps the most significant long-term aspect of the Palestine situation, pointed out by the committee as both a trigger to communal strife and a mechanism for possible insurgency, was 'the extent to which the Zionist Commission had assumed the role of a full-blown Administration'. By 1920 the *Yishuv* already had its own courts of law. Based on the old Jewish system of arbitration, these had expanded (as the Dail Arbitration courts were threatening to do in Ireland at the same time) into 'a complete system of judicature within the country'. Worse, as with the Dail courts, there was 'reason to suspect that sub-mission to these courts is not always voluntary'. There was an effort to establish supervision over Jewish recruits to the police, and to set up a Jewish militia. The Zionist intelligence organiz-ation was far more developed and efficient than the govern-ment's, and there was even a separate Zionist public health administration deploying American funds. Taken altogether, the pattern of growth of a Jewish state within the state fully justified the committee's stark warning that such a development represented a 'grave danger to the public peace' and prejudice to the government. The situation was, it declared, 'in truth, intolerable'.

It was to be tolerated, one way and another, for over twenty-five years, but its fatal outcome was clearly foreseeable from the beginning. Nothing was done to avert this outcome. Indeed, the reverse was the case: the civil government which was established after the winding-up of OETA pursued, *faute de mieux*, the creation of parallel institutions for Arabs and Jews. The in-tention was to reconcile Arabs to the Mandate by providing a measure of self-government, but its effect was to accentuate the gulf between the two communities.[11]

The 1920 disorders doomed the military government to belated extinction. A High Commissioner took office at the end of June 1920, though the basis of his authority remained a military one until the Mandate was regularized in 1923. The outgoing Chief Military Administrator, Sir Louis Bols, had rounded on the Palestinian community leaders with rough words – 'I am supported by so powerful a military force that I can crush any disturbance of the peace, and I tell you that in future I shall use these strong forces without restraint . . . force will be met by force.'[12] The first High Commissioner, Sir

Herbert Samuel, arrived to pursue a different line, seeking compromise and reconciliation. As a Jew himself he was expected by the Government to be able to restrain Zionist enthusiasm, but this hope, like so many others, proved groundless. The impression of calm, orderly progress fostered by the Cairo Conference in March 1921, which followed eight months of Samuel's conciliatory proconsulship, was rudely shattered in May, when the May Day demonstration of the Jewish 'Bolshevik' organization (MPS) in Tel Aviv-Jaffa brought on riots even more violent and widespread than those of the previous year.

On the first day of rioting, 3 Arabs and 27 Jews were killed – 17 of the latter beaten to death – and 34 Arabs and 104 Jews wounded (13 by gunshot, 4 by bomb-blast, 44 by knives and 43 by stones or sticks). The Commission of Inquiry judged that, as in 1920, the Arabs were 'the first to turn this quarrel into a race conflict', and 'behaved with a savagery which cannot be condoned'.[13] Jaffa was brought under control by the imposition of martial law on 3 May, but conflict broke out at other settlements, Petah Tiqvah, Kfar Saba and Rehovot, where Arab attacks were opposed by troops with air support. An Arab crowd assembling to attack Hebron was broken up and driven off by aircraft.

The disturbances were a disastrous setback to Samuel's policy, but he assured Zionist leaders on 8 May that 'coercion could not be applied to this country, otherwise we should have a second Ireland'.[14] Instead he confronted the issue of Jewish immigration, and decided to suspend it temporarily. The resulting determination of Zionist extremists to use force if necessary against the government was something totally unanticipated by British policy. Signs of a real crisis of will within the government now appeared, and were never altogether to disappear. The C-in-C Middle East told Churchill that unless policy was radically altered, 'sooner or later the whole country will be in a state of insurrection' which would be beyond the control of the available military forces.[15] Samuel advised the granting of a representative assembly in Palestine in line with the promises made to Arabs elsewhere, a proposal which brought Zionist leaders to the brink of despair. Churchill, however, sternly replied that 'to make such a concession under pressure would be to rob it of half its value', and reasserted the conventional piety: 'We must firmly maintain law and order and make concessions on the merits and not under duress'.[16]

This statesmanlike formula was easier to voice than to realize. As in Ireland, it seemed to mean in effect that constructive policy, however much merited, could not proceed while it might look like concession to violence. Without any political action, the means of maintaining law and order remained doubtful. The delay in declaring martial law in Jaffa – Samuel only gave way reluctantly to the urging of the District Governor – was discussed by the Commission of Inquiry. Sensibly, if rather patronizingly, it observed that even though the government might have felt that no measurable advantage would be secured by declaring martial law, 'soldiers are not lawyers, and they will not ordinarily incur the very serious risks . . . of taking the means necessary to deal with violence unless protected by a declaration of martial law'.[17] This modest contribution to the longstanding debate on emergency powers was to be ignored in future crises. Efforts were made to strengthen the police and to build up a *gendarmerie* to cope with serious disorder.

Palestine was to serve as a testing ground for the theory, if not the practice, of the 'third force'. The obvious brittleness of the part-Arab, part-Jewish police quieted any traditional British doubts about the desirability of *gendarmeries*, and Colonel Wyndham Deedes set about organizing a mixed force on semi-military lines. (The original idea had been, at the insistence of the MED's military adviser, Colonel Richard Meinertzhagen, a segregated force. But as Deedes wrote after the May troubles, such a system 'seemed to emphasize the division in the community and to promise something in the nature of a civil war in the event of further troubles'.)[18] Eventually, apprehensions about the reliability of any 'native' recruits led to the formation of 'a picked force of white gendarmerie'. These were none other than General Tudor's Black and Tans brought across from Ireland, where they had recently been made redundant by their failure to preserve the United Kingdom. Tudor undertook to provide 7–800 'absolutely reliable men' of the RIC Auxiliary Division, and was confident that many more of the doomed RIC would be happy to transfer, bringing with them their own equipment and a number of vehicles. This was a specialist counterinsurgency force on the cheap. Meinertzhagen thought 'they are a magnificent lot of men and should acquit themselves well'. Churchill expressed confidence that 'the spectacle of these men riding about the country' would have a major impact.[19]

This remarkable development did not pass entirely without comment. The permanent secretary of the new Middle East Department felt that it was 'a matter of political importance that the force should not be transferred as a unit to Palestine'.[20] But the likely effect of the Black and Tan ethos on the infant police system in Palestine does not seem to have been discussed. It was, predictably, considerable. Together with the ever-present financial stringency, which led to repeated reductions and reconstructions of the police over the next twenty-five years, it stood in the way of building an ordinary civil police organization and outlook in circumstances that were never less than difficult.

The fumbling arrangements made to cope with civil emergency after 1921 were not tested for a long time. Thanks to factors outside the government's control – economic depression and a marked reduction in the number of Jews trying to enter Palestine – a period of quiet followed the 1921 explosion. Four years of calm in Palestine was a long time, and when Field-Marshal Plumer succeeded Samuel as High Commissioner in 1925, he was confident that all regular military forces could be removed from the country. The Palestine Gendarmerie, already knocked about by financial pruning, was unceremoniously broken up – its etiolated British section transferred to the Palestine police, its native section to the newly-formed Trans-jordan Frontier Force.[21]

3 Transjordan

Churchill's decision to detach Transjordan from Palestine was vigorously but unsuccessfully opposed by Samuel as well as by extreme Zionists, who saw it as dividing *eretz Israel*. The separation created a doubly curious administrative framework, with both the High Commissioner and the military C-in-C (or Air Officer Commanding) responsible for the whole area, yet in practice increasingly distant from the state which began to form at Amman. Feisal's brother, Abdullah, became Emir with quasi-independent status; his civil and military advisers, the

Chief British Representative and the AOC at Amman, likewise drifted away from their superiors in Jerusalem. Abdullah's own police force, the Arab Legion under a British commander, Peake Pasha, was something of a law unto itself.

Partly as a result of Churchill's decision, which abruptly halted the inflow of Jewish settlers, the new sub-state had relatively few internal security problems. Those which did arise were less intractable than those in Palestine, and proved amenable to the RAF's new air policing techniques. Air control, primarily tailored, as will be seen, for Mesopotamia, was well adapted to dealing with periodic tribal disturbances or incursions of external invaders, of whom the most ferocious and persistent were the fundamentalist Islamic sect of Wahabis. The formidable irruption of 3000 Wahabis in August 1924 struck terror into the settled tribes, but was turned back from Amman with surprising ease and cut to ribbons by a small RAF armoured car force. Despite the crushing success of the riposte, some unease was felt at the slow channel of decision which had to run back from Amman to Jerusalem, and at the fact that the Wahabis had got so close to the capital in such strength without the Arab Legion 'knowing anything about it or being able to operate in any way'.[22] The formation of a new *gendarmerie*, the Transjordan Frontier Force (TJFF), provided the effective ground support on which the air control scheme depended, and thereafter no major disorder was experienced. The awesome Wahabis remained a threat to public security in spite of Trenchard's efforts to denounce their *jihad* as a looting campaign. The fear of slaughter of all males, adults and children alike, paralysed the development of a settled community. But after 1924 the state had no occasion to see them as a challenge at the political level.

4 Iraq: insurrection and air control

The three provinces (*vilayats*) of the Ottoman empire which made up the land known as Mesopotamia were richly varied in nature. Kurdistan (Mosul) was sometimes compared with the Scottish Highlands, in both physical and socio-economic terms. The riverine area of the Tigris and Euphrates had produced settled cultivation and some urban development, while the desert in the west was still the sphere of nomads. Altogether the extent and range of territory presented a formidable problem of control.

The British ambition to control Mesopotamia was evident from the time of Townshend's campaign, but equally marked was a concern with financial economy. The particular difficulties created by the endemic disturbance of the tribal territories were to produce a dramatic shift in internal security methods after 1920. As early as April 1920, while still Secretary for War and Air, Churchill threw his weight into an attack on the cost of traditional military methods of control. His fertile imagination had already pictured a system both economical and spectacular. His memorandum on 'Mesopotamian Expenditure' protested against the 'vicious system' by which the Foreign Office could more or less dictate the distribution of military garrisons, so that 'a score of mud villages, sandwiched between a swampy river and a blistering desert, inhabited by a few hundred half naked native families' were occupied by regular troops 'on a scale which in India would maintain order in wealthy provinces of millions of people'.[23] The only way of achieving economy would be to hand over control of Mesopotamia to the Colonial Office, which should then specify a fixed annual expenditure. It could take a giant step towards reducing expenditure by transferring military responsibility from the army to the air force.

Churchill's vision of air control, which crystallized in conversations with the Chief of the Air Staff, Sir Hugh Trenchard, was almost revolutionary. Seizing on the unprecedented mobility of aircraft, they held that even a vast land like Mesopotamia could be garrisoned at two or at most three centres. 'An ample system of landing grounds judiciously selected,' Churchill mused to Trenchard, 'would enable these air forces to operate in every part of the protectorate and to enforce control, now here, now there, without the need of maintaining long lines of communication'.[24] Not only would such a garrison be more economical than traditional ground forces, it would also be more effective than such forces in the sort of operations with which Britain was already familiar on the North-West Frontier. The speed with which tribal insurrections were generated could only be matched by the speed of reaction of aircraft.

Air operations, moreover, would not offer the tribesmen their favourite target – the cumbersome 'punitive column' with its line of communication which all too often proved a source of weapons and booty for the insurgents. Aircraft could strike but could not (it was thought) be struck. Even this priceless quality of invulnerability did not exhaust the catalogue of assets. A crowning advantage of the scheme was the suitability of air forces for operations in extreme heat. The damage to the human material of marching columns in such conditions was always severe. The efficiency of even the best units was rapidly impaired. But the endurance and reliability of machines should be much greater, and the physical fitness of aircrew could be maintained in ways previously inconceivable. At the central aerodromes there would be 'good buildings and . . . modern amenities such as electric fans and light, good food carefully prepared by expert professional cooks, served in comfortable central halls, under the guidance of expert caterers . . .' The air enthusiasts looked into the future, and it was bright. The reality over the next decade – as T.E. Lawrence's experiences attested – was remote from the vision; but the vision remained none the less powerful for all that.[25]

A month after Churchill's memorandum, an unpleasant reminder of the past was provided when most of Mesopotamia was engulfed in sudden insurrection. A couple of apparently trivial incidents led to the mobilization of over 100,000 tribesmen, at least half of whom were armed with modern rifles. This was open rebellion rather than insurgency, but the Arab fighters' methods were unconventional enough to bemuse the Imperial soldiers who poured into the country to suppress the outbreak. For the benefit of newly arrived troops the General Staff in Mesopotamia prepared 'Notes on Modern Arab Warfare', which opened with the observation that 'the Arab is most treacherous', but went on to express reluctant admiration for the military capacities of the tribesmen. 'They flock to the banner of their shaikh and then to the sound of the guns, moving and collecting with a rapidity little short of marvellous . . . They make very skilful defensive dispositions, and show considerable cunning in the selection of time and place to interfere with water supply, railway, or line of march.' They were always short of ammunition (which explained the relative immunity of military camps from sniping), careful shots, on the lookout for opportunities to overwhelm small detachments and seize their weapons. Their 'inherent dislike of getting killed' could on occasion be overcome by religious fanaticism or greed for loot. Their real weakness in formal combat was their lack of a command structure: 'they can rarely alter plans once made or make new ones to meet a new situation'.[26]

The insurrection was systematically crushed by General Sir Aylmer Haldane, but only after he had been reinforced with two divisions. Punitive columns brought every village to submission (often by reducing it to ashes), and extracted collective fines totalling 817,000 rupees, 63,435 rifles (21,154 of them modern), and 3,185,000 rounds of ammunition. It galled Churchill to have to supply such large forces so soon after complaining about the cost of the garrison, and he tried every shift to avoid reinforcing Haldane.[27] At one point he reflected that 'it was an extraordinary thing that the British civil administration should have succeeded in such a short time in alienating the whole country to such an extent that the Arabs have laid aside the blood feuds they have nursed for centuries . . .' But in the end the methodical suppression of the rising was so complete that financial retrenchment could be resumed with gratifying speed.

The key to this was the political strategy of placing King Feisal – now baulked by the French of his Syrian ambitions – on the throne of Iraq. (The Arabic name for the country derived from the low cliff that formed its western desert boundary.) General Haldane, after his brief hour of absolute authority, returned to a less than cordial relationship with the High Commissioner, Sir Percy Cox. Haldane was unimpressed by both his celebrated civil colleagues, Cox and his predecessor, Sir Arnold Wilson. He observed that even a military officer 'seems to lose all sense of military principles soon after he joins the civil administration. If permitted, he would like to scatter broadcast the forces, often small in number, which are available for the maintenance of order.' Nonetheless Haldane came, like Wilson, to endorse the feasibility of Churchill's concept of air control. In January 1921 he was still convinced that air power could not be substituted for ground troops, but by June he had changed his view. He was now convinced, on the basis of careful tests and observation, 'that disturbances can be checked or prevented from arising by aircraft, and that unless, which is improbable, rebellion were to arise in every corner at once, the sudden arrival of aeroplanes on several days should act as a preventative'. He now thought, indeed, 'that had I had sufficient aircraft last year I might have prevented the insurrection spreading beyond the first incident at Rumaithah'.[28]

In the meantime Sir Arnold Wilson had prepared an even more enthusiastic paper on the effect of air power, holding that it would soon enable the government to dispense with all ground forces except the local levies. These views were re-inforced by local opinions – the Divisional Adviser at Nasiriyeh reported that 'Aeroplanes are now really feared'; the Political Officer at Sulaimani noted that 'throughout the whole of the disturbances here, the aeroplanes have been most successful. It is astonishing how frightened the tribesmen are of them'.[29]

Churchill's old department did not give up without a fight. When he presented a memorandum to the Cabinet on 'Policy and Finance in Mesopotamia' in August 1921, arguing that only air control could provide a reasonable degree of internal and external security 'within the financial limits, which are inviolate', the War Office riposted roughly. Churchill's successor, Worthington-Evans, held that 'the only weapons which can be used by the Air Force are bombs and machine guns'. These might suffice to repel external attack, but the forces in Mesopotamia were 'intended to keep order and gradually to reconcile hostile tribes to a civilized rule'. For this task 'the only means at the disposal of the Air Force, and the means in fact now used, are the bombing of women and children in the villages'. He wound up icily, 'If the Arab population realize that the peaceful control of Mesopotamia ultimately depends on our intention of bombing women and children, I am very doubtful if we shall gain that acquiescence . . . to which the Secretary of State for the Colonies looks forward.'[30] This powerful fusion of ethical and pragmatic objections was to reappear many times in the future, in the mouth of senior military officers as well as liberal opinion. But it did not prevail against the argument of financial economy.

All that remained for the RAF to do was to elaborate an operational repertoire by which air control could be made a reality, and to produce evidence of its success. These tasks were satisfactorily completed after it took control of Mesopotamia in October 1922. There was some recognition amongst airmen of moral issues such as those raised by the Secretary of State for War. The air weapon, although portrayed as a rapier in contrast to the bludgeon of the traditional military punitive column, was nevertheless a sledgehammer in its impact on its victims. There was an obvious need to develop techniques short of, and perhaps also beyond, bombing and machine-gunning. The refinement of tactical doctrine to meet this need fell – fortunately for the RAF – to the brightest of its rising stars, Air Vice Marshal Sir John Salmond.

Salmond's first approach was to take a frankly terrorist line, to break the nerve of those who challenged the government. The word 'frightfulness', so recently associated with German war crimes, was used in RAF internal memoranda. The idea was that occasional demonstrations of terrifying destructive power, using delayed-action bombs, phosphorus bombs, 'liquid fire', shrapnel, smoke and gas, would establish the credibility and moral ascendancy of aircraft. Normally a mere overflight ('demonstration flight') would be enough to deter tribesmen planning to take up arms. Efficient watchfulness – i.e. frequent patrolling – would maximize this demonstrative effect. (Although there were some who argued that the moral effect of aircraft would inexorably diminish as the Arabs became familiar with both their powers and their limitations.) Salmond recognized the 'stigma' attached to air action, the 'cruel necessity of killing not only non-combatants but people innocent of any complicity'; but he always insisted that the short, sharp shock administered from the air was in the end the most merciful method.[31]

In the first flush of enthusiasm, some time was spent on the prospect of developing gas bombs for internal security use. The airmen thought that these would have an 'excellent moral effect', though their ardour was dampened by the feeling that the League of Nations might not approve of such weapons being used by a mandatory power. Pragmatic objections were raised as well: Meinertzhagen noted that in Morocco the Moors were killing one Spanish prisoner for every gas bomb dropped, and such retaliation was 'infectious'.[32] Gradually, the RAF worked out a method which did not depend on killing at all. (At least of humans; animals were to remain an attractive target.) Salmond pointed out in 1924 that it was already 'a commonplace here that aircraft achieve their result by their effect on morale, and by the material damage they do . . . and not through the infliction (*sic*) of casualties'. He produced a vivid image of the power of air action to 'knock the roofs of huts about and prevent their repair, a considerable inconvenience in wintertime'. It could 'seriously interfere with ploughing or harvesting – a vital matter; or burn up the stores of fuel laboriously piled up and garnered for the winter; by attack on livestock, which is the main form of capital and source of wealth to the less settled tribes, it can impose in effect a considerable fine, or seriously interfere with the actual food source of the tribe'. In the end, he noted, 'the tribesman finds it is much the best to obey the Government'.[33]

The complacent conclusion was vindicated, at the technical level, by the elaboration of this local interdiction method, which came to be called 'air blockade'. The parallel with long-established naval precedent was obvious, and was always used by the RAF to counter allegations of inhumanity. The air force made good its claim to manage Iraq. Not only was internal turbulence gradually suppressed, but when a Turkish invasion threatened to detach the province of Mosul from the control of Baghdad, only the air weapon (wielded with neo-Nelsonian independence by Salmond) could restore the situation.[34] For good or ill, therefore, the RAF was the midwife of modern Iraq.

5 Palestine 1929–39

The success of the air control scheme in Iraq was an important element in Trenchard's strategy for establishing the identity of the RAF as a separate service. It led him to press on the claim of air power to substitute for conventional military garrisons throughout the Empire on a scale that was perhaps imprudent. At the crest of Trenchard's wave, in 1929, the RAF suffered a severe setback in Palestine, and its position was subsequently more equivocal. The setback was not altogether the fault of the RAF itself. Airmen had always recognized that Palestine did not offer the same scope for air control as other Middle Eastern territories. The problems encountered there were not those of vast empty spaces: this was a small country with a relatively large urban population. The RAF made it clear from the start that the role of air power in countering urban riots would be limited. But it believed that a reliable local *gendarmerie* could be created which would practically obviate the need for regular troops. Lord Plumer, backed by the Colonial Secretary, Leo Amery, went further than the RAF intended in the mid-1920s by dismantling the Palestine Gendarmerie without ensuring that the Palestine police force reached a level of effectiveness which would make it a match for serious communal disturbance.

The makings of such disturbance were easy enough to see. The problem, as with all endemic conflict, was to identify the moment at which it would erupt. The mechanics of crowd action are notoriously difficult to analyse, and in 1929, as in 1920 and 1921, the precise process by which tension shifts to open violence remained concealed. But it is clear that the possibilities of intervention to prevent or inhibit the spread of the riots were severely limited by the weakness of the Palestine Government's security forces as well as its political position. The crucial moment of decision was probably 15 August, when the Government decided not to ban a Jewish demonstration at the Western Wall (or 'Wailing Wall') in Jerusalem. This demonstration was an intentionally provocative assertion of the Jews' right of access to the wall – an issue whose intractability could be taken to stand for the Palestine problem as a whole. The intractability was both cultural and physical, since the Western Wall of the old Jewish temple was the foundation of the *Haram ash-Sharif*, the third most holy place of Islam.

The Government's decision was taken in the light of the knowledge that the police force was too weak, and also too unreliable, to enforce a ban. The issue of the wall itself, unlike, say, the issue of immigration, was outside the scope of government power. The attempt to preserve the old Turkish status quo (giving Jews a customary but not prescriptive right of access to the open space at the foot of the wall, and no right to bring religious furniture there) had already infuriated Zionists. An attempt to impose conditions on the demonstration would certainly have been seen by Moslems as virtually giving official approval to the Jewish claim. So the government neither granted

nor withheld permission for the demonstration, which culminated predictably in the raising of the Zionist flag and singing of
the *Hatikvah*, the national anthem of the putative Zionist state,
by the would-be national soldiers of the *Haganah*. The inevitable Arab counter-demonstration on the following day pushed
tensions to breaking-point. Open violence broke out on 23
August and spread from Jerusalem as far as Hebron in the
south and Safed in the north.

The police, with a few notable exceptions – like ex-RIC
Inspector Cafferata, the 'man of lead' who tried single-handed
to defend the Hebron Jews against what the *Daily Mail* called
'20,000 fanatical Arabs, many of them inflamed by blood lust' –
collapsed.[35] The RAF armoured cars, without infantry support,
were ineffective in built-up areas. (A lesson which had to be
relearnt with grim consequences in Peshawar the following
year.) The catastrophe would certainly have been worse but for
the rapid transfer of two infantry platoons (South Wales
Borderers) from Egypt to Jerusalem by air on 25 August. The
main body of military reinforcements under Brigadier General
Dobbie did not arrive in Jerusalem until late the next day. Haifa
was not brought under military control until the 26th. A formidable task remained throughout the country to prevent further
attacks on Jewish settlements, to suppress looting of the settlements which had been evacuated, and finally to restore order.

The military forces available for these tasks were eventually
considerable: besides Dobbie's brigade (the South Wales
Borderers, Green Howards and South Staffords) and the TJFF,
there were Royal Marines from HMS *Sussex* at Jaffa and from
HMS *Barham* at Haifa. The speed with which they moved to
stifle the outbreaks of violence was seen by many Jews as
culpably inadequate, but by the army as unusually fast thanks to
the existence of a *de facto* state of martial law. On 26 August
the responsible civil and military authorities (the deputy High
Commissioner and the Air Officer Commanding) agreed infor-
mally to hand over control to the newly arrived Dobbie – an
unusual arrangement which does not appear to have been
sanctioned from London.[36] Such an *ad hoc* reaction is a classic
instance of the old idea of martial law, forced into being by the
breakdown of the ordinary machinery of government. Dobbie's
own account, however, laid emphasis on the fact that martial

law was never actually proclaimed, and suggested that it was 'infinitely preferable that the Civil Government should continue to function, so long as that was possible'. The civil authorities did not openly abdicate, but made no effort to influence Dobbie's operational plans. In the view of many Jews, they deferred too readily to a man who had no knowledge of Palestine.

The first phase of military operations was essentially defensive – a hectic form of guard duty. Detachments were rushed from settlement to settlement to fend off Arab attacks, increasing their mobility by wholesale requisitioning (in official terminology 'hiring') of cars and trucks. By 29 August Dobbie believed that 'pacification' had been achieved. The second stage, as he put it with soldierly simplicity, was 'to punish the offenders . . . so as to prevent a repetition of the outrages'. As he saw it, the army could not take it upon itself to administer punishments; it could only create the conditions in which the police could gather evidence and arrest suspects. But the raids by which this process was fostered were definitely military operations, and seem to have borne a punitive aspect: Dobbie judged that they 'had a salutary effect, and acted as a deterrent to further disorders'. By early September it was possible to bring in detachments and to begin removing some units from Palestine.

The 1929 riots confirmed the potential ungovernability of Palestine. In their extent and duration they verged on insurrection, while away from the towns a new phenomenon clearly foreshadowed the guerrilla insurgency of the next decade. A force known as the 'Green Hand Gang' began to operate, supplying itself from the rural villages. The police inevitably labelled it a terrorist group, and maintained that although it claimed to be waging holy war (*jihad*) – and though the villagers provided it with food and contributions – 'they were not prepared to go further, and only the more fanatically-minded villagers regarded them as "holy fighters"'.[37] Yet the admitted fact that there was active popular support for the group as *mujahideen*, and that the passive support essential to a guerrilla campaign was also being freely given, was ominous.

The Government did not altogether fail to heed the renewed warning of 1929. Trenchard frankly asked the Air Staff to analyse the records of the decade to see 'where we had gone wrong in dealing with Palestine'.[38] Not surprisingly, the resulting blame tended to fall on the hapless officers of the Palestine police (whose force had crumpled under pressure that was admittedly severe, but in Trenchard's view not irresistible), the Treasury 'screaming for economies' and denying Plumer the two extra flights he asked for, the inadequate intelligence service, and Plumer himself. The High Commissioner had put the local military commander (an Air Commodore) in an impossible position by interfering in military policy – he was a Field Marshal, 'and one was never allowed to forget it!!', as Trenchard noted. The moral seemed to be, he added, 'when you want to fill a civil appointment, fill it with a civilian'. If this was indeed the lesson of Palestine, it was to be conspicuously flouted.

There was at least no question after 1929 of withdrawing all British troops. Two battalions were retained indefinitely, while the British component of the police was expanded. The *gendarmerie* question was raised once again in a triangular correspondence between the Foreign Office (which favoured recreating the Palestine Gendarmerie), the Palestine Government (which wanted to keep the British infantry battalions), and the Air Officer Commanding (who strongly advised enlarging the TJFF to garrison the whole of Palestine).[39] The debate petered out inconclusively with the High Commissioners, as upholders of the new status quo, winning more or less through the force of inertia. The lack of urgency shown in dealing with this vital issue, in spite of the AOC's forceful arguments, was another dangerous sign.

The High Commissioner from 1931 to 1938, Lieutenant General Sir Arthur Wauchope, was appointed as 'a general who does it with his head not his feet', in Ramsay MacDonald's words. He outranked all the service officers in Palestine even after the arrival of Dill as putative Military Governor in September 1936, and his attitudes were decisive in the management of the crisis which broke in the mid-1930s. One of the Air Staff's most serious complaints against the High Commissioner in 1929 (Sir John Chancellor) had been that whilst sharing the – in their view – alarmist fears of General Dobbie that a full-scale *jihad* was breaking out, and apparently taking the view that the disturbances were not merely riots but an organized rising against the British government, he had still refused to permit the bombing of hostile villages. He had, it recorded impatiently, 'trotted out all the time honoured shibboleths such as "women and children" and "legacy of hate" etc.' Such 'depths of ignorance' showed the urgent need for 'the education of the civil authorities in this sort of country in the use of air power'.[40] This was not of course purely a civil-military problem. Like many senior army officers, Dobbie had shared (or, the Air Staff suspected, fostered) the aversion to bombing villages. But the discord underlined the basic problem of decision making in crisis. The military idea of rapid, decisive deterrent action could be fatally undermined by excessive caution on the part of the civil authority.

Such caution was widely perceived to have been the main reason for the failure to stifle the 1936 disturbances and prevent them from developing into a large-scale insurgency. The identification of an insurgent challenge is of course the precondition of all efforts at counterinsurgency. The situation in Palestine was a perfect illustration of the difficulty of finding an appropriate response to an oppositional movement which remained in the indefinite zone between passive resistance and open warfare. Up until the fourth or fifth week of the national strike organized by the Arab High Committee, the dominant form of resistance was civil disobedience, and its main focus was, as in previous emergencies, the towns. Towards the end of May 1936, the focus shifted to the countryside. In Samaria, soon to become notorious in military circles as the 'Nablus-Jenin-Tulkarm triangle', a recognizably modern guerrilla campaign took shape. The main forms of action were arson, sabotage of railway lines and installations, cutting of telegraph lines, minor disturbances and attacks on individuals. Sniping of police stations and military camps became more noticeable than in earlier emergencies, indicating either an improvement in ammunition supplies or an awareness of the value of a mass of minor attacks in creating a cumulative impression of governmental disintegration. There were, occasionally, serious attempts to ambush patrols, even those strengthened with armoured cars.[41]

Until 24 May government instructions prohibited any offensive action against armed Arab groups. Then, after a close encounter between the AOC and a large rebel force near Tulkarm, the High Commissioner agreed to 'the unification of control of the Civil Administration, the Police and the Military under the Military Area Commander [of No.1 Area] in so far as plans for the restoration of order were concerned'. Restrictions on opening fire were removed, but the effort to secure unity of control foundered on what the AOC called the 'inherent reluctance' of political officers to employ punitive measures, even though the High Commissioner saw the situation at the end of May as 'a state of incipient revolution'.[42]

The service commanders regarded punitive measures as the only means of 'regaining the initiative'. A series of village searches was initiated in the areas of greatest dissident activity, ostensibly to find arms and suspects, but actually 'punitive and effective'. At this stage the level of military intervention was confined to assisting the police, mainly by providing cordons to seal off villages for searching by police. But early in June the inevitable collapse of the Arab section of the police set in: punitive action against 'their own people' was, the AOC recorded, 'repugnant to them'. Whether this was because they had failed to absorb the police ethos, or because the punitive measures organized by their officers were a good deal too rough and ready, is not clear. In any case military involvement became more intense when it was decided that government control must be reasserted over Jaffa, which by the end of May had become effectively independent. The 'no go area' of the inner city was all but impossible to search. A maze of precipitous narrow streets with interlocked buildings on different levels created a complex trench system with vertical sides reaching thirty or forty feet in height.

The solution adopted was a drastic display of military environmental logic. After all sniper fire had been silenced by a deluge of 'sustained retaliation', two motor roads were driven through the old city on north-south and east-west axes. The wholesale demolitions required major military forces, and between 3 and 8 June reinforcements poured into Palestine. Each battalion expanded into a brigade (the Northern Brigade, with headquarters at Haifa, containing the 1st Loyals, 1st Yorks and Lancs, and 1st Seaforth Highlanders; the Southern Brigade, based on Jerusalem, with the 2nd Dorsets, 1st Royal Scots Fusiliers, and 2nd Cameron Highlanders). However, the Government – the High Commissioner with the direct approval of the Colonial Secretary – still refused either to adopt a positive political policy of suspending Jewish immigration, or a positive security policy of suppressing Arab resistance.

The service commanders were now pressing for martial law, but the High Commissioner adhered to a policy of 'endeavouring to protect life and property without adopting severe repressive measures'. In the military view such a passive policy was doomed to failure, and it is not easy to see what political advantages it offered. Whatever its intentions, it did not have the effect of minimizing antagonism. Wauchope agreed to the promulgation of new Emergency Regulations on 12 June, defining new offences (such as sabotage), and giving the army powers of search and arrest.[43] But efforts to improve military intelligence were making little headway, and searches were becoming gradually more ineffectual. Since they produced widespread allegations of military brutality, a gift to nationalist propaganda, and were as always extremely unpopular with the troops themselves, they were finally abandoned in July.

Other military measures under the Emergency Regulations proved powerless to inhibit the development of the guerrilla campaign. A distinct hardening of the resistance movement was noticeable in June. The average strength of the bands operating in the 'triangle' increased from 15–20 to 50–70, and they showed much more fight in ambushes or encounter battles. The AOC now recognized that they were not out for loot but were engaged in a 'patriotic war'. His effort to encircle and capture the most active bands by a big cordon and sweep operation near Nablus on 5–7 July was, like most such drives under such conditions, a failure. As usual, the consolation drawn was that the secondary object of 'showing the flag and operating in a country previously unvisited by military forces for years' was successfully attained. The effect of such transient visits was of course minimal. In August the Arab campaign reached a new level of coherence with the arrival from Iraq of the great fighter Fawzi al-Qawuqji: an improvement in tactics became noticeable, alongside an intensification of terrorist action to secure universal compliance with the national strike.[44]

For a time the army made no progress, and even suffered a setback, in its efforts to secure greater freedom of action. During the July sweep some newly arrived mechanized troops (of the 8th Hussars), under the mistaken impression that they were on active service, shot down some Arabs evading the cordon. The resulting public outcry led the High Commissioner once again to tighten up the regulations on opening fire, in a way that the AOC considered seriously restrictive. An agreed form of instruction was not achieved until 3 September. By then the AOC took the view that 'do what we could with the military "in aid of the civil power", we were not now holding the situation', and once more advised the declaration of martial law.[45]

By this time the Cabinet was prepared to listen to this advice and to override the High Commissioner's policy. The Colonial Secretary held that it was 'imperative that the authority and prestige of the Government of Palestine should be reasserted without any delay', and the Cabinet agreed on 2 September that a complete extra division should be sent to Palestine to make possible the application of martial law 'at an appropriate moment'. Lieutenant General Dill was put in command of the massively expanded Palestine garrison, and took over from the AOC on 15 September in the daily expectation of becoming military governor. But even at this eleventh hour the Cabinet had left itself some political leeway. The appropriate moment never arrived. Instead, the mere threat of martial law, and the very visible military reinforcements, coupled with the promise of a Royal Commission under Lord Peel, seemed enough to induce the Arab High Committee to call off the national strike.[46]

The army felt that by pulling off this last minute compromise the High Commissioner had subverted the Cabinet's decision, and that scarce forces had been diverted to Palestine under false pretences. A few weeks after his arrival Dill was complaining that the expansion of the garrison was due not to 'the military requirements of the situation but rather to the disinclination of the civil authorities to make full use of their powers . . . because they feared that strong repressive measures would cause bitterness'.[47] Unusually, in this case the military view was supported by both the British commission of inquiry (the Peel Commission) and the League of Nations, which censured Britain for failing to apply martial law to nip the disturbances in the bud in June. But the basic conflict of military and civil views persisted. The magical tranquillizing effect of the Peel Commission was rapidly wearing off by the time Wavell succeeded Dill as C-in-C in August 1937. At the end of September the assassination of the Nazareth District Commissioner signalled a renewal of guerrilla activity.

This second insurgency was to last well into 1939, and was never decisively mastered by British military methods. Wavell, the very model of a modern major general, tried to implement the latest ideas of mobility. These at least rejuvenated the theoretical basis of the traditional military argument against dispersion of force. The critical link in the modern method was air support. Improved techniques of coordination, above all improved wireless communication, made possible the 'fixing' of rebel forces by 'air cordon' while mechanized infantry sped out from central bases to crush them. Reality did not always live up to the theory, but there was an increased incidence of success in encounter fights as a result of air support. There was also a real effort to engage the popular base of the guerrilla campaign through the policy of 'village occupation', aimed at 'denying food and shelter to the bands and driving them into open country'.[48]

As always the crucial factors were military strength and military powers. Wavell had two brigades where Dill had had two divisions. Under his successor, Haining, the garrison was again increased to corps strength, and this in itself had a definite effect in a country as small as Palestine. Even so, there is little evidence (in spite of Montgomery's bluster) that the day-to-day problem of small scale intimidation was ever solved, or the skein of relationships between the fighters and the Arab population decisively ruptured. The roots of insurgency remained untouched. The question of military powers continued to hang in the air. Wavell laid much stress on improving civil–military relations, and seemed well placed to succeed because of his long-standing friendship with Wauchope. In this complex sphere, however, cordiality at the top – though better than nothing – is not enough, and even this seems to have evaporated after Wavell's departure as his successor struggled to secure the powers he believed vital to crush the rebellion.

From mid-1938, when the new High Commissioner, Sir Harold MacMichael, told the Cabinet that unless there was a major change of policy (on immigration and partition) there would be no alternative to martial law, Haining argued that any further reformulation of emergency powers simply could not work. He was convinced that the delegation of powers from a virtually defunct civil authority was a legal fiction, 'more academic than practical'. It seemed designed to avoid martial law rather than to meet the real needs of the situation. The situation was one in which civil government was utterly paralysed, and where only force could avail. But politicians were using the illusory fact that civil government, propped up by military force, had not actually collapsed, to suggest that although the situation might be critical, it was not quite one of civil war. At the end of the year, after months of infighting, Haining wrote a report on the progress of operations in which he held that civil-military friction was the biggest single impediment to success.[49]

By this stage the government had tacitly turned a blind eye to the very tough action taken by the army, including some quite rough collective punishments. This squeamish compromise, a sort of unofficial martial law, did not overcome the resistance of the local civil administration, much of which was now in total opposition to the military view. As one senior political officer told the High Commissioner, there were – 'sentimentalists' aside –

> many British people of *balanced* mentality in this country . . . who feel very strongly that punitive measures, adopted against persons against whom there are no reasonably good grounds for suspicion . . . are wrong even if these measures are not accompanied by 'regrettable incidents' (and with feelings running high these incidents are bound to occur).

He went on, 'is it right to punish people so harshly for refusing to commit virtual suicide by giving information and assistance against their own flesh and blood?' He angrily repudiated the military principle of 'collective responsibility', holding that 'there *is* none in present circumstances, and we cannot expect it unless we give protection in return'. Here was the nub of the problem of public security. 'There is no longer any cohesion or free public opinion in the villages nor any authority except that of the rebels'. The fault, as he rather despairingly concluded, lay in the unmendable past – 'a spirit of corporate responsibility cannot be *created* in times like these'.[50]

But what in fact was to be done? The situation was unquestionably deteriorating alarmingly. September 1938 was, according to the High Commissioner, the worst month so far. It was not just that 188 people had been killed; the disturbances had 'more than ever assumed the character of open rebellion', and 'spread more widely over the country than ever before'. He thought there was 'little doubt that the Arabs fear the terrorists far more than they respect the government', and mentioned as an instance of the insurgents' authority the docility with which their order prohibiting the wearing of the *tarbush* had been obeyed throughout Palestine.[51] The civil authority depended on the troops, but believed that the army's robust approach would make a settlement impossible. The military and air authorities took a simpler view. The AOC, Air Commodore Harris (future leader of the bomber offensive in the Second World War), roundly declared – in private – that 'one 250lb or 500lb bomb in each village that speaks out of turn' would solve the problem. Although he was unusual in committing the view to paper, he was not alone in believing that 'the only thing the Arab understands is the heavy hand, and sooner or later it will have to be applied'.[52]

Harris followed RAF tradition in arguing for a properly established local *gendarmerie*. The army was 'a sledge hammer used to miss a fly'. Air action was also less effective than could be wished.

Apart from the few occasions when an aircraft manages to get stuck into worthwhile targets (and the oozlebart is getting cleverer daily at avoiding this) the best anti-oozlebart work is done by 'special' night squads (very secret) composed of a selected officer and up to say thirty mixed volunteer soldiers and sworn in local (mostly Jew) toughs. These squads are no more and no less than gendarmerie and their success proves to the hilt what is really lacking in the internal security provisions locally.[53]

In fact the Special Night Squads, in which Orde Wingate first displayed his talent for unconventional warfare, were developed under the aegis of the army. Their ruthlessness – which Harris delicately refrained from mentioning even in private – became a major point of civil-military contention. Contrary to Harris's implication, the army was certainly not hostile to the recreation of a *gendarmerie*, which it saw as the only way of stiffening the civil power quickly enough to allow the army to hand back areas which had been pacified by military force.[54]

Harris departed from RAF tradition, however, in his venomous hostility to the TJFF. Keeping the force in being was 'incredibly foolish', he thought, 'arming our probable enemies'. (He evidently did not foresee any danger in arming Jews.) He obviously believed that the appalling situation in the 'triangle', where the TJFF was stationed, was partly caused by the force's disloyalty, though no evidence of this was ever produced.[55] The triangle was always the storm centre of the insurgency and the supreme test of counterinsurgency methods. This was amply recognized by the special adviser brought in from Bengal to rebuild the battered police force, Sir Charles Tegart. He concluded from the interrogation of captured rebels that in the triangle 'bandits roamed around the villages, getting food, shelter and recruits, and were not encountered by the police dispositions'. To re-establish control here and elsewhere in Palestine, Tegart fell back on the idea of the blockhouse, which had originated in the Boer War. His fortified police posts were comparatively humble structures, however, and without the backing of massive infantry strength were too often ineffective. At the same time they emphasized the already serious isolation of the police from the community.[56]

Besides the 'Tegart forts' a more novel form of static defensive work was erected. A border fence, a triple line of barbed wire booby-trapped at intervals and patrolled by police, was laid out at a cost of £1400 per kilometre to cut off supplies and recruits from across the Jordan. The army believed that no such fence could stop really determined men, and was critical of particular design features and patrol arrangements, but agreed that it was worth a try. In principle, sealing the border was a significant step, but since nobody had any exact knowledge of the dependence of the insurgents on outside supplies (which is habitually exaggerated by governments), the practical impact of this costly measure could not be calculated.

The belief that insurgency is supplied or run from outside is often a corollary of the belief that the 'bandits' or 'gangs' are criminal terrorists rather than national fighters. This belief by no means disappeared in 1936. It was re-expressed with unparalleled force by Major General Bernard Montgomery after he assumed command of 8th Division in 1938. With characteristic, dangerous straightforwardness he attacked the general idea (accepted by GHQ Palestine as well as the Palestine Government) that the Arab campaign was a national movement. He announced that he had made a full investigation, and found that it was a campaign of 'professional bandits'. The enemy's 'esprit de corps' was 'a gang one'. He evidently saw the proof of this assertion in the fact that they had no units larger than 50–150 men.[57] Even allowing for the intensely fissiparous nature of the Arab campaign, which was indeed its most serious weakness, this showed an egregious failure to grasp the essence of guerrilla warfare. Montgomery saw no contradiction between his curt statement that 'we are definitely at war' and his prescription for securing public support – by showing them that they 'will get a fair deal from us but be killed if they rebel'.

Montgomery's private letters in early 1939 painted a desolate picture of a shattered civil administration ('officials never visit the country districts and know nothing about what is going on in the villages') and a disintegrating police (senior officers 'absolutely and completely useless', junior officers 'take no interest in the men; the men are drinking heavily'). Yet he continued to believe that the tireless exertion of military pressure could crush the 'bandits who are terrorizing the decent people'. By July he was able to announce that the Arab rebellion was 'now definitely and finally smashed'. How had this astonishing result been achieved? Few observers would have shared Montgomery's conviction that it was the outcome of his actions.[58] Rather it seemed that, as in 1936, the insurgency had died away – in the nick of time for Britain, as international tension screwed up to the pitch of imminent European war. The commitment of two divisions had horrified the CIGS:

How can we be expected to despatch half of our meagre land forces to carry out a role of internal security – and internal security in the sense of preventing Arabs and Jews slitting each others' throats? . . . sending troops to Palestine is like pouring water onto the desert sands . . . They really cannot expect us to lock up 20 battalions on this futile business. God, what a mess we have made of the whole of this Palestine affair![59]

This was perhaps a fitting epitaph on the Arab rebellion, and an advance obituary on the quarter century of British rule in Palestine.

6 Palestine: the Jewish insurgency 1943–8.

The final, most dramatic act in the struggle to carry through the Palestine Mandate began in 1943 with the first use of violence by Jewish fighting organizations against the government. Once unthinkable to Jews and government alike, this violence had a long gestation. As early as 1920, as we have seen, the establishment of Jewish defence forces as part of the apparatus of a Jewish quasi-state created a possible framework for insurgency. The double terror of Nazi persecution and Arab attack in the 1930s submitted the moderate *Yishuv* to fearful stress. Throughout the crisis of 1936–9, the majority succeeded in maintaining a policy of self-restraint and non-retaliation (*havlaga*). The Jewish defence force (the *Haganah*) remained neutral, though some of its members found an outlet for action in the Special Night Squads. The policy of *havlaga* was ruptured only by small dissident groups, which began a series of avowedly terrorist attacks on Arabs with the object of provoking reprisals and arousing Jewish fighting spirit.

The British attempt to pacify Arab fears by maintaining strict immigration controls became ever more incomprehensible to Jews as the full enormity of the Nazi *Endlosung* became apparent. Gradually the conviction that force must be used to prise off the British grip on Palestine, to allow unlimited immigration and the establishment of a Jewish state, took active shape. By late 1941 the Palestine Government was alerting London to the danger of a Jewish insurrection.[60] The most hostile dissident organizations were the Irgun Zvai Leumi (IZL) and the so-called 'Stern Gang' (whose own title was Lohamei Heruth

Israel – Lehi – or in English, Fighters for the Freedom of Israel, FFI). Both pursued a classic guerrilla strategy of employing inferior physical force to maximum pyschological effect, attacking the weaknesses of the government and aiming to convince British public opinion that holding Palestine was not worth the cost. (The Irgun leader Menachem Begin refused to accept that the British presence in Palestine was anything more than old-fashioned colonialism.)[61]

The fact that these groups were labelled 'terrorists' not only by the government but also by the moderate Zionist leaders tended to suggest that in this case the label was not merely official propaganda. Many believed that the 'freedom fighters' were insignificant and altogether unrepresentative, lacking any public support and relying on intimidation. Even so, and even in view of the avowedly terrorist origins of the groups during the Arab rebellion, the use of the term 'terrorist' was rather misleading. After 1943 nearly all their violent acts were directed against the British armed forces and police, and, as the army remarked, there should be no suggestion that British soldiers were terrified by such attacks. (Indeed the army made an effort to ban internal use of the word terrorist early in 1947.)[62] And in fact, although armed action led to an unprecedented polarization of the Jewish community, and even to intra-communal violence as the *Haganah* sought to exert control over the IZL and FFI, there could be no doubt of the extent of passive public support for the fighters. Certainly the British troops who pursued them recognized that without the wholehearted assistance of the Jewish settlements the 'gangs' could not have survived.

The conclusion that Britain was faced with a Jewish insurgency was one that was too uncomfortable for the government to draw. Yet there could be no doubting the significance of the picture drawn by the Ulster police chief who was brought in to advise on Palestine in 1946:

Jewish terrorist organizations have seriously weakened the prestige of the Government, done much damage to life and property, thrown thousands of Government forces on to the defensive and caused the withdrawal of the police from duty on the streets . . . Against this no repressive or offensive measures have met with any marked success.[63]

As so many military and civil officials had said in the past, only a major shift of political direction could have a material effect on such a situation. In his final despatch in 1944 the departing High Commissioner, MacMichael, bluntly stated that his advocacy of partition was the 'logical outcome of the dubiety with which the ulterior intentions of the Balfour declaration were originally shrouded and of the permutations and uncertainties of policy which have followed.'[64] A despairing military commander leaving Palestine in November 1936 protested that 'no action that can be taken by the military alone can stop terrorism': action 'must be in support of some political policy which is not existent at present . . . We have apparently not made sufficient use of our political weapons nor does it seem that we ever intend to do so'.[65]

The last High Commissioner of Palestine, another civilianized general, Sir Alan Cunningham, was fated to re-enact the sterile civil-military contentions of the 1930s in his attempt to uphold 'law and order' by methods compatible with British political tradition. His antagonist was an army driven to the end of its tether by a persistent and ruthless guerrilla campaign. The ruthlessness was most shockingly displayed in the Irgun's milk-churn bomb attack on the King David Hotel (which served as both military headquarters and government secretariat) in Jerusalem in July 1946. The persistence was probably more telling still. Troops were subject not only to incessant harrying to which, as usual in such conflicts, they could produce no really effective military response, but as the struggle darkened into the semblance of a blood feud, to kidnapping, flogging and execution in retaliation for the judicial punishment of captured 'terrorists'. The climax of the struggle came in July 1947 when two NCOs were hanged by the Irgun.

The army's corner was most determinedly fought by Montgomery, who became CIGS in June 1946. Using the same simple reasoning which he had perfected as a divisional commander before the war, he demanded an all-out offensive to crush the Jewish terrorists. The army was being improperly used, he said, confined to defensive tasks rather than being freed for the offensive actions which were the only way of gaining the initiative. The first fruit of Montgomery's hustling was a massive combing-out of Tel Aviv, Operation 'Agatha', at the end of June. The King David Hotel attack was the IZL's response to this. Otherwise its effects were hard to quantify, but Montgomery pressed on with his demands. In January 1947 he called for intensive searches throughout the length and breadth of Palestine, 'turning the place upside down', setting aside the cumbersome need for direct evidence of local complicity in terrorist outrages. He was confident that 'no real harm would be done to the population and in time they would tire of being upset and would cooperate in putting an end to terrorism'.[66]

Cunningham, far from sharing this confidence, held that such action would entail a 'serious risk of violent Jewish reaction amounting to a general conflagration which would destroy all hope of a political settlement'. For a brief moment these venerable sentiments seemed to lose their charm. The Cabinet allowed Montgomery to draft revised instructions governing the use of military forces to restore order, and the army believed that it had virtually got martial law powers. The characteristic sting in the tail of the Cabinet decision came with the revival of the proviso first made on 13 October 1938, that military action 'which may produce major political repercussions' must still have the High Commissioner's consent.

Cunningham never accepted that he was restricting the army's freedom of action. Although this charge had been firmly laid by General D'Arcy in 1946 – the High Commissioner had delayed Operation 'Agatha', and repeatedly vetoed 'vigorous' offensive, retaliatory or punitive actions requested by the army, on the grounds of the 'major political factors involved and the extreme difficulty of hitting the section of the community responsible' – Cunningham was able to turn the tables completely in 1947. When the question of martial law was under discussion he wrote:

> Beneath the suggestion presumably lies the implication, which seems to die hard, that the administration or myself in some way hamper the military in their operations against terrorists . . . The boot is on the other leg, the pressure is being put on the Army by me and I am willing to agree to any measure which will bring about results.[67]

As a *coup de grâce* he added that he had recently become greatly concerned at 'the apparent inability of the Army to protect even themselves', let alone the public, and had pointed out to them the wider damage done by the terrorist successes against troops.

The nub of the issue lay in Cunningham's phrase 'any measure which will bring about results'. The argument over martial law in 1946–7 was only in part about whether it was legally justifiable or politically advisable. The paralysis of the civil government was obviously so severe as to make it dependent on military support. The circumstances were exceptional, and un-British. The real question was whether military rule could actually work. The acid test of this was the big double operation 'Elephant'/'Hippopotamus' mounted in the first half of March 1947. Tel Aviv and Jerusalem were both placed under martial law and sealed off, as a giant form of collective punishment for a spate of IZL attacks in the two cities on 1 March. In the event, the Palestine Government became as dismayed as the *Yishuv* by the economic chaos resulting from the military blockade. After fifteen days martial law was lifted. Cunningham reported, somewhat paradoxically, that 'by its very nature martial law in this form cannot be kept on for more than a short period without degenerating into riots and disorders'.[68] (If he was right, then the administration was indeed bankrupt. But in another report he remarked a different irony, that because the military authorities had had to take responsibility for food distribution, they had come to seem benevolent rather than terrifying. This was a fault that could be corrected.) He made it clear that military action by itself could not 'get at' terrorists. Only the cooperation of the ordinary people would permit this, and martial law could only work if it imposed the sort of pressure that would elicit such help.

The Cabinet and the Chiefs-of-Staff Committee were disconcerted at the haste with which martial law had been withdrawn, and the apparent failure of the measure to inhibit terrorist activity. They urged that a more effective system should be prepared for any future use of martial law. They questioned the need for such thoroughgoing restrictions as the closing down of banks and the suspension of essential services, and pointed out that martial law could, in theory, be the most flexible of all forms of administration. (In this they came near a highly un-English idealization of military rule.) It was obvious from the debate which followed that there was still alarming disagreement about what martial law actually meant. What was the difference between statutory martial law and martial law 'proper'? The Colonial Office legal advisers discounted the value of the latter concept. The Cabinet, in a masterly display of terminological obfuscation, reasserted the English way by deciding to prohibit the use of the phrase 'statutory martial law'. Instead measures taken under the Palestine Defence Order were to be referred to as 'controlled areas'.[69] But as the ungovernability of Palestine became ever more complete, the High Commissioner showed the soldier under his civilian skin by insisting that if, in the last resort, martial law was what was needed, no 'statutory' form would work. 'I am very strongly of the opinion . . . that Military Government thus set up would lack the political and psychological weight of martial law proper, the import of which is generally understood throughout the world.'[70] At bottom the terminological question was, to the end, a political one. As a Colonial Office official noted, the declaration of martial law proper would be 'tantamount to throwing in our administrative hand in Palestine'; 'our prestige would suffer' and the machinery of civil administration would be irreparably damaged.

To most onlookers, however, it seemed that such damage had already been done. As early as January 1947 administrative officers were withdrawn into defended compounds, a major public confession of governmental weakness. (The biggest, in Jerusalem, was mockingly nicknamed 'Bevingrad' by Jews.) At the same time, the operations of the police showed an ominous slide into illegality. With utter disregard for earlier Irish experience, the 'special night squads' were revived in a new form. Orde Wingate was dead, but his Chindit right-hand man, Bernard Fergusson, came to Palestine as Assistant Inspector General to establish secret anti-terrorist groups. In his view it was essential that the officers in command of these groups 'should have experience and knowledge of terrorist methods' (from having used such methods in the Chindits or SOE), and unimportant whether or not they had police experience. Such an idea was absolutely contrary to the advice given by Sir Charles Wickham, the Ulster police chief called in as adviser in 1946, and threw the Colonial Office into a quandary.[71] Its implication, that only state terrorists could combat dissident terrorists, was indeed alarming. The inevitable disaster was not long in coming: on 6 May 1947 an 'operation' led by an ex-SOE officer, involving the abduction of an FFI poster-sticker, ended with the murder (accidental or otherwise) of the unarmed activist and the arrest of the officer. As too often before, the attempt at counter-terrorism, albeit disguised in fashionable military jargon – the 'counter-gang' principle – reaped a political whirlwind.[72]

A more humdrum symptom of moral degeneration appeared after the discovery of the hanged and booby-trapped bodies of the two NCOs in July, a grisly incident in which the officer who cut them down was injured. Violent reprisals by troops and police in Tel Aviv culminated in the machine-gunning of Jewish shops and cafés by police armoured cars. Five people were killed and ten wounded. The absolute alienation of government from community could scarcely have been more graphically displayed. Not for nothing had Sir Charles Wickham warned against the 'militarization of the police' through the creation of specialist anti-terrorist units, and laid down the axiom that 'an armoured car performs no useful police duty'.

Reprisals were the inevitable outcome of the frustration of armed forces unable to make any visible headway against outrageous and calculated provocation. The bafflement of the troops is evident in a painstaking account of the operations of 6th Airborne Division, written shortly after the final evacuation. The troops retained a keen sense of their own operational superiority on the rare occasions when they could bring IZL or FFI units to battle, and a strong sense of their own rectitude in their efforts to persuade the Jewish community to cooperate in the restoration of 'order'. They were genuinely distressed by the undisguised hostility they met when carrying out their endless, and too often fruitless, cordon-and-search actions in Jewish settlements. The vituperation, often spat out by young children, and the passive resistance 'so determined that it could only be broken by force', were beyond their comprehension. If only, the writer wistfully reflected, the law-abiding majority 'had realized what a cancer they had in their midst and been determined to cut it out, relations with the troops would have been so different'.[73]

'And been determined' – there was the rub. Without the persuasion that Jewish citizens should feel closer to British troops than to Jewish guerrillas, the most efficient military operations could do no more than contain the expansion of the IZL and FFI campaigns. Against the dynamism of insurgency, containment is a negative achievement. The most striking guerrilla operation of all, the attack on Acre prison on 4 May 1947, was a near-disaster for the Irgun in a military sense, but politically it was a spectacular symbolic triumph. Despite all military efforts, the insurgents' capacity continued to grow – not so much in the number as in the power of individual attacks. The sophistication of explosives technology resulted in the 'barrel bomb', the biggest of which was used to shatter the police headquarters at Haifa on 29 September 1947, killing nine police and wounding twenty-seven.

By that time Britain had finally recognized its incapacity to prolong this 'obscure and repugnant campaign'. The impossibility of maintaining public security or of restoring law and order were the most obvious reasons for laying down the Mandate and handing Palestine back – not, of course, to the defunct League of Nations, but to its spiritual successor, the United Nations Organization. But Britain had put up with disorder for a long time before acknowledging its failure to implement the terms of the Mandate. It is hard to escape the conclusion that in 1947 the fundamental *raison d'être* of the British presence in Palestine had begun to disappear. India was being abandoned. Henceforth, as Churchill bluntly put it, 'no British interest is involved in our retention of the Palestine Mandate'.

Notes to Chapter III: The Middle East

1. High Commissioner [HC] Palestine, despatch and 'Note on Jewish illegal organizations', 16 October 1941. FO 371 31378.
2. B. Wasserstein, *The British in Palestine: The Mandatory Government and the Arab-Jewish Conflict 1917–1929*, London 1978, pp.9, 32–3.
3. Committee of Imperial Defence [CID] memo., 'The Strategical Importance of Palestine', 2 July 1923, with appendices: Middle East Department [MED] memo., 14 May; Air Staff memo., 13 June; General Staff memo., 18 June. AIR 5 586.
4. S.H. Slater, 'Iraq', *The Nineteenth Century and After*, April 1926, p.480.
5. M. Gilbert, *Winston S. Churchill*, Vol.IV., London 1975, p.571.
6. M12c to DDMI, 22 July 1920. WO 32 9614.
7. R. Storrs, *Orientations*, London 1937, p.387.
8. Military committee of inquiry, report, 1 July 1920. WO 32 9614.
9. Wasserstein, *The British in Palestine*, p.66.
10. A subject still skimped in work such as Y. Alexander, 'From Terrorism to War: the Anatomy of the Birth of Israel', in Y. Alexander (ed.), *International Terrorism*, New York 1976, pp.218–9.
11. Wasserstein, *The British in Palestine*, p.131.
12. Storrs papers III, 2. Pembroke College, Cambridge. Samuel to Lloyd George, 25 April 1920. Viscount Samuel, *Memoirs*. London 1945, pp.150–1.
13. *Palestine: Disturbances in May 1921*. Reports of the Commission of Inquiry, October 1921. Cmd.1540, pp.33, 44.
14. Central Zionist Archive [CZA], Jerusalem, A226/31/2, quoted Wasserstein, *The British in Palestine*, p.104.
15. GOC-in-C Middle East Land Forces [MELF] to Sec. of State, 30 May 1921. CO 733 3.
16. Sec. of State, Colonies, to HC Palestine, 14 May 1921. CO 733 3.
17. Cmd.1540, p.33.
18. Deedes to Young, 2 August 1921. CO 537 849.
19. Churchill to Sinclair, 5 April 1922. Gilbert, *Churchill*, IV, p.647.
20. Sir John Shuckburgh at Middle East Committee, 5th meeting, 22 December 1921. CO 537 831.
21. Note on Palestine Police by MED. CO 537 2269.
22. Minute by DDOI. AIR 5 203.
23. Cabinet memo. by Sec. of State, Colonies, 'Mesopotamian Expenditure', 1 May 1920. C.P.3197, CAB 24 106.
24. Sec. of State, War, to Chief of Air Staff [CAS], 29 February 1920. AIR 5 224.

25. Sir A.T. Wilson, 'Note of Use of Air Force in Mesopotamia', 26 February 1921. AIR 5 476. T.E. Lawrence, *The Mint*, unexpurgated edition, London 1955.

26. Lt.Gen. Sir J.A.L. Haldane, *The Insurrection in Mesopotamia 1920*. Edinburgh 1922. App.IX, pp.332–41.

27. Gilbert, *Churchill*, IV, pp.494–6.

28. Haldane, *Insurrection in Mesopotamia*, p.92. Haldane to Churchill, 25 June 1921. AIR 5 476.

29. Wilson, 'Note'. D.A. Nasiriyeh to HC Palestine, 22 May 1921, AIR 5 251. P.O. Suleimani to HC Iraq, 20 August 1921. AIR 5 1287.

30. Cabinet memo. by Sec. of State, War, 'Policy and Finance in Mesopotamia', 17 August 1921. C.P.3240, CAB 24 127.

31. 'Forms of Frightfulness', DDOI to DCAS, 16 February 1922. AIR 5 264. A.C.M. Sir J. Salmond, 'Use of Air Force in Iraq', 1923, and 'Note on the Employment of the Air Arm in Iraq', 1924. AIR 5 338.

32. Air Council to Colonial Office, 15 August 1921. CO 537 825. Minute by Meinertzhagen, 20 August, loc.cit.

33. Statement by A.C.M. Sir J. Salmond (Air Staff memo. No.16), 1924. AIR 5 476.

34. There is a lively account in John Laffin, *Swifter than Eagles: the biography of Marshal of the Royal Air Force Sir John Maitland Salmond*, Edinburgh 1964, ch.XIII.

35. Cafferata papers, Middle East Centre [MEC], St Antony's College, Oxford.

36. The clearest analysis of military action is Sir Charles Gwynn, *Imperial Policing*, London 1934, ch.IX. The primary source is Brig. W.G.S. Dobbie, 'Palestine Emergency. Narrative of Operations between 24th August and 12th September 1929', 7 October 1929. AIR 5 1243.

37. Palestine Police, 'Notes on Terrorism'. Tegart papers I, 3. MEC. Also reports on activities of Safad gang; HC Palestine to Colonial Office, 22 February 1930. CO 733 190/5.

38. Note on conversation with CAS, 3 September 1929. AIR 9 19.

39. Memo. on formation of a Gendarmerie or Semi-military Force for Palestine, App.A. WO 106 5720.

40. Air Staff, Planning Section, 'Rough notes on some points arising out of the Palestine disturbances, 1929'. AIR 9 19.

41. Report by Air Vice Marshal R.E.C. Peirse, 'Disturbances in Palestine, 19 April-14 September 1936', pp.22–3. WO 32 4177.

42. HC Palestine to Colonial Office, 2 June 1936. CO 733 297.

43. *Palestine (Defence) Order in Council 1931, Emergency Regulations 1936*. Cf. *Palestine Martial Law (Defence) Order in Council 1936*. WO 32 9618.

44. Though the army considered early in 1937 that the main feature of the campaign had been the 'lack of enterprise' shown by the rebels, even under Fawzi, and their 'apparently complete lack of appreciation of the trouble they were in a position to cause'. Gen. Staff, Jerusalem, 'Preliminary Notes on the Tactical Lessons of the Palestine Rebellion 1936', 5 February 1937. WO 191 75.

45. AOC Palestine, Appreciation, 20 August 1936, and 'Note on Martial Law'. WO 32 4177.

46. Cabinet 56(36), 2 September 1936. CAB 23 85.

47. GOC-in-C Palestine and Transjordan to War Office, 30 October 1936. WO 32 9401.

48. There were eleven mobile columns, each of around 100 men; seven operating in 16 (Northern) Bde. area and four in 14 (Southern) Bde. area. Lt Gen. A.P. Wavell, Report on Operations in Aid of the Civil Power, 12 September 1937–31 March 1938. AIR 5 1244.

49. GOC-in-C P/TJ to CIGS, 6 October 1938. WO 106 2033. Sec. of State, Colonies, to GOC-in-C P/TJ, 15 October 1938. Haining papers, MEC. GOC-in-C P/TJ to DMO&I, War Office, 2 December 1938. WO 106 1594.

50. Memo. for HC Palestine by DC MacGillivray, 14 September 1938. MacGillivray papers, MEC.

51. HC Palestine, Narrative Despatch, 24 October 1938. CO 935 21.

52. AOC Palestine to AOC Middle East (secret and personal), 5 September 1938. AIR 23 765.

53. Ibid.

54. GOC-in-C P/TJ to DMO&I, 20 November 1936. WO 106 2033.

55. J. Lunt, *Imperial Sunset: Frontier Soldiering in the 20th Century*, London 1981, pp.50–70, gives a compact account of the TJFF's service.

56. Tegart papers III, 2.

57. GOC 8th Div. to CIGS, December 1938. WO 216 111.

58. Montgomery to Tegart, 10 December 1938. Tegart papers III, 4. B.L. Montgomery, 'Brief Notes on Palestine', 21 July 1939. WO 216 46. HC Palestine, Narrative Despatch, 1 September 1939. CO 935 22.

59. Diary of Sir Henry Pownall, 29 August 1938. B. Bond, *British Military Policy between the Two World Wars*, Oxford 1980, pp.268–9.

60. HC Palestine, despatch, 16 October 1941. FO 371 31378.

61. M. Begin, *The Revolt*, London 1951, pp.29–31.

62. R.D. Wilson, *Cordon and Search: With the 6th Airborne Division in Palestine*, Aldershot 1949, p.13.

63. Report by Sir Charles Wickham, 2 December 1946. CO 537 2269.

64. HC Palestine, final despatch, July 1944. WO 216 121.

65. GOC-in-C P/TJ to GOC-in-C MELF. 21 November 1946. Cunningham papers I, 3. MEC.

66. Cabinet Defence Cttee, 19 December 1946. 'Palestine: Use of the Armed Forces'. DO(46)145. FO 371 52567. Brief for Sec. of State, Colonies, on new Directive for HC Palestine on Use of Armed Forces. (Cabinet, 15 January 1947.) CO 537 3870.

67. HC Palestine to Sec. of State, Colonies, 16 March 1947. CO 537 2299.

68. HC Palestine to Sec. of State, Colonies, 14 March 1947. Loc.cit.

69. Joint Planning Staff, Chiefs of Staff Cttee., memo., 20 March 1947. CP(47)107. Cabinet, 20, 27 March. CM(47)30th, 33rd conclusions. CAB 128 9.

70. HC Palestine to Sec. of State, Colonies, 10 August 1947. CO 537 2299.

71. Asst.IG, Operations and Training, Palestine Police, to Colonial Office, 12 February; and CO minute, 'Secret Police', 13 February 1947. CO 537 2270.

72. M.J. Cohen, *Palestine and the Great Powers 1945–1948*, Princeton 1982, pp.237–8.

73. Wilson, *Cordon and Search*, p.60.

Notes on Further Reading

In the fecundity of the writing it has generated, the Palestine problem can be compared only to Northern Ireland. There is a very good general political history, based on original sources, in A.W. Kayyali, *Palestine, A Modern History* (Croom Helm, London 1978), and a sensibly perplexed British account in N. Bethell, *The Palestine Triangle* (Putnam, New York 1979). Detailed analyses of the vital early years of the Mandate period can be found in D. Ingrams, *Palestine Papers* (London 1972), and B. Wasserstein, *The British in Palestine* (Royal Historical Society, London 1978). The later period has produced two fine volumes by M.J. Cohen, *Palestine: Retreat from the Mandate* (Elek, London 1978), and *Palestine and the Great Powers* (Princeton University Press 1982). The postwar years are the subject of a massive but fascinating investigation in W.R. Louis, *The British Empire in the Middle East* (Oxford University Press 1984). There is no general work on the Arab insurgency, though G. Antonius, *The Arab Awakening* (Hamish Hamilton, London 1938), remains an important treatise on Arab nationalism. Specific studies of the Jewish insurgency have been rather disappointing (e.g. J. Bowyer Bell, *Terror out of Zion*, St Martin's Press, New York 1977), though there is a successful fusion of historical and journalistic technique in T. Clarke, *By Blood and Fire: the Attack on the King David Hotel* (Putnam, New York 1981). The most vivid account of the war remains Menachem Begin's memoir *The Revolt* (W.H. Allen, London 1951), well complemented by G. Cohen, *Woman of Violence: Memoirs of a Young Terrorist 1943–1948* (Rupert Hart-Davis, London 1966). There are good (though very different) memoirs from the British side; for the army, R.D. Wilson, *Cordon and Search* (Gale and Polden, Aldershot 1949); for the administration, Sir Alec Kirkbride, *A Crackle of Thorns* (John Murray, London 1956); and, for the early years, Sir Ronald Storrs, *Orientations* (Nicolson & Watson, London 1937).

Iraq has been much less written about in English. There are one or two sound general histories, but the most relevant work on mandatory policy is in P. Sluglett, *Britain in Iraq* (Ithaca Press, London 1976). The two volumes of memoirs by Sir Arnold Wilson, *Loyalties: Mesopotamia 1914–1917*, and *Mesopotamia 1917–1920: A Clash of Loyalties* (Oxford University Press, London 1931), are uniquely immediate sources. For a different perspective, see E. Burgoyne, *Gertrude Bell from her Personal Papers*, vol.II, 1914–26, E. Benn, London 1961.

IV

Asia

---

1 Violence and non-violence

Britain's attempt to control the subcontinent of South Asia was
a commitment on an unique scale – heroic, arrogant, or absurd,
according to the viewpoint of the observer. Broadly speaking,
British opinion saw Britain's role in India as a mission to protect
and emancipate the masses of a caste-ridden society from the
tyranny of corrupt and oppressive ruling groups. Few Indians,
even amongst the westernized, English-speaking élites like the
Bengali *bhadralok*, were able to view the British presence in
this light. From the early years of the twentieth century until
1947 the Raj was wracked by a suppressed but acute conflict
over the pace, shape and direction of political development
towards Indian self-government (*swaraj*). Britain's self-image
as protector of the people, interposing efficient British administration between them and their traditional rulers, produced
mounting tensions as the latter evolved into standard-bearers of
a modern nationalism. Reluctance to hand back power to the
traditional élites began to look more and more like a convenient
excuse for delaying self-government as long as possible.

Since these élites were the only politicized element of Indian
society, and represented the only viable source of recruitment
into an Indian administration for the foreseeable future (Gandhi
was an outstanding exception, but no less exceptional for that),
British governors were driven to the conclusion that Britain
might have to retain control indefinitely.[1] That this control
resulted from altruism as much as from self-interest was not
appreciated by those subject to the pervasive racialism of
British rule.

The element of self-interest could not be entirely disguised,
even if it looks in retrospect to have been more imaginary than

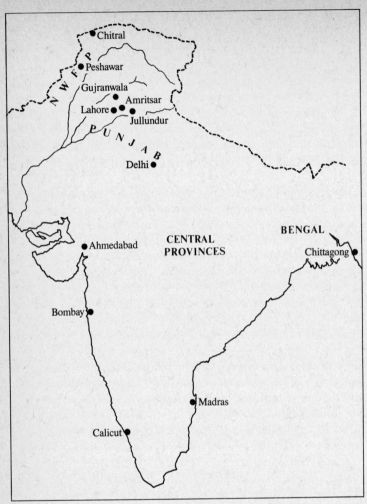

India

real. At the beginning of the twentieth century, India was not merely 'the jewel in the Crown', but the keystone of the Empire both structurally and spiritually. Without India much of the Empire would have been meaningless, and the Empire as a whole would have lacked its inner ethical purpose. In a sense, India made the Empire as Ireland made the United Kingdom; the integrity of both could not be tampered with except at the price of destroying the whole structure. India made Britain a world power, the model of the status to which Germany aspired. Few people, even British radicals opposed to the entire Imperial idea, could believe that in real terms India was a net drain on British economic strength. The reverse seemed self-evident. To the nationalists of the nascent Congress movement, taking up the 'white man's burden' involved no hardship or self-sacrifice.

But as the nationalist movement squared up to the problem of how to shift the burden of rule back on to Indian shoulders, it was seriously divided. Although resistance to the British Raj was widespread, it was conditioned by complex regional differences and above all by the ever-present religious division of the subcontinent. Communal conflict between Hindu and Moslem was a precipitant of endemic disorder and collective violence, and was eventually to engulf India in mass slaughter. But even where co-operation in for the struggle against Britain could be achieved, a fundamental difference over method remained. Put simply, this was the issue of violence as against non-violence – or, in the terms made familiar in Ireland, physical force as against moral force.

In practice the issue, as in Ireland, was blurred. The gradations of force are almost infinite, and clear lines between the threat, the fear, and the use of violence are impossible to draw. Even the most disciplined and quiet crowd of protesters may arouse the fear of violence in some people. But the broad moral and practical distinction is comprehensible and important. Gandhi's international reputation was founded on his thorough-going commitment to non-violent methods. The moral insurgency which he led employed the technique of mass civil disobedience or non-cooperation (*satyagraha*). As in the original Sinn Féin programme, passive resistance was coupled with dedication to cultural, not merely political or economic, autonomy. The cultural basis for the working of non-violence was immeasurably stronger in India than in Ireland: Gandhi could mobilize the low-caste Hindu religious principle of self-abasement and sacrifice to give *satyagraha* a mass backbone.

Gandhi's principles were, however, unavoidably compromised in practice. It is probably impossible to imagine an absolutely non-violent mass movement. One recent writer has indeed suggested that there was no tenable distinction of principle between moral and physical force – 'force, whether moral or physical, is force, and to the extent it succeeds in breaking the will and the resistance of the adversary it is terrorism, even if it is only moral terrorism'.[2] Such a view points up a significant aspect of social pressure, but it is not necessary to go quite as far as this to recognize that the means of giving expression to the communal will – marches, mass meetings, ostracism, and so on – are inherently intimidatory and frequently lead to collective violence. From the governmental standpoint, the *satyagraha* 'encouraged a disrespect for the law that was bound to be exemplified in disorder'.[3] The transition from protest demonstration to riot can be rapid, and was repeatedly made in India.

The periodic upsurge of violence both before and after the beginning of the non-cooperation movement in 1917 had other sources too. A very different strain of Hinduism, the conscious repudiation of lower-caste submissiveness, and the exaltation of violence, inspired the terrorist secret societies (*samitis*) formed amongst the *bhadralok* of Bengal. These groups adopted violence not as a byproduct of other strategies but as a weapon specifically designed to assert a national claim. The label 'terrorist' was of course primarily an official one, but it tallied better with the outlook of the *samitis* than is often the case with official descriptions. (Unfortunately, administrators usually failed to resist the temptation to go for terminological overkill by adding the adjective 'anarchist'.) In effect these were revolutionary groups using targeted violence, including several assassinations of British officials, and a significant number of armed robberies (dacoities), to heighten public awareness and to build up their organization.

The London-based India House group issued a pamphlet around 1909 declaring, 'Terrorize the officials, English and Indian, and the collapse of the whole machinery of oppression

faber and faber

review copy

BRITAIN'S CIVIL WARS
Counter-insurgency in the Twentieth
Century

by Charles Townshend

Publication Date: March 1986

ISBN: 0-571-13802-0
$35.00 cloth
5 1/2 X 8 3/4, 224 pages

In this fascinating and lucid book,
Dr. Townshend examines Britain's
methods of dealing with insurgency
since 1900 in Ireland, the Middle
East, Asia and Africa. He describes
the problem British law has in treat-
ing the gray area of violent rebellion
less intense than open war.

---

ff

faber and faber, 50 cross street, winchester, ma 01890 (617) 721-1427
Please send us two copies of your review

is not very far . . . This campaign of separate assassinations is the best conceivable method of paralysing the bureaucracy and of arousing the people'. The *Jugantar* (New Era) group at about the same time pointed out that mass killing could feasibly wipe out the small English population of India altogether.[4] The timescale was unclear, but it was obvious that since the terrorist groups were small their struggle would have to be protracted, an insurgency rather than an insurrection.

Because 'terrorism' could not pose an immediate threat to the state, the British response to the first terrorist campaign (1906–17) was inevitably hesitant. Just as the motives for maintaining British rule were complex, so the manifestations of control could be complicated to the point of contradiction. The Bengal insurgency revealed the problems created by the overlapping fields of force of three levels of government: the Government of Bengal, the Government of India, and the Imperial Government. The first spate of terrorist violence in Bengal was a reaction against the partitioning of the province, which was seen by the *bhadralok* as a deliberate attack on their paramountcy, since it left them in a minority in both the resulting provinces.[5] General lack of public support for terrorist action at the outset allowed a vigorous governmental repression to succeed quite rapidly. Even so, the legal basis for repression was the Criminal Law Amendment Act XIV of 1908, which allowed scheduled offences to be tried without jury. This was tacit recognition that, despite the success of the police investigations in penetrating the *samitis*, intimidation of witnesses and juries was a real threat to the normal judicial process.

With the passage of time this threat increased rather than decreased. Bengali public opinion, or at least the *bhadralok* class, educationally and politically the most westernized, showed an unmistakable admiration for the idealistic youths who risked their lives in attacks on the foreigners. Gradually the terrorists were accepted as quasi-heroic figures whose bravery was expunging the slur of cowardice which had been widely cast on the Bengali *babu*. This dangerous development could be answered in one of two ways: by full-blooded repression or by wholehearted concession. The complicated political structure, however, prevented the consistent adoption of either strategy. The atmosphere of the Morley–Minto reforms showed that the

Imperial Government inclined to the latter, as did the urbane, liberal Governor of Bengal, Lord Carmichael, who saw terrorism as resulting from the frustration of the *bhadralok's* legitimate political aspirations.[6]

But the Government of India took the opposite view. Its Home Member (in effect, home secretary), Reginald Craddock, saw terrorism as an irrational manifestation of evil. Using the trusty conservative metaphor of 'disease' in the 'body politic', he viewed Bengal as 'a strange world, a topsy-turvy arrangement under which all the maleficient influences are hailed as deliverances, and all the benevolent (i.e. British) influences are howled down as tyrannical'. Identifying the situation as 'an absolute inversion of right and wrong', Craddock set the Government of India's face resolutely against the modern age. Nationalism was to him a mere sham, a vehicle for the selfish pursuit of power by unrepresentative elites. India's true interests were represented by British government.

The Great War tilted the balance against Carmichael's conciliatory approach, and confirmed the stern emphasis on law and order. The Defence of India Act, modelled on the Defence of the Realm Act and ostensibly framed to counter external threats, became in practice civil emergency legislation. In the Government of India's view, the security of all India was menaced by the unruliness of Bengal. By 1914 Bengali violence was perceived not as sporadic political discontent but as 'a well-developed criminal conspiracy aimed at the destruction of British rule'.[7] No concessions were to be made to the relatively advanced level of Bengali political society: uniform central standards were to be imposed. The definitive statement of this view came from the 'Sedition Committee' under Justice Rowlatt, which produced its epoch-making report in July 1918.

Starting from the dramatic assertion that before the war 'the forces of law and order working through the ordinary channels were beaten', it concluded that the powers furnished by the Defence of India Act must be kept in perpetuity. In particular it specified that emergency powers should be applicable to disturbed areas in three stages: first, abandoning trial by jury, and making statements recorded by dead or absent witnesses admissible as evidence; second, giving powers to control the movements and activities of suspects; and third, giving powers to detain suspects without trial and to search without warrant.

These were extreme remedies, noticeably at variance with the British legal tradition. But it has been remarked that the proposed powers were already familiar from the Defence of India Act, and many of them also from the much older Regulation III of 1818, which had been used periodically to detain state prisoners for political reasons. It was the speed with which the Government of India moved to implement the 'Rowlatt legislation' (under the misapprehension that the DIA powers would lapse six months after the end of the war, rather than – like DORA – six months after the signing of the last peace treaty, an eventuality which could be deferred until 1921) that magnified its shock effect.

The Anarchical and Revolutionary Crimes Act (popularly called the 'Rowlatt Act') was pushed through the legislature on 18 March 1919 by the votes of the official majority. Gandhi's counterstroke was the 'Rowlatt Act *satyagraha*', the first attempt at mass mobilization on a purely political issue such as legislation. The Viceroy, Lord Chelmsford, believed that feeling did not run deep enough to cause a real crisis, and decided that Gandhi's bluff could be called. This proved to be a major miscalculation. The 'day of humiliation' on 6 April initiated a moral insurrection which soon became more alarming than any upheaval since the Great Mutiny. 'The civil disobedience campaign opened with a threat to law and order so serious that it can only be described as an incipient rebellion.'[8] From the start the organizers' grip on the whole movement was marred by misunderstandings that led to the first *hartals* (strikes) beginning on 30 March, a week early. The decision to arrest Gandhi on 8 April to prevent him moving from Bombay to North India certainly had the opposite of its intended effect. Riots broke out in Bombay and Ahmedabad, Gandhi's home town, and an electric atmosphere of tension ran across the north. An unprecedented degree of cooperation between religious groups in the civil disobedience campaign was made more ominous for Britain by the *Khilafat* movement, which manifested the alarm of Moslems throughout central Asia as Turkey was defeated by Britain and the only independent Islamic state was threatened with destruction. The stage was set for a truly awful event.

2 Amritsar

'. . . we shall have to be ready to try conclusions to the end to see who governs Amritsar.' (Miles Irving, 8 April 1919)

Does the belief that a general rebellion is imminent, and that only exemplary force can prevent it, justify the use of such force? This was the crucial question raised by Brigadier General Dyer's action at Amritsar on 13 April 1919. The common law permits and requires the responsible officer to use the exact degree of force necessary to restore order – not one blow more, not one bullet less. That necessary degree must be judged, in good faith, by the officer himself. The possible consequences of this doctrine were never more fearsomely demonstrated than in the judgment of Dyer and the massacre which resulted.

The situation in Amritsar on the day Dyer took command of the city (11 April) was undoubtedly serious, and perhaps critical. The whole of the Punjab was intensely excited and disturbed since the premature *hartal* of 30 March and the second on 6 April. Moslem feelings ran higher as the scale of British and French ambitions in the Middle East became apparent. In Lahore and Jullundur an explosion seemed imminent, and in Amritsar it seemed to detonate. More precisely, it seemed to be detonated by the authorities. On 8 April the Deputy Commissioner at Amritsar, Miles Irving, sent an alarming message to the Punjab government at Lahore, calling for military reinforcements and declaring that in event of a major riot, nine-tenths of the city of 160,000 would have to be abandoned. The small military force available in Amritsar, about 180 infantry (Somerset L.I.) and forty or fifty mounted artillerymen, could do no more than defend the civil lines on the northern outskirts of the city.

Irving also declared that he had abandoned hope of negotiating with the local Congress leaders, and recommended that they should be arrested. The Lieutenant Governor of the Punjab, Sir Michael O'Dwyer, authorized the arrests, but without sending the military reinforcements. This was a hazardous line, to say the least. It indicated a powerful faith in the theory that the agitation was not spontaneous, but was got up by a handful of 'ringleaders'. And even so, it seemed to ignore the inevitably provocative effect of arresting such leaders – unless it represented a tacit desire to push the crisis to a head.

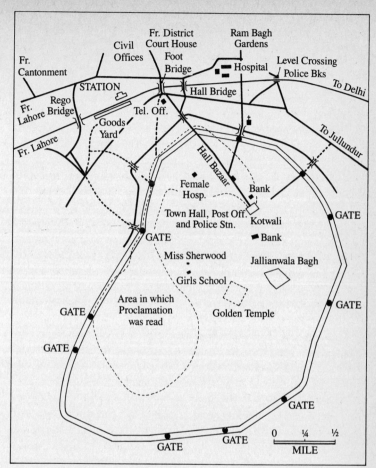

Amritsar City 1919

If so, the arrests were spectacularly successful. They were effected without incident on the morning of 10 April, but the defensive scheme for the city (as Irving had warned) made no provision for dealing with the huge crowds that gathered in the centre as the news of the arrests spread. By midday most shops had closed and some 30,000 people were on the streets, moving towards the civil lines where the small garrison was positioned. At the railway bridges inadequate picquets – inexplicably composed of mounted men whose horses, untrained for crowd control, soon became a liability – were nearly overwhelmed by a barrage of stones. To protect themselves they opened fire, killing ten people. Simultaneously a general assault on Europeans began within the city. In a series of attacks on banks, which the Indian police conspicuously failed to control, an official of the Alliance Bank was beaten to death, and two officials of the National Bank were killed and burned with their building. Still more electrifying to the European community was the attack on a missionary teacher, Miss Sherwood, who was beaten unconscious and left for dead in a street where she had sought refuge amongst Hindu friends.

In India, as a judicious writer put it later, 'when rioting results from an organized movement, the Mutiny becomes present to all European minds'.[9] It is impossible to measure the effect of this folk memory on the decisions that followed, but impossible not to sense its ubiquity. The Mutiny was a collective nightmare, just as the ferocity of its suppression was a perpetual reminder of what one English liberal called 'the tiger in our race'. That tiger was once again momentarily uncaged when Dyer arrived from Jullundur to take command of the reinforced garrison of Amritsar on the night of 11-12 April.

That day was fairly quiet, in spite of the potential for violence at the funerals of those killed the previous day. The 12th, too, passed off quietly, although vigorous security operations began. The police, escorted by troops, carried out a number of arrests, and a strong military column made a demonstration march around the outer wall of the city. There was, according to Dyer, sporadic firing at the column, but he refrained from replying. Instead he published a proclamation forbidding all movement in or out of the city except by written pass, and imposing a curfew from 8 p.m. The proclamation, read out by Dyer at various points in the northern part of Amritsar on the morning of the 13th, announced that 'any processions or gatherings of four men will be looked upon as an unlawful assembly and dispersed by force if necessary'.

These rough-and-ready regulations amounted to a state of martial law. Martial law had not yet been proclaimed by the Punjab Government, but the Deputy Commissioner had handed over authority to Dyer on his arrival by a document stating that 'the troops have orders to restore order in Amritsar and to use all force necessary'.[10] This offhand formulation of the common-law doctrine looks to have been gratuitously slanted towards the expectation that force would have to be used. With Irving obviously relieved to abdicate, and no guidance from O'Dwyer, responsibility devolved on Dyer alone. He took no advice. According to his own testimony he retired to his office after reading out the proclamations, and brooded on his course. Continuing sabotage of railway and telegraph lines outside the city convinced him that a full-scale insurrection was imminent. When he heard that a mass meeting had been called at 4.30 p.m. in the Jallianwala Bagh, in defiance of his regulations, he disposed his available force (407 British and 793 Indian troops) to control the northern city, and took a detachment of 25 Baluchis and 65 Gurkhas (40 of these armed only with *kukris*) with two armoured cars to disperse the meeting.

The Bagh was not, as its name would suggest, a public garden, but a large derelict square or tank with a floor four feet below ground level. This low floor, enhanced by the buildings which rose up on all sides, and the few narrow exits, turned it into a deathtrap for the vast crowd – maybe as many as 20,000 – gathered there. (Dyer's defenders describe the sides of the depression as 'low enough for a man to leap over'.) What were Dyer's intentions as he marched his force into the northern entrance to the Bagh will never be known. His explanation at the subsequent inquiry was certainly influenced by the fierce controversy that had welled up in the meantime. What he did was to line up his fifty riflemen and open fire without giving any warning or calling on the crowd to disperse. Fire was continued for about ten minutes; 1650 rounds were expended; at least 380 people were killed, and an unknown number wounded. Dyer then rapidly marched off his troops without making any arrangements to deal with the dead and injured.

This ruthless action had a stunning effect. Amritsar was cowed, and the whole Punjab agitation subsided – a process perhaps hastened by the equally shocking use of aircraft to bomb rioters in Gujranwala.[11] Dyer was hailed by many as the 'saviour of India', who had prevented a second Mutiny. His evidence to the committee of inquiry (the Hunter Committee) fully acted up to this heroic image. He declared bluntly that he had deliberately decided to produce an unforgettable moral effect. He had not warned the crowd to disperse because his proclamations had already given ample warning. 'If I had fired a little,' he said, 'I should have been wrong in firing at all,' and he added that if he had been able to get the armoured cars through the narrow entrance to the Bagh he would have used their machine guns too. He had not been aware that the crowd was unable to disperse quickly, and may have seen its failure to do so as defiance or as a threat to his force. (He told his superior, General Beynon, 'I realized that my force was small, and to hesitate might induce attack,' and when Beynon visited the Jallianwala Bagh on 24 April and still could not understand 'why you shot so many,' Dyer said he had had the impression that the crowd, as it surged back from attempted escape down a cul-de-sac, was gathering for a rush.)[12] But his statement made it clear that there was no direct resistance to justify such intense firing. Dyer's justification was the situation in northern India as a whole rather than in the Bagh or even Amritsar itself.

In fact the composition of his force, nearly half of which was armed only with close-quarter weapons, suggests that he originally envisaged a less abnormal crowd-control operation. His force was small, but was well equipped to defend itself against a crowd using primitive weapons. (The crowd in the Bagh was, as it happened, not even armed with the studded sticks, *lathis*, that were commonly carried in the region.) Whether or not Dyer was right in his estimate of the general situation – and though he reached his view alone he was by no means alone in it – his action was clearly unjustified by immediate necessity, and thus illegal, even under martial law. The pseudo-legal argument of his apologists that those who gathered in the Bagh 'were substantially the same crowd as those who had murdered the bank managers and looted the bank godowns' certainly does nothing to strengthen his case.[13]

Still more ill-advised, if possible, was his action following the formal proclamation of martial law, to avenge the attack on Miss Sherwood. The lane in which she had fallen was closed at each end by picquets on 19 April with instructions that anyone who wanted to pass down it must go 'on all fours'. As Dyer's later testimony made clear, this was literally intended and literally enforced, even on residents of the lane who were not suspected of complicity in the assault. This 'crawling order' was in force until O'Dwyer heard of it on the 24th and immediately 'asked for' it to be rescinded. Other 'fancy punishments' later disavowed by O'Dwyer were imposed in the Punjab on the authority of junior officers, and the whole administration of martial law seemed to confirm the worst political image of military tyranny. (Whilst for their part soldiers found confirmation of their fear that 'an officer who takes strong action which he genuinely considers is necessitated by the circumstances cannot rely on the support of the Government, and that his career will be ruined'.)[14]

The political damage done by the military action in Amritsar was incalculable. Nationalist leaders throughout India reacted with outrage not only against the massacre and the 'crawling order', but also against the wave of public adulation of Dyer in Anglo-India and Britain. Dyer's 'monstrous deed' (Churchill's phrase) may possibly have 'saved India' from insurrection in 1919; but it surely injected a lethal poison into the British hope of steadily emancipating India under British tutelage. Echoing the most infamous use of military force in aid of the civil power, a recent historian has suggested that 'Jallianwala Bagh was the Indian Peterloo'.[15]

3 The Malabar rising of 1921–2

It may be felt that Amritsar merely emphasized the inherent contradiction in the self-image of the British as beneficent rulers. If such severe action was widely regarded as vital to maintain the authority of government, it was obvious that government still rested on naked force to an extent wholly alien to the 'British way'. The instinctually close relationship between military and civil authorities – of which the accord between

Irving and Dyer on 11 April was a typical example – blurred the distinction zealously maintained in Britain.[16] A government so quasi-military in character faced insuperable problems in its efforts to move from benevolent despotism towards a partici-patory political system.

The belief that insurrection could only be prevented by demonstrative force received support from events in Malabar in 1921, where governmental hesitancy allowed a small resistance movement to grow into a full-scale insurgency whose extent was limited by ethnic boundaries rather than by state power. The situation in Malabar was admittedly unusual. The Mappillas, a Moslem religious group forming nearly a third of the population, were a curious centre of turbulence in the comparatively tran-quil climate of the Madras Presidency. To them the adjective 'fanatical', so liberally applied to Moslem peoples, seemed particularly appropriate. They were descended from Arab traders who had fought a sporadic *jihad* against the Portuguese through the seventeenth and eighteenth centuries. Armed struggle was deeply ingrained in their way of life. Throughout the period of British rule a sequence of 'outbreaks' had oc-curred, in which groups of Mappillas would launch a miniature holy war, forcibly converting the surrounding Hindu popu-lation, and eventually dying to the last man in battle against the forces of government. It is easy to see how such a holy war tradition could, in twentieth century terms, produce a formid-ably resilient guerrilla insurgency.

Such in fact occurred in 1921 when the deep-rooted tradition of sacrificial *jihad* was fused with the wider political awareness of the pan-Moslem *Khilafat* movement. The authorities were unprepared to cope with the explosive results of this fusion. In comparison with the north, south India had presented few internal security problems, and ever since the assumption of direct British rule after 1857 the military garrison had been steadily reduced. Though the recurrent Mappilla outbreaks had led to special legislation (the Moplah Outrages Acts) and to the creation in 1884 of a special police force, there was confidence – perhaps more serene in the Government of India than at Madras – that military forces were not needed. This confidence was increased by the success of the Malappuram Special Force in dealing with Mappilla disturbances in 1915 and 1919.

The outbreak of 1921 overwhelmed these slender resources with alarming rapidity. The creation of a paramilitary group of 'Khilafat Volunteers' led by a religious teacher, Ali Musaliar of Tirurangadi, was the first sign. By Ramadan (8 June) this partly-uniformed force, wearing crossbelts and carrying knives, was 300–400 strong, and sufficiently confident to proclaim the dawn of the 'Khilafat Raj'. The real roots of its strength lay in the endemic conflict between Mappilla tenants and Hindu landlords, especially in the district (*taluk*) of Ernad. But the political dimensions of the challenge were much wider. 'We cannot go on as we are, with peace only so long as we remain inert,' wrote the District Collector: firm action must be taken, as a Special Commissioner sent from Madras reported on 14 August, to dispel the rapidly spreading idea 'that the British Raj is finished and the Mappilla Raj has taken its place'.[17]

The action decided on was the arrest of twenty-four leaders, mostly in Tirurangadi. The police, reinforced by all available troops (a company of the Leinster Regiment) swooped at dawn on 20 August, but found that information about the raid had leaked. Only four of the wanted men could be arrested, and the Mappilla inhabitants of Tirurangadi reacted with violent rioting. The raiding column only got back to its headquarters in Calicut with great difficulty and some losses. On 23 August the District Collector at Calicut declared that the situation was 'now beyond civil powers', and asked that the military should take charge.

Faced with the most serious insurrection since 1857, the authorities seemed to be in no doubt about the necessity for military intervention. The Governor of Madras, Lord Willingdon, wired Delhi that 'a state of open rebellion exists, and that Martial Law should be established in the Taluks of Ponnani, Walluvanad and Ernad. We are of opinion that conditions now correspond to the state of affairs described in Chapter 2 of the Martial Law Manual, and that regular action, as contemplated in Chapter 3 of the Manual, should be taken. It is therefore suggested that Martial Law be introduced by Ordinance by the Governor General.'[18] The Government of India's reaction at this point is significant. The new Viceroy, Lord Reading, reported to London, 'It has been suggested that it is preferable to continue dealing with the situation by means of *de facto* martial law, now apparently in force without any Ordinance, the operations of the military being confined to suppression of disorder and dispersal of unlawful assemblies.' But Reading rejected this course: the ghost of Amritsar unmistakably haunted his argument that an ordinance was necessary for

> (1) validating proceedings of summary courts; (2) providing for legal method of punishing acts which, though not offences against the ordinary law, are breaches of martial law regulations, and incompatible with maintenance of order; (3) preventing irregular or improper punishments for breaches of military rules; (4) indemnifying officers for acts done in good faith and in reasonable belief that they are necessary . . .

That the third point was the crucial one was underlined by the further gloss: 'Government of India consider it essential that trials and punishments should be left as little as possible in hands of military officers.'[19]

The resulting martial law ordinance was framed to preserve both the nature and the structure of the civil courts, merely adding supplementary courts to deal with offences created by the martial law regulations. The military, in short, could make regulations and make arrests for breach of those regulations, but could not impose punishments. This was, as Willingdon protested to the Secretary of State, a 'travesty of martial law', all the more remarkable in that everyone recognized that the civil power and the judiciary in Malabar had utterly collapsed.[20] He wrote still more bitterly to Reading,

> You may think me a brutal and militant person; you may feel we are not to be trusted with summary powers; but I am certain that in any other country the chief offenders would have been dealt with in summary fashion after such an outbreak; I suppose this excessive caution is due to the trouble over the Punjab but I am sorry, very sorry, you found it necessary to water the original ordinance down.[21]

Nonetheless, by September the situation seemed to be under control. The small military force at Calicut rapidly seized the initiative and marched on Malappuram, defeating a large Mappilla concentration there. Rebel casualties were enormous. Their disregard of death – expressed often in the belief that as holy warriors they were invulnerable to bullets – led them into ferocious, suicidal attacks. Their numbers had sufficed to overwhelm the unsteady Malappuram Special Force with its obsolete armament of single-shot Martini-Henry carbines; but even armed with these captured weapons the Mappillas never had a chance in open combat against regular troops.

After relieving Malappuram the troops advanced on the centre of the insurgency, Tirurangadi, and secured the surrender of Ali Musaliar (an achievement primarily due to loyal Mappilla police officers). The rebellion seemed to have been scotched. But, in the army's view, the opportunity to capitalize on the initiative of the Calicut garrison was thrown away by the Government of India's obstructiveness. In fact, it seems likely that in any case the determination of the Mappillas would have led them to resort to guerrilla methods, for which the south Malabar countryside was ideal. By late September the GOC Madras, Major General Burnett-Stuart, estimated that 10,000 Mappillas were fighting in guerrilla bands, avoiding open combat but plundering, terrorizing and forcibly converting Hindus, sabotaging communications, and continuing to proclaim the Khilafat Raj.

This was a formidable situation, and Burnett-Stuart did not mince words in calling it 'actual war, and famine, and widespread devastation'. It could only be dealt with as war. The civil authorities made an effort to put their house in order by rebuilding the armed police: a Malabar Special Police force 300 strong, equipped with magazine Lee-Enfields, was created on 30 September, and doubled in strength a month later. By then, however, the Government of India had belatedly accepted the martial law ordinance was seriously hampering the counter-insurgency campaign. In particular the military authorities protested that the delays of the civil courts defused the atmosphere of alarm which was a vital aspect of martial law (an argument which had become familiar in Ireland earlier that year), and which was especially vital in the gathering of intelligence information.

On 10 October a new ordinance was issued to meet the

Madras Government's objection that 'the absence of all pro-vision for speedy trial has materially fortified the rebels in their resolute defence'. It authorized 'systematic military measures with adequate forces', and the use of military courts. The available military force was brought up to five battalions. But even with enlarged powers the military faced an intractable problem; as Burnett-Stuart put it, 'In the military sense the situation is not out of hand, but tendency will be for bulk of population to become part-time as opposed to whole-time rebels, for active bands to become smaller, more elusive and numerous, and for dacoity to increase . . .' He thought it im-possible to make 'any prophccy as to when the rebellion can be expected to end. It may go on in some districts until every Moplah is either exterminated or arrested.'[22]

The genocidal undertones of this last sentence seemed to be made explicit on 19 November, when seventy out of ninety-seven Mappilla prisoners locked in a train from Malappuram to Bellary died of asphyxiation. Albeit accidental, a grim event such as this had serious political repercussions, and once again pointed up the crudity of martial law administration. Military measures against the rebels seemed ineffective. The reinforce-ments were used to mount a major operation, a 'drive' of Ernad and Walluvanad districts, but this ambitious and costly effort had little tangible result, and as usual the achievements were listed as 'showing the flag' and demonstrating the government's determination.

Only after this unsatisfactory operation were the five battalions given responsibility for the control of five separate areas, within which they gradually wore down the guerrilla bands and eroded their basis of support amongst the Mappilla peasantry. This was a slow process, and was not officially pronounced complete until 25 February 1922. By then 2339 rebels had been killed and 1652 wounded, while 5955 had been captured and over 39,000 voluntarily surrendered. Whilst regretting the heavy loss of life, Burnett-Stuart was 'satisfied that punishment has fallen on the guilty and that no lesser chastisement would have sufficed to bring the misguided and fanatical rebel community to their senses'.[23]

4 Civil disobedience and Bengal terrorism, 1930–6

At the trial of Ali Musaliar by Special Tribunal in Calicut, the judges ruled that the rebellion was not the result of 'mere fanaticism' nor of agararian conflict. 'Their intention was, absurd as it may seem, to subvert the British Government and substitute a Khilafat Government by force of arms.'[24] This subversive dimension was to be increasingly evident in Indian disturbances between the wars. In south India, admittedly, the situation never again became as critical as in 1921–2. Successful experimentation with armed police forces, though sometimes involving failures like the ill-disciplined East Coast Special Police which was modelled on the MSP, produced a flexible structure responsive to local conditions. Though the Madras Police Report for 1930 observed that 'an orgy of mass violence' had accompanied the non-violent Congress agitation, it did not amount to insurrection. Military forces were again reduced, and the level of force used to control demonstrations was carefully monitored. Most riot control duties devolved on the district reserve police, who were armed with *lathis* and smoothbore muskets with the specific intention of reducing their lethal capacity (and also the potential value to rebels of captured police weapons).

In north India the situation was markedly different. The sense of political challenge was far more acute; terrorist campaigns in Bengal, however small in scale, mesmerized the government – when it was not engrossed by the perpetual threat of the North-West Frontier. Bengali terrorism was an active menace for over half the twentieth century life of the Raj. The three recognized campaigns totalled some twenty-five years, and each seemed more serious than the last. For terrorism, as for civil resistance, 1930 was the climactic year. The second terrorist campaign, from 1923 to 1927, showed that a radical wing of Congress was definitely committed to violence, and was only prepared to suspend it for limited periods to test the effectiveness of Gandhi's non-cooperation strategy. The Bengal Congress party was strongly influenced by exponents of violence under the leadership of Subhas Chandra Bose, who formed the New Violence Party in 1927 and the Bengal Volunteer Group in 1928.

By this time the second terrorist campaign, whose path had been eased by the repeal of the Rowlatt legislation in 1922, had succumbed to the pressure of a new emergency law, the Bengal Criminal Law Amendment Act 1925. But the idea of physical force was if anything strengthened through the 1920s as its intellectual justification was more highly developed. How far it could be accurately described as 'terrorism' remained a problem. The *Jugantar* publicists drew their main inspiration from Ireland, and in the late 1920s the New Violence Party exhorted Bengali youths to study the methods of the IRA and the writings of Pearse and Breen. This linking of the self-sacrificial idealist and the pragmatic rebel (neither of whom was a terrorist in any strict sense) provides a clue to the nature of Bengali terrorism. Its objectives were expressed in the *Philosophy of the Bomb* as to

> instil fear in the hearts of the oppressors, bring hopes of revenge and redemption to the oppressed masses, give courage and self-confidence to the wavering, shatter the spell of the supremacy of the ruling class and raise the status of the subject race in the eyes of the world, because it is the most convincing proof of a nation's hunger for freedom.[25]

There was some retreat, perhaps, from the exterminationist hopes expressed before the war – 'the number of Englishmen in the entire country is not more than a lakh and a half . . . with a firm resolve you can bring English rule to an end in a single day' – but few can have believed that the English would be frightened into leaving India by violence short of this. Terror seems to have remained a means of electrifying public opinion as a prelude to insurrection, rather than a strategy of protracted psychological attrition.

In the event there was to be no insurrection, but the psychological impact on the British was remarkable. Public attention was first riveted by a dramatic operation which preceded the official reopening of the *Jugantar* campaign in 1930. On 18 April the police and auxiliary force armouries and the European club at Chittagong were raided by a band of 100 *Jugantar* fighters. The armouries produced a disappointing haul – less than sixty rifles and twenty-two revolvers – and the planned massacre of Europeans was thwarted by the Good Friday emptiness of the club. Nonetheless the scale of the raid was unprecedented, and the military organization of the raiders gripped the public imagination. From late 1930 terrorist incidents increased sharply, and public security was seen – by Europeans at least – to be endangered. By the early summer of 1931 the situation appeared to be sliding out of control. The emergence of female assassins – seen by the chief of police as a 'sinister development' – such as the two young women who shot the District Magistrate of Tipperah on 14 December 1931, represented a revolutionary dimension that the British were loth to recognize.

The first response of the authorities was the posting of punitive police in fifty-two villages in the Chittagong district at the end of July. A mobile police striking force of ninety-six men was formed, and a battery of special powers ran from the Bengal Emergency Powers Ordinance of 1931 through the temporary Suppression of Terrorist Outrages Act to the Public Security Act (aimed at the civil disobedience campaign renewed in 1932) and the permanent Bengal Criminal Law (Arms and Explosives) Act 1932. Under emergency powers it became an offence to aid 'absconders' (a term including not only those wanted for criminal offences, but also anyone evading internment under the Criminal Law Amendment Act, and anyone who had 'elected to go into hiding') or to refuse to give information to the authorities. The police obtained powers to search all suspects and to intercept mail, and District Magistrates had remarkable powers to control the residence and activities of individuals.[26] Internment was freely used: the police expressed strongly, if inelegantly, the belief that 'next to shooting a terrorist dead, nothing can be comparable in importance as an instrument for paralysing him to one by which one can lock him up'.[27] But, as so often, internment produced political difficulties, aggravated by the fact that internees could not be removed from Bengal, and the camps provided a focus of anti-government feeling.

As had often been proved elsewhere, however, powers alone are of limited effect without the will to use them. Administrations require a controlling vision to cope with insurgency.

The appointment as Governor of Bengal of Sir John Anderson, whose Irish experience was only part of his formidable administrative record, brought the intangible but unmistakable quality of firmness to a demoralized provincial government. There were still no rapid solutions. The fear of full-blown insurrection persisted; large-scale military assistance to the police was unavoidable, and in 1932 troops were finally authorized to carry out searches. Larger scale operations, such as the drive of a 700 square mile area around Chittagong by 400 armed police and 1000 troops between December 1931 and March 1932, were predictably unimpressive. After a hundred house-to-house searches each month, and the liberal application of curfews and collective fines, the net result was the arrest of a single absconder.

The Bengal police chief, Sir Charles Tegart, recognized that 'as the ordinary law proved entirely inadequate to deal with the situation, so did the ordinary police machine'.[28] He believed it was less important to expand the numbers of the police than to build up an effective intelligence service. But as always when financial stringency had run down such services, rebuilding was a painfully slow process. In 1932 it was necessary to hold the situation by numbers alone, and seven infantry battalions were operating in aid of the civil power by August that year. Gradually the refinement of intelligence and the maximization of search effort in the most disaffected villages produced results. Terrorist actions declined by over 30 per cent from 1932 to 1933, and by over 60 per cent from 1933 to 1934. By then the general improvement was seen as justifying the withdrawal of punitive police and collective fines.

By 1936, when terrorist incidents fell to a mere four, the insurgency could be pronounced defeated. Yet its capacity to alarm government and excite public opinion had never depended on the sheer quantity of incidents. Midnapore had been seen as a particularly 'bad area' even though only four incidents had occurred over six years – but three of these had been assassinations of successive district magistrates.[29] In this way terror had a real impact, even if it did not live up to the hopes of terrorist intellectuals. It challenged the credibility of government, and the Raj was exceptionally sensitive to such challenges. What distressed successive governors of Bengal was the degree of public sympathy for, or acceptance of, terrorists, as shown in assistance to absconders. Anderson's predecessor Sir Stanley Jackson (himself the victim of an attempted assassination by a female student) recognized that 'the one way in which this serious trouble can be dealt with is by getting public opinion against it', but also recognized that his efforts in this direction were a failure. The problem was to convince the public that terrorism was a real threat to public security and not just to the state or its British officials. Anderson told the Bengal legislative Council that 'it is not enough to meet force by force or to answer lawlessness by asserting the majesty and power of the law. An atmosphere must be created in which the seeds of disorder will not germinate.'[30] The people must be directly interested in law and order, and this could only happen if government pursued constructive social and economic policies. By the mid-1930s it can be said that the Raj had done too little in this direction, too late.

It is significant that whereas in the Middle East resistance almost miraculously subsided on the outbreak of the world war, Indian opposition was maintained. It was not merely a matter of the extremist actions of Bose, which the government was able to denigrate as inspired by Nazi Germany, but the far deeper and wider 'Quit India' movement of 1942–3, which yet again confronted the Delhi government with the most severe crisis since the Mutiny. At the height of the disturbances the equivalent of fifty-seven battalions of troops were employed to aid the police.[31] Despite comprehensive efforts by the government to write this near insurrection – and the rough-and-ready methods used to suppress it – out of history, its scale confirmed the rootlessness of the British system in India and its unchanging dependence on force.

5 The North-West Frontier

We have sought to conciliate these people, but it were as well to attempt the conciliation of a brood of tiger cats. Forty years or more of alternate conciliation and punishment has left these tribes as truculent and irreconcilable as ever.

Thus Lord Kitchener wrote of the North-West Frontier of India, a region whose singularity was marked even amidst the bewildering variety of the sub-continent. From the British governmental point of view its overriding peculiarity was its status as a sort of administrative no-man's-land. The territories between the river Indus and the border of Afghanistan (the Durand line) were the home of warlike Pathan tribes – Afridis, Mahsuds, Mohmands, Wazirs – whose skill, determination, and persistence as guerrilla fighters mocked all British efforts to impose the *Pax Indiana*. The loosely drawn line of British control ran with no ethnic – and little military – logic through the middle of the Pathan lands.

For this reason it was impossible to separate 'internal' from 'external' security problems. Though an unmistakably internal emergency was to break out at Peshawar in 1930, the near-continuous military struggle in Waziristan may be seen either as an attempted counterinsurgency or as a campaign of conquest. Transfrontier tribes, formed into loosely organized and free-moving military bodies called *lashkars*, raided the administered zone for both economic and ideological (i.e. religious) reasons. In an overwhelmingly Islamic region there was ample fuel for a succession of minor *jihads*, of which the most protracted was the campaign of the indomitable Faqir of Ipi through the 1930s and 1940s.

The frontier was a shifting and restless play of forces. Because of its strategic location it had special importance for Britain, being seen as the frontier not only with Afghanistan (the 'Minor Danger', as it was called), but also with the vaster and vaguer power of Russia (the 'Major Danger'). The 'great game' played out here focused much of the psychic energy of the Empire, even though British administrators were mournfully aware that Indians refused to share the excitement of defending 'their' frontier. The minor epics of heroism in the Khyber Pass which rang through the British popular presses found no echo in India.[32]

What were the British doing there? This was not an easy question to answer, and, perhaps for that reason, was seldom if ever asked. But because it was not asked, the destiny of the frontier was left in the hands of the men on the spot. 'This great blood-sucking Frontier, which has drained us of men and money for nearly a hundred years,' the Chief Commissioner of the North-West Frontier Province (NWFP) wrote in 1922, 'is still the playground of chance decisions, personal predilections, and professional ambitions'.[33] The result of this was more or less inevitable: a gradual inching forward of the administered zone as local authorities sought to punish and prevent the raids of the recalcitrant tribes beyond.

This 'forward policy' could well have succeeded if the Government of India had backed it fully and applied all the military resources needed. Baluchistan to the south was in fact brought under control by a determined policy in the late nineteenth century. But as long as the forward policy remained casual and intermittent it made no impact on the Pathans. Indeed the pinpricks of punitive columns seemed to have the opposite effect, solidifying resistance and increasing the military capacity of the tribes. By 1940 there were estimated to be 414,000 fighting men and 233,562 breech-loading rifles available to them.[34]

Lord Kitchener's complaint formed part of the army's efforts to get adequate resources for the forward policy. At the time he wrote, the policy had been overtly abandoned by the Viceroy, Lord Curzon, and replaced by a low-profile occupation in which policing was carried out by the tribes themselves, recruited into local levies called *Khassadars*. This 'close border system' was in turn gradually eroded from 1908 onwards, and was swept away by the First World War. In 1919 the army made a bid for a full-scale forward move. Dismissing the idea of tribal responsibility as assuming a 'power of self-government and self-restraint throughout the tribes that does not exist', it confidently predicted that 'a few columns properly equipped with every modern convenience of war are all that are required to reduce such "robber bands" to submission'.[35]

The army was traditionally well placed to implement such a move with or without high-level political approval. Throughout the period of British rule there was a general acceptance that any reverse suffered by British troops on the frontier represented a blow to Imperial prestige that could only be expunged by a punitive expedition. Thus by 'trailing their coat' in Pathan territory the soldiers could, if they wished, more or less guarantee such an outcome. But in the postwar atmosphere of financial retrenchment the fearful cost of such expeditions was increasingly unattractive to government. As in the Middle East, the

RAF pressed its claim that air action could achieve the same –
or a better – result, at a fraction of the cost. As Trenchard wrote
to the C-in-C India, Lord Rawlinson, in 1921, he 'could bring
war with Afghanistan to a conclusion by aeroplanes alone
without your moving a soldier, and at half the cost and without
casualties. But I am afraid you and the Army will never admit
this.'[36]

Trenchard was right. India was to prove the main bastion of
resistance to the airmen's ideas. 'At the headquarters of the
Government of India the most conservative and influential
opinions regarding the unprovenness and inhumanity of the air
method are most strongly entrenched.'[37] With no Churchill to
cut through the Gordian knot of traditional procedures, the
RAF had to fight for nearly two decades for the right to give its
methods a fair trial; and it lost. At first, in the early 1920s, the
omens seemed good. Rawlinson professed himself ready to
reconsider his position if the Iraq experiment was successful. Sir
John Maffey in the NWFP put up to the Viceroy an unconventional memorandum arguing for a wholehearted reversion to
Curzon's 'close frontier' system, and condemning the renewed
military effort to gain 'control' as ill-conceived and dangerous.
Arguing persuasively that since the mid-nineteenth century
Britain had got involved in the tribal territories with a vague
notion that somehow 'our position there would strengthen our
arm against the major and more distant danger', Maffey
pointed out that on the contrary this entanglement had weakened the British ability to cope with the major danger. Now it
threatened to engulf all the available forces. 'We have fought
our way stubbornly into the midst of this terrible and inhospit-
able country. It is now realized that without vastly greater
efforts control is not possible.' Such efforts were now beyond
Britain's resources. The frontier was a 'juggernaut which is
breaking the heart of the regimental soldier and the tax payer'.
Air power, Maffey implied, offered a way out of the morass.[38]

Air Marshal Sir John Salmond toured India in 1922
before taking up his Iraq command, and secured permission to
test the air control method operationally. It was used against
the Mahsuds with apparent success in 1925, but military trad-
itionalism quickly reasserted itself. Although the Government
of India's Tribal Control and Defence Committee urged in 1931

that greater use should be made of air power, which had 'placed in the hands of government an offensive weapon of the greatest importance', effective 'even against the most inaccessible tribe', the RAF continued to chafe at its subordination to the army's outdated prejudices.[39]

Its greatest opportunity was snatched from it soon after the commencement of operations against the Mohmand tribe in 1935. At the outset the army accepted the air force dictum that 'no satisfactory test can be carried out so long as ground troops are employed in combination'. But within days a ground column was sent into Mohmand territory, so that instead of being steadily demoralized by the pressure of air blockade, the tribesmen were able to rally and strike directly against a tangible enemy.[40] Maffey had protested in 1922 against the policy of driving roads into tribal territory, which in his view merely gave the tribesmen an easier target, but the army seemed wedded to this method. Towards the end of 1935 the RAF saw 'clear evidence that the most strenuous efforts are being made to push on with the most expensive road making programme'. The military authorities no longer had to wait days or weeks for permission from the Government of India: columns were 'rushed off down the motor roads within a few hours'. The net result of this reduction in reaction time was not the imposition of law and order, but a dramatic increase in the level of armed conflict.

The struggle between air force and army modes of control went the army's way until the Second World War made the issue more or less irrelevant. In 1939 the Viceroy, Lord Linlithgow, reviewed the problem and came down in favour of the prevailing military dispositions, which placed large numbers of regular troops in advanced positions inside the unadministered zone.[41] It still seemed self-evident to the Government of India that the sort of control which ground forces could exert could not be duplicated by any other means.

The hostility to air control had an ethical dimension as well. The traditional view obviously served the army's professional interests, but soldiers' dislike of air action seems to have been sincere. Rawlinson angered Trenchard by talking of 'baby bombing', and senior military officers consistently took the view that people subjected to air bombing would not only learn how to survive it but would become justifiably more antagonized and embittered. Field Marshal Chetwode, C-in-C India in 1935, put the military attitude eloquently.

> I loathe bombing, and never agree to it without a guilty conscience. That, in order that 2000 or 3000 young ruffians should be dis- couraged from their activities, dozens of villages inhabited by many thousand women, children and old men, to say nothing of those who have refused to join the *lashkars*, should be bombed, and their inhabitants driven into the wilderness, while the Air Force conduct a leisurely 'month or more' bombing . . . is to me a revolting method of making war, especially by a Great Power against tribesmen.[42]

To the air force this was a wilful misunderstanding of the air method, which presupposed accurate intelligence and the blockading – without human casualties – of the villages from which the *lashkars* came. But the essence of the dispute was not whether air action could effectively interdict the *lashkars*, or whether military punitive columns were, as the RAF alleged, far more damaging to the innocent than air action was. It was at root a question of propriety: was air attack a proper way of dealing with these indomitable and, after their fashion, honour- able warriors?

Adhesion to traditional standards, however admirable in intention, bore a high cost. Not only was order never imposed in the unadministered zone, but the strain of defending outposts like Chitral (branded by Maffey as ludicrous) demonstrably weakened the security of the administered zone. The potential dangers were clear during the 1930 emergency in Peshawar. The bloody clash in the city itself was a textbook example of the misapplication of military force in aid of the civil power. The magistrate who decided to take a section of armoured cars to face the rioters, in the belief that they would be the most economical and invulnerable weapon with which to overawe the crowd, was technically most to blame. But the real culprit was the Indian system, under which the army was assumed to be at the disposal of the civil authority. As a result the military commander saw no need to advise the magistrate on the oper- ational methods and limitations of his armoured cars, and seems to have thought he had no duty to do so.[43] The ease with which a mass demonstration was turned into a riot, and thence into an insurrection, was a grisly augury for the future of British India.

6 The Malayan Emergency, 1948–60

We stand for law and order. It is perhaps the greatest gift inherited that we can bestow on these peoples, and if we suspend the law because we are too incompetent to secure order, that is the end of us, our mission and our ideals.

Oliver Lyttelton

The twelve-year Communist insurgency in Malaya, dated from the declaration in 1948 to the lifting in 1960 of the State of Emergency, was the most protracted conflict faced by Britain – outside Ulster – in the twentieth century. It was also a new kind of conflict, which might be called the first postcolonial war. That is, although it originated as an old-style colonial war, the struggle against Communism soon came to eclipse in the British view traditional colonial postures. Far from resisting Malayan independence, Britain came to foster it as an additional weapon against Communism. In fact a quiet transition to self-government was achieved in 1957, and the 'Emergency' was terminated under the auspices of the new Federation of Malaya.

This was possible primarily because of the ethnic divisions of Malaya, which reduced or removed the possibility of a single nationalist movement, and limited the scope of the Communist insurgency. From the start its mass base was with few exceptions confined to the Chinese community in Malaya and in Singapore. Although the wartime forerunner of the Malayan Communist Party guerrilla organization, the Malayan People's Anti-Japanese Army, had been accepted as a national movement, Malays generally saw the later MCP-MRLA (Malayan Races Liberation Army) campaign as an alien insurrection, to be resisted on racial as well as political grounds.[44] And though the MCP's strength was initially demonstrated in its power to paralyse the Singapore docks, its campaign in Malaya never had a secure urban base once Singapore was detached from the embryonic Malayan state (a step designed to ensure that Malays remained the majority community). It quickly fell back to the

155

Malaya

figurative and literal periphery of the country – the rural areas and, finally, the deep jungle. The jungle gave it the means to endure, but it never attained sufficient weight to threaten any but the weakest government posts or forces.

In these circumstances, the government's failure to destroy the Communist guerrillas in the early years of the insurgency may seem more remarkable than its eventual success. The resilience of the Communist military organization was due to its absolute dedication and its ruthless terrorization of the so-called 'squatter' community, but its inability to achieve real momentum gave the Government room to make mistakes and take half measures without fatally imperilling its position. The British counterinsurgency could develop at a leisurely pace, and be kept under the aegis of the civil power. The struggle was never described as a war: it was always 'the Emergency', even though a twelve-year emergency stretched the sense of the term. Various reasons were advanced for this political fiction. The Colonial Secretary, reassuring the Pahang Planters' Association in 1950, argued that 'if we called this war we should presumably have to deal with our prisoners under International Conventions, which would not allow us to be as ruthless as we are now.' This curious argument may be set alongside the reason given by one of the racier chroniclers of the struggle, that insurance policies would have been invalidated by recognition that a state of war existed.[45]

If this was not a war, or a rebellion (though official reports sometimes spoke of a revolt), it was fought not by rebels but by 'bandits' or 'Communist Terrorists' – CTs. Not everyone was happy with the civil definition of the conflict. Towards the end of 1950 the Director of Anti-Bandit Operations reported that it was becoming increasingly obvious that 'unless the Federal Government is placed on a War Footing . . . a still graver emergency will arise, straining the morale of Malaya beyond breaking point'. GHQ of Far East Land Forces complained that the civil administration was 'still far too slow in many respects for quick action' and that 'more drastic measures' must be considered.[46]

But the arguments against any supersession of the civil power were maintained with great clarity and conviction from the first. Shortly after the State of Emergency was declared on 22 July

1948 the newly arrived High Commissioner, Sir Henry Gurney (previously Chief Secretary in Palestine), accelerated the compilation of a wide-ranging set of Emergency Regulations to provide all the necessary powers. Drawing directly on his Palestine experience, Gurney observed that it was possible to make these powers so comprehensive as in effect to empower the High Commissioner to take any action he saw fit. But he held that 'the withdrawal of the civil power and the substitution of military control represent the first victory for the terrorists'.[47] The declaration of faith in the ordinary law by the Colonial Secretary, Oliver Lyttelton, confirmed this premise.

What came about in Malaya was the development of a novel and fluid form of emergency power, of the sort foreshadowed in Palestine in the last year of the mandate. The essence of martial law as envisaged by successive generations of soldiers, the concentration of authority and the use of force at discretion, was achieved without the pernicious political effects of openly avowed military rule. It was a skilful balancing act which blurred the distinction between civil and military spheres. The crossing of traditional boundaries took place at two levels. At the level of high authority, there was a steady movement towards the acceptance of a civil-military 'supremo' (the exotic term conveying the foreignness of the idea). To begin with, the Commissioner of Police, Colonel Nicol Gray – another old Palestine hand – became *de facto* controller of operations, though his post gave him no direct authority over the troops who were needed to assist the police in all rural searches. Early in 1950 Gurney proposed the appointment of 'an experienced military officer for a new *civil* post', preparing and executing a general counterinsurgency plan. 'In consultation with heads of police and fighting services he would decide priorities between tasks and the general timing and sequence of their execution.'[48]

This was truly a new departure. The role was acceptable to traditional outlooks because it was carefully described as one of coordination – rather like the role of Foch as *generalissimo* of the Allied armies on the Western Front in 1918 – but in fact it also involved the formulation of political policy. The new post of Director of Anti-Bandit Operations was given to a retired lieutenant general, Sir Harold Briggs, who produced his plan of campaign very shortly after his appointment in April. The

'Briggs Plan' was obviously in large part Gurney's work, and stressed the political dimension of the problem. Its overriding aim was the defence and integration of the rural ('squatter') Chinese community by means of resettlement in new villages which would rupture the logistic machinery of the guerrillas. At the same time a clear structure of national and regional authority to implement the plan and control the security forces was laid out. Altogether the plan was a milestone in British counter-insurgency policy. Never before had issues been clarified, remedies specified, and powers harmonized with such precision.

It was, of course, too good to be true. As we shall see, its aims were too ambitious for the capacities of the Malayan administration: both the resettlement programme and the framework of offensive operations based on food denial required skills which the police and army did not, at first, possess. By the end of 1950 there was manifest disappointment at the limited progress made, and in 1951 the MCP guerrilla campaign rose to its highest intensity. The final triumphant emergence of the civil-military supremo came after dramatic changes. In October 1951 Gurney was ambushed and killed. At the end of the year Briggs resigned, and died shortly afterwards. The Colonial Secretary of the incoming Conservative Government completed the sweep by dismissing the Commissioner of Police.

The death of Gurney, whose 'evident grasp of essentials' had gained him the absolute confidence of the Colonial Office, seemed a major disaster. There was no clear sense of direction afterwards. The Commissioner-General for South-East Asia, Malcolm MacDonald, opposed the idea of a 'supremo' and held that the tradition of dual control should be maintained. (He cited the unbalancing impact of the brilliant General de Lattre de Tassigny at that time in French Indochina.) But the new government was predisposed towards replacing Gurney with a soldier, and eventually picked Field Marshal Sir Gerald Templer.

As High Commissioner, Templer had no concrete powers that had not been possessed by Gurney and Briggs. It was rather his abrasive personal style, his determination to act and to be seen to act, that created a new atmosphere. In the words of one commentator, he 'energized' the situation. He reaffirmed the necessity – in which Gurney's belief had seemed to falter – of integrating the Chinese community into a united 'Malayan nation', and of creating 'truly responsible local government'. At the same time he took demonstrative and well publicized coercive action. His rough treatment of the unfortunate inhabitants of Tanjong Malim, near the scene of an ambush, including a violent public castigation, the imposition of a 22-hour curfew, and the exaction of swingeing collective fines, helped to reinforce the Government's prestige.

Under Templer the Malayan police organization reached its final shape. This was the other level at which traditional boundaries were crossed. Gurney's original insistence on maintaining the civil power was linked with the argument that the government's principal instrument must be the police force. 'The day is past in which a clear dividing line could be drawn between the responsibilities of the police for maintaining law and order and the role of local military forces in internal security or defence against external attack.' Flying directly in the face of the recommendations made by professional police advisers in Palestine, Gurney held that 'the old concept that the police must do the policing and the armed forces the fighting is both dangerous and dead (or should be)'.[49] The inevitable result of such an outlook was the expansion and militarization of the police to meet the emergency.

The first of these processes was carried so far that the overblown force threatened to collapse under its own weight. Worse, the Commissioner of Police's attempt to promote his fellow 'Palestinians' to senior commands in the expanded force led to severe internal stresses. Despite Gurney's professed faith that Gray commanded universal confidence as operational planner, Gray was brought to the point of resignation in October 1950 on the grounds that 'political considerations . . . are impeding the improvement of the Force at a high level'.[50] Briggs initially took the view that Gray was irreplaceable, but eventually came round to the opinion (also held by the Officer Administering the Government, deputizing during Gurney's absence in London) that the police would never 'come right' while Gray was in post: there was a 'wall of resistance' and he was not really getting his orders carried out.[51]

The militarization of the police was also fraught with problems. It was effectively symbolized by the question of whether police vehicles should be armoured. Gray, though a militarizer in many respects, stood out against the use of armour on traditionalist police grounds. The argument in favour of armouring at least the cabs, if not the bodies, of police trucks was that the high incidence of police casualties in ambushes was primarily due to the immobilization of their vehicles when their drivers were killed in the first burst of fire. If trucks could be driven out of the ambush position, there would be a much greater chance of mounting an effective counterattack. Against this Gray put forward a series of arguments, some of which were technical – that armour simply reduced mobility, critically so on unmade roads – and some tactical – that armour would discourage the men from getting out of their vehicles and attacking the ambushers. But his strongest arguments were moral. Armour would alter the public perception of the police, and might place a fatal psychological gulf between them. Gray even went so far as to suggest that the vulnerability of police patrols was an indirect means of protecting the public – 'the more the police are protected the more likely are bandits to be driven to civilian targets'.[52]

Few others could accept that such arguments outweighed the frequent and demoralizing success of the insurgents in killing police and capturing weapons. The Negri Sembilan State Security Committee pointed out that 'soldiers can have this measure of protection without impairing their offensive spirit'. In the end armouring went ahead, though too late to prevent a sequence of minor tragedies. The armour issue played a part in the gradual erosion of Gray's position, and influenced Lyttelton's formal decision to remove him. His successor, Arthur Young, ex-Commissioner of the London Metropolitan Police, cut back the size of the force drastically and urged the adoption of British police methods. Operation 'Service' pressed the Malayan police to emulate the ways of the English bobby, not entirely without success. But the most thoroughgoing reform took place in the intelligence sphere.

Briggs saw clearly enough that the quality of the intelligence service would be the hinge of the counterinsurgency effort, and that the Malayan CID was not up to the task. He brought in Sir William Jenkin, a retired Indian Police officer, as adviser on reorganization in May 1950, though another internal crisis had to be weathered before Jenkin could be formally appointed

Director of Intelligence, with access to the High Commissioner and executive control over the CID and the strengthened Special Branch, in November.[53] The Special Branch was overhauled in August, and eventually came to fulfil the function envisaged by Briggs, directing and coordinating the whole intelligence machinery of the security forces. Military intelligence was permanently linked with it at the level of each state, where intelligence was under the control of a Head of Special Branch; and was temporarily linked for particular operations at local level through the Circle Special Branch Officers. The merging of all intelligence-gathering and processing under a single agency was seen by most participants as the crucial element in the counterinsurgency. Mistakes remained to be made, and it is obvious that the best intentions could never entirely overcome differences of outlook and procedure. (The experience of Frank Kitson, coming to Malaya quite late in the Emergency, undoubtedly shows that the army's capacity to utilize police information remained limited.)[54] But the Special Branch sped up the slow process of learning, and replacing haphazard methods by those with a clearly conceived purpose.

At the operational level the campaign was a gradual elaboration of the two effective methods of engaging the MCP, resettlement and 'food denial'. Resettlement, as we have seen, was grasped in principle from the outset, but the administrative effort needed to make it workable was enormous. The Briggs Plan aimed to put half a million squatters beyond the reach of the guerrillas by concentrating them in 'New Villages' defended by police and community guards. To do this successfully the government needed to apply overwhelming force at the point of each movement. By and large the initial success rate was high. The Chinese community accepted the advantages which the new settlements offered, though not until Templer's arrival were they offered security of land tenure in them. The problem lay in policing – preventing the guerrillas from penetrating the villages either while they were being established or afterwards. This required an infrastructure which could not be created as fast as it was needed. The security measures involved, such as twice-daily body searches, were burdensome, and the overgrown police force was often incompetent or corrupt.

The administrative framework had been in existence for a

long time before steady refinement made it reasonably efficient. But from the very start it established a mechanism for engaging the phenomenally elusive communist guerrillas, by focusing their activity in areas defined by the authorities. Without such focusing the security forces had no means of coming into contact with the rebels except fortuitously, through being ambushed. Planned searches as usual produced little result. Once again the army took a long time to relearn the lesson that large-scale formal operations could not justify the energy they consumed. As late as the winter of 1952–3, the aggressively-codenamed Operation 'Hammer' in the Kuala Langat area of Selangor failed because – the police thought – the military planners wanted swift and spectacular results. Poor coordination with Special Branch both before and during the operation led to a mismatch between the search area and the area of the target MCP organization. As a result the guerrillas were able to evacuate the search area and still remain in reach of their elaborate supply and intelligence organization. After the first onslaught, 'little information of operational value was forthcoming'.[55]

Eventually military efforts came to be concentrated on a combination of local patrolling with larger-scale 'food denial' operations. As the new villages became well established – and by 1954 this process had gone far enough for Templer to 'reward' some parts of the country by declaring them 'white areas' in which nearly all restrictive Emergency Regulations were lifted – the insurgents retreated further into deep jungle. Throughout the conflict the MCP/MRLA organization was subjected to a certain degree of strain by Special Branch work against its complex jungle communications system. A gradual trickle of surrenders occurred, and the careful treatment of Surrendered Enemy Personnel (SEPs) produced steady success in discovering guerrilla bases. This time-consuming work had some effect in reducing the insurgents' offensive capacity, but could not achieve anything like wholesale elimination. The near-superhuman patience and dedication required is vividly illustrated in Kitson's account of his efforts to find a technique for developing 'background' into 'contact' information.[56] It is doubtful whether any regular military force could be expected to maintain such techniques consistently.

The only alternative was to put pressure on the insurgents by denial of food supplies. The principle involved was simple enough, and had, again, been obvious from the outset; the difficulty was to develop a sufficiently sophisticated procedure to guarantee the result. Such a development was not achieved until the mid-1950s, and despite the skill eventually shown in these elaborate operations it is probably fair to say that they would not have succeeded if the insurgency had not already been on the wane. Their sheer complexity offered enormous scope for disruption by insurgent action.[57] But the MRLA no longer possessed the military energy it had shown in 1950–1. In the earlier period the concentration of such large forces in a small area would have been politically impossible, since it would have exposed the rest of the country to unacceptable risks.

The conclusion that must be drawn is that the Communist insurgency in Malaya was effectively neutralized by 1954. Such small hope as it had ever had of uniting the Malayan peoples against the British had vanished. The battle for the 'hearts and minds' of the people, a phrase that became a watchword of the Emergency, was won by the government primarily, it seems, because it never lost its legitimacy. The emphasis on maintaining civil authority, and the high profile given to social reconstruction within the overall counterinsurgency plan, were not in themselves novel. What was important was that they were both practicable in Malaya. The civil power *could* cope, and reconstruction *could* produce satisfaction. The latter circumstance was perhaps fortuitous: a similar aspiration in Palestine had proved ineffectual. But the preservation of legitimacy was largely the result of conscious effort and a clear grasp of issues.

The marked determination to maintain the outward show of civil authority was reasserted after Templer's two-year reign by once more separating the functions of High Commissioner and Director of Operations (only the latter being a soldier). Much store was set by the avoidance of martial law, though it must be said that the legal system created to meet the Emergency could only be described as the 'ordinary law' by a considerable stretch of the imagination. The special powers taken by the civil authority were far-reaching. Detention without trial was ubiquitous – some 35,000 people were interned – while 15,000 more were deported under the very extraordinary Emergency Regulation 17D, which was framed to deal with squatters before resettlement was fully implemented. Collective punishments were commonplace, and on at least two occasions (at Kachau and Batang Kali) there were cold-blooded massacres of innocent civilians. Reprisals of lesser severity, and a high level of casual violence by both troops and police, were effectively camouflaged by the Government, and in general it is astonishing how successfully the authorities preserved the impression of regularity.

As Sir Robert Thompson observes, the publication of laws and their impartial application – the belief that the 'rule of law' binds the government as well as the people – is the basis of reciprocal obligation. In Malaya this crucial reciprocity was grasped with unusual percipience. When Oliver Lyttelton rebutted the planters' demands for drastic action against so-called 'collaborators', he did so with the argument that 'until the Government could deliver its part of the bargain, which was to protect the citizen on his lawful occasions, it was mere cynicism to prosecute those who were protecting themselves in the only way open to them.' He said, 'At the point of a gun you would pay rather than be murdered, and so would I, and you know it.' Once the Government could provide 'reasonable protection' collaborators would be treated as traitors, but not before.[58] Such wisdom bespoke a confidence that came more easily to secretaries of state than to those directly embroiled in an insurgency, but it was nonetheless wise.

Notes to Chapter IV: Asia

1. Viceroy (Linlithgow) to Secretary of State for India (Amery), 3 September 1942. N. Mansergh and E.W.R. Lumby (eds), *The Transfer of Power*, HMSO 1971, vol.II, no.401.
2. S. Qureshi, 'Political Violence in the South Asian Subcontinent', Y. Alexander (ed), *International Terrorism*, New York 1976, p.178.
3. Sir A. Rumbold, *Watershed in India 1914–1922*, London 1979, p.140.
4. Sir C. Tegart, 'Terrorism in India', Address to the Royal Empire Society, 1 November 1932. *United Empire*, XXIII, 1932, pp.661–3.
5. J.H. Broomfield, *Elite Conflict in a Plural Society: Twentieth Century Bengal*, Berkeley 1968.
6. Governor of Bengal, minute, 24 April 1913. Broomfield, op.cit., p.75.
7. Govt of India, Home Department, to Sec. of State, 26 March 1914. Rumbold, op.cit., p.16.
8. Sir P. Griffiths, *To Guard my People: The History of the Indian Police*, London 1971, p.242.
9. Maj.Gen. Sir C. Gwynn, *Imperial Policing*, London 1934, p.37.
10. I. Colvin, *The Life of General Dyer*, Edinburgh 1929, p.165.
11. AOC Middle East to Chief of Air Staff, 24 November 1919. Trenchard papers C.II/18, MFC 76/1/57.
12. Sir M. O'Dwyer, *India as I Knew It*, London, 1927, p.283. Colvin, op.cit., p.194.
13. Colvin, op.cit. p.176.
14. Gwynn, op.cit., p.63.
15. D. Arnold, 'The Armed Police and Colonial Rule in South India, 1914–1947', *Modern Asian Studies*, II, 1977, p.105.
16. A small but quite significant peculiarity of the Indian regulations governing military aid to the civil power was that when the civil authorities called for military aid the military were bound to provide it, and were bound to fire when called on to do so by the civil official present. Thus a substantial discretionary element in the British law was removed.
17. R.L. Hardgrave, Jr, 'The Mappilla Rebellion, 1921: Peasant Revolt in Malabar', *Modern Asian Studies*, II, 1977, pp.75–6.
18. Viceroy to India Office, telegram, 24 August 1921. CP 3265, CAB 24 127.
19. Ibid.
20. Governor of Madras to Sec.of State, 10 October 1921. Montagu papers, India Office Library MSS Eur.F.136.
21. Governor of Madras to Viceroy, 6 September 1921. IOR, MSS Eur.F.93.

22. GOC Madras to GHQ India, 24 October 1921. Hardgrave, op.cit., pp.88–9.
23. GOC Madras, Final Report on the Operations in Malabar, 14 March 1922. Hardgrave, op.cit., p.91. For a semi-official account, see R.H. Hitchcock, *A History of the Malabar Rebellion*, Madras 1925.
24. Hardgrave, op.cit., p.95.
25. *The Philosophy of the Bomb*, drafted for the Hindustan Socialist Republic Association by Bhagwati Charan.
26. Note on the Policy of the Terrorist Parties in Bengal, by Special Superintendent R.E.A. Ray, CID, Bengal, 13 January 1932. C.P.148(32), CAB 24 229.
27. Ray, quoted in Griffiths, op.cit., p.268.
28. Tegart, 'Terrorism in India', p.670.
29. D. Clark, 'The Colonial Police and Anti-Terrorism', Oxford University D.Phil. thesis, 1983, p.123.
30. Broomfield, *Elite Conflict*.
31. Govt of India, Home Department, to Sec.of State, 12 September 1942. Mansergh and Lumby (eds), *Transfer of Power*, vol.II, no.735.
32. Sir J. Maffey, 'Unsolicited Views on an Unsolved Problem', 2 August 1922. Trenchard papers, MFC 76/1/39.
33. Ibid.
34. WO 208 773, 774.
35. General Staff, India. Note on Military Policy Towards the Tribes of the North-West Frontier, 1919. AIR 5 1323.
36. Trenchard to Rawlinson, 8 December 1921. Trenchard papers, MFC 76/1/136.
37. Notes on Air Power on the North-West Frontier, 16 October 1935. AIR 5 1325.
38. Maffey, op.cit.
39. Report of the Tribal Control and Defence Cttee, Govt of India, 1931. AIR 23 684. Notes for DDOps, 16 October 1935. AIR 5 1325.
40. Notes for Deputy Chief of Air Staff on Mohmand operations 1935, 14 October 1938. AIR 5 1323.
41. Memorandum on Frontier Policy, 22 July 1939. IOR, L/P&S 12/3265.
42. C-in-C India to Viceroy, 20 August 1935. AIR 23 687. (The C-in-C withdrew the letter 'after strong protest by the Air Officer Commanding'.)
43. Gwynn, *Imperial Policing*, pp.253–75.
44. A. Short, *The Communist Insurrection in Malaya 1948–1960*, London 1975, p.271.
45. Notes of meeting, CO 537 5991. N. Barber, *The War of the Running Dogs*, London 1971.

46. 'Appreciation of the Military and Political Situation in Malaya as on 25 October 1950.' GHQ FARELF to Ministry of Defence, 13 November 1950. CO 537 5975.

47. HC Malaya to Sec.of State for Colonies, 30 May 1949. CO 537 4773.

48. Chiefs of Staff Cttee, 2 March 1950. CO 537 5974.

49. HC Malaya to Sec.of State for Colonies, 30 May 1949. CO 537 4773.

50. HC Malaya to Sec.of State for Colonies, 28 February 1949. CO 537 4750. Commr of Police to Chief Sec. Malaya, 21 October 1950, and to OAG, 3 November 1950. CO 537 5973.

51. Notes on 'Police Command' by H.R. Briggs, 25 October 1950; OAG (Sutton) to HC (Gurney), 3 and 15 November 1950. Loc.cit.

52. Short, *Communist Insurrection in Malaya*, p.279.

53. Jenkin to Acting Chief Sec.Malaya, 10 November; Sutton to Gurney, 15 November 1950. CO 537 5973.

54. F. Kitson, *Bunch of Five*, London 1977, pp.79–151.

55. Short, op.cit., pp.365–6.

56. Kitson, op.cit., pp.88ff.

57. For a detailed description of these operations see R. Clutterbuck, *Riot and Revolution in Singapore and Malaya*, pp.220–50.

58. Short, op.cit., p.332.

Notes on Further Reading

The successful suppression of the history of Indian insurgency is one of the more surprising achievements of the British Raj, enduring long after its death. Whilst the North-West Frontier was a byword for unremittingly fierce conflict – a classic *genre* piece here is Winston Churchill's *The Story of the Malakand Field Force* (Longmans, London 1898) – India was blanketed under the *Pax Britannica*. The most striking example of massive censorship is the non-history of the 1942 resistance movement: only recently have occasional scholarly studies (e.g. F.G. Hutchins, *India's Revolution* (Harvard University Press, Cambridge, Mass. 1973), unsurprisingly unsympathetic to the British authorities) and S.A.G. Rizvi, *Linlithgow and India* (Royal Historical Society, London 1978) begun to appear. The abolition of the event is most apparent in the great document collection *The Transfer of Power* edited by P.N.S. Mansergh and E.W.R. Lumby (14 vols, HMSO London 1970–1984). The Mappilla rebellion and Bengal insurgency remain shrouded in obscurity. The uncharacteristic exception is Amritsar, which has been the subject of two useful books, R. Furneaux, *Massacre at Amritsar* (Allen & Unwin, London 1963), and A. Draper, *Amritsar* (Cassell, London 1981). The context is clearly explored in Sir Algernon Rumbold, *Watershed in India* (Athlone Press, London 1979). Dyer, the quintessential imperial soldier/policeman, has not yet had a modern biography. I. Colvin, *The Life of General Dyer* (Edinburgh 1929), is vigorous but intensely partisan. The autobiography of Sir Michael O'Dwyer, *India as I knew it* (Constable, London 1925), is the same, but lays bare the presuppositions of the Raj administration. There is a lucid and sympathetic panorama of the Indian civil service and army in P. Mason (Woodruff), *The Men who Ruled India* (2 vols, Jonathan Cape, London 1953–4), and *A Matter of Honour* (Jonathan Cape, London 1974). The same, rather more one-dimensionally, is done for the Indian police in Sir Percival Griffiths, *To Guard my People* (E. Benn, London 1971). Their opponents are now beginning to receive first-class scholarly attention. Judith M. Brown's *Gandhi's Rise to Power* (Cambridge University Press 1972), and *Gandhi and Civil Disobedience* (Cambridge University Press 1977), will be revelatory to many readers, not least those who have seen the Attenborough film.

Malaya cannot claim the same range or quality of works, but there is a very substantial analysis of the Emergency in A. Short, *The Communist Insurrection in Malaya* (Muller, London 1975), which can be complemented by R. Clutterbuck, *The Long, Long War* (Cassell, London 1967), and *Riot and Revolution in Singapore and Malaya* (Faber & Faber, London 1973). N. Barber, *The War of the Running Dogs* (Collins, London 1971) is a ripping yarn, and a good example of how journalists dramatize events which hover on the brink of crisis without ever quite going over. Sir Robert Thompson, *Defeating Communist Insurgency* (Chatto & Windus, London 1966) is the definitive official memoir.

V

Africa

1 Order and rebellion in sub-Saharan Africa

Rebellion was rare in British Africa. Between the convulsions
of the conquest in the late nineteenth century, which culminated in the great Boer War, and decolonization after 1945, of
which the most savage was Mau Mau, British rule was maintained by a happy mixture of bluff and consent.[1] Modern
historians of Africa tend to emphasize the continuity of African
resistance to colonial power, whether the 'indirect' control
favoured by Britain in most of its African possessions, or the
rarer colonization involving white settlement. But it is easy
to distinguish different modes of resistance. The initial or
'primary' resistance was a reflex reaction to outside intrusion,
mostly uncoordinated and easily crushed by small amateur
armies of Europeans with modern weapons. The most substantial resistance was offered by the Asante (Ashanti) in Nigeria,
the Shona and Ndebele (Matabele) in Rhodesia, and the Zulu
in southern Africa.[2]

After the crushing of these tribes, there followed a generation
of transition. Absence of open revolt was accompanied by the
creation of political movements using modern European
nationalist concepts. Finally, renewed overt 'secondary' resistance was marshalled under the banner of nationalism (however
awkwardly this ideal fitted the arbitrary political boundaries
which had been established by European colonial competition).[3]
Even in this final phase, though, internal emergencies requiring large-scale military action remained unusual. British colonies
never saw a national insurrection as formidable as the Maji
Maji wars in German Tanganyika. Troops were used to suppress disorders in Nigeria in 1929, Sierra Leone in 1931, the
Copperbelt in 1935, and in the 1950s even Nyasaland slid into

serious disturbances. None of these crises could be described as an insurgency; nonetheless, the response of the colonial authorities was habitually brusque.[4] Martial law was seldom required, because the emergency regulations which became 'normal' in the twentieth century provided powers which were adequate and less provocative. The general crisis of colonialism did not set in until the 1950s, and then the wind of change began to blow so strongly that all but the most obtuse settlers bowed before it. Nationalist movements were able to come to power in many states without the need to resort to armed struggle.

The apparent ease with which decolonization occurred, however, should not obscure the fact that the colonial administrations in Africa were tough. If they rested on bluff for their day-to-day working, the underlying threat of force was easily credible. Early pacifications had often shown the special violence peculiar to small ruling groups faced by huge subject populations. It is noteworthy that dum-dum ammunition, with its horrific effects, was considered appropriate for use against natives even after the Hague Convention, by which time its use against Europeans (for instance by the Boers) provoked virulent denunciation. Such violence was necessary for rulers who remained alien in background and outlook, even when they spoke of the 'paramountcy of African interests'. Consensus could not be achieved; quiescence could not be exactly equated with 'order'; and it might be said that Africa in the transitional phase between primary and secondary resistance was in a state of veiled insurgency and endemic emergency.

2 South Africa I: The Boer guerrilla struggle

In scale and significance, the Boer War of 1899–1902 dwarfed all other British conflicts – the two world wars apart – in modern times. It made a grimly prophetic opening to the twentieth century. Its scale was vast: fighting extended not only across the open expanses of the two Boer republics, the Orange Free State and the Transvaal, but also spread through much of the British Cape Colony and part of Natal. By late 1900 some 240,000 British troops were deployed on combat and internal security duties, in an attempt to overcome the commitment of the Boer community to total war.

172

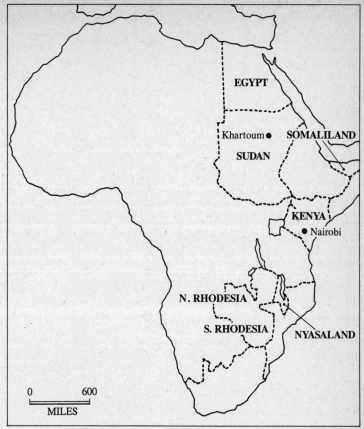

EGYPT

Khartoum● SOMALILAND

SUDAN

KENYA
● Nairobi

N. RHODESIA

S. RHODESIA   NYASALAND

0   600
MILES

Africa: British Territories

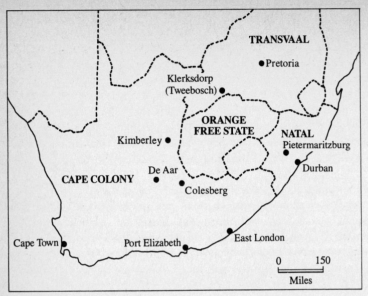

South Africa

The war's significance lay not so much in its political results as in its military lessons – though these were widely misinterpreted at the time. The early phase of open combat was remarkable, but the most enduring lesson lay in the more confused period of irregular warfare which followed. The first, spectacular phase of sieges (Ladysmith, Kimberley, Mafeking) and setbacks (Magersfontein, Colenso, Spion Kop) was over in little more than six months. Indeed, Cronje's surrender at Paardeberg in February 1900 took place barely four months after the start of hostilities; Prinsloo's surrender in July set the full stop to conventional military operations. By contrast the second phase, of fluid and dispersed fighting, lasted almost two years.

The first phase demonstrated the power of modern rifle arms to transform the nature of battle by imposing awful penalties on attackers, and creating what has been called the 'empty battlefield'. In this, though, it did no more than confirm the lessons of the Turkish defence of Plevna against the Russians in 1877. Likewise, in demonstrating that staff work was the lifeblood of modern armies, it merely taught the British a lesson that had already been learnt by most continental states. The second phase was considerably more novel. In effect it saw the delineation of modern guerrilla warfare, the war of the militarily weak against the strong, in which political motivation counts for more than military organization. The Boers demonstrated that with sufficient determination and support, dispersed irregulars can turn the very strengths of their opponents into weaknesses, and impose disproportionate costs on an occupying power.

This lesson was to hold good in other circumstances, confounding the British hope that the oddities of Boer geography and society would make the war a treacherous guide to the future. In many ways the burghers provided a limpid illustration of the ideal type of 'people's war'.[5] The spontaneous cohesion of their variable military units (*commandos*) was rooted in their powerful sense of community. The dispersion of their main armies under Lord Roberts' steamroller advance was accompanied by a refinement in the fighting quality of those who kept the field, as faint hearts and indecisive leaders were cast off.

The Boer guerrilla campaign resulted from the independence and self-sufficiency of the burghers who went on fighting after the fall of Pretoria. The number of *bittereinders* was never precisely known, because formations were so fluid, but it was anywhere between 20,000 and 40,000. Their campaign was shaped primarily by their spirit of independence, but it also had from the start hardheaded and charismatic leaders with definite ideas about its potential.[6] The ideas of commanders like De La Rey, De Wet, Botha and Smuts, were of two sorts. The first was the belief that unremitting resistance within the republics would eventually convince the British that occupation was not worth the cost. The second was the hope that spreading the war to the disaffected Afrikaner population of Cape Colony would create a rebellion which the British could not control. Neither of these objects proved attainable in the event, but they remained valid in principle.

It was the close relationship between the Boers of the free republics and the Afrikaners of Cape Colony which took the *Tweede Vryheidsoorlog* (or Second War of Independence) across the boundary between international war and insurgency. The British were faced with a struggle that was never, even in its early phase, a purely conventional war. As time went by, its warlike qualities became increasingly unrecognizable, and it evolved into a struggle for the control of the civil population. The conflicting logics of conquest and pacification set up tensions within the British leadership, as an internal security scheme of unprecedented scope was gradually elaborated.

As so often, the tension centred on the use of martial law. At the time, and in the circumstances, this was more or less inevitable. The formal involvement of British government and army precluded the sort of rough-and-ready methods used in Rhodesia and elsewhere. Yet at this early point in the century no alternative legal forms of emergency powers were available, so that martial law, with all its drawbacks, had to be employed.[7] There was no doubt of the need for emergency measures. What came to be a matter for dispute was the extent of these measures. Martial law of course applied automatically in the zone of combat, and few people disputed its extension to places like Dundee, Mafeking, Kimberley, De Aar and Colesberg in mid-October 1899. But the further extension of martial law throughout Natal and most of Cape Colony by the end of that month rested on different justification.

This was both military and political. The military justification was that the increasingly complex nature of modern warfare had made old legal definitions of the theatre of war, based on seventeenth-century conditions, inappropriate. In particular, the old legal test – whether the civil courts were still sitting – no longer provided a useful guide to the existence of a 'state of war' in any district.[8] This was a persuasive argument, and it was to be powerfully reinforced after 1914 by the inescapable 'totalization' of war. Yet it had the weakness of novelty in 1899. The political justification was connected with it, though different: it was the contention that a large proportion of the Cape Colony population was disloyal, and likely to assist the enemy.

This was certainly true, though it is impossible to be sure how serious the threat to British control was. For once, the authorities were less alarmist than they might have been, in the light of Boer optimism. Many Boers, from commando leaders like Jan Smuts to lone troopers like Deneys Reitz, were convinced that a full-scale insurrection would start among the Cape Dutch if only a sufficient stimulus could be applied.[9] They kept on trying, all the way through until 1902, but without success. They attributed their failure to the ruthless British internal security measures. The British seem to have had a more realistic view of the difficulties in the way of open insurrection. Admittedly the ineffectual Governor of Cape Colony, Sir Walter Hely-Hutchinson, reported as late as October 1901 that half the white population were 'more or less' pro-Boer; he thought that most of the Colony was 'in a half-suppressed state of secret rebellion', and the incursion of Smuts could precipitate 'a war of revolution'. The highly aggressive High Commissioner for South Africa, Sir Alfred Milner, admitted at the same time that the British writ did not run beyond the towns and railway lines.[10] Yet it was obvious by then that the Colony had withstood a long 'invasion' by commandos under Kritzinger and Hertzog without suffering open revolt.

This fact inevitably complicated the authorities' position. The army was demanding the extension of martial law throughout the Colony, with comprehensive controls over the civilian population, not only to eliminate opposition but also to eliminate 'fence-sitting' and enforce active cooperation. The Cape Colony Government resisted the military demands more or less openly. The British authorities, Milner in South Africa and

Joseph Chamberlain in London, had to consider whether the army's way of winning the war might result in losing the peace.

The main tussle was over the 'five ports', Cape Town, Wynberg, Simonstown, Port Elizabeth and East London, which in 1901 remained outside the scope of martial law. The army, using the military argument already outlined, held that vital supplies were reaching the commandos through this huge chink in the British armour. The Cape Government countered by charging that martial law was oppressive and unjustifiable: to apply such brutish controls to the finely-tuned centres of trade would bring economic ruin. They pointed to the maladministration of martial law, in the hands of incompetent and insolent junior officers, across the Colony at large. Extensive dossiers of military inefficiency and oppression were compiled.[11] The army, perhaps unwisely, tried to refute the allegations *in toto*, and became increasingly isolated. By September 1901 Lord Kitchener was telling the Secretary of State for War that 'the attitude taken up by the Cape Government is nothing less than one of actual hostility to His Majesty's Forces, and the same is going on throughout the Colony'.[12] 'Martial law,' he later added, 'is always a difficulty but it is rendered ten times more so if every unfounded complaint is taken up by an irresponsible official.'

The most irresponsible official, in Kitchener's view, was the Attorney General of Cape Colony, John Rose Innes. Until his appointment there had been 'peace between the civil and military'. In the opinion of the former Attorney General (now Kitchener's legal adviser in the occupied republics) Innes was 'off his head'.[13] It is clear that Innes took an extremely combative stance on martial law. In August 1901 he declared that 'whole areas of the Colony are gradually but surely being ruined, with the result that disaffected persons are gravitating to the enemy, while well affected citizens are becoming sullen, indifferent and lukewarm'. To this serious charge he added a personal note when he told Hely-Hutchinson, 'When two people ride the same horse one of them must be in front – we cannot work martial law on even terms with the military – either they or we must be in front. I am not going to ride behind.'[14]

This was of course an absolute negation of martial law. But were Innes' charges groundless, as Kitchener maintained? His

most serious allegation was that the army had illegally compelled civilians to join *ad hoc* defence units ('Town Guards').
The army never satisfactorily rebutted this charge, and when it
tried to deflect criticism by branding all allegations as the
malicious propaganda of disloyal Afrikaners, it looked to be
protesting too much. There is plenty of evidence that military
rule was both inefficient and unpleasant. Civil officials complained of the 'improper, not to say insulting treatment' they
received from local military authorities, and a more neutral
witness, who in fact later became a Deputy Judge Advocate in
the martial law administration, reported from De Aar that
martial law was 'most disagreeable . . . A civilian is treated like
a dog and requires a pass at every turn.'[15] The Secretary of
State for War, St John Brodrick, who gently prodded Kitchener
on this matter throughout the war, wrote at the end that he was
still receiving reports from various quarters that martial law was
'unintelligently administered'.[16]

The spectre of domineering junior officers wielding tyrannical powers was the tip of the iceberg of the British campaign as
a whole. The failure of early attempts to hunt down the elusive
commandos was followed by the methodical creation of the vast
internal-control machine which has ever since been linked with
Kitchener's name. The problem facing the army was indeed
baffling. The 'pacification' of wide expanses of *veld* across
which armed men shifted, dispersed, or coalesced into commandos anything from a few dozen to several hundred strong
for attacks on supply depots and convoys, or even military
columns, defied conventional wisdom. The vulnerable communication system, especially the railway lines, provided
opportunities for sabotage by quite small fighting bands, and
forced a massive dispersion of troops on defensive duties. The
commandos always seemed to have warning of the approach of
a British force, while the troops could get no information about
their opponents.

The basic problem, it was widely recognized, was one of
mobility. The burghers, even when occasionally caught at a
disadvantage, were able to outrun the pursuing forces – this
despite the fact that they took with them the lumbering ox-
wagons which were often their only remaining personal property (their farmsteads, as we shall see, having been burned by

the British). After each encounter fight there was a duel of dust-clouds, in which the British horsemen could usually be relied on to lose their way or halt to rest their mounts first. At root, as the *Times History* afterwards insisted, it was a matter of individual skills of horsemastership and wagonmastership. The Boers 'were born cattle drivers and they practised instinctively the art of concealing their transport at a long distance in the rear of their fighting line, and of covering its movements, if necessary, by sham demonstrations'.[17]

The first attempt at an answer to the problem was to create flying columns which could match the skills of the commandos. This was, as always, the most attractive solution in a military sense. Unfortunately the standards required proved all but impossible to attain. A few columns became very effective, but the bulk of the mounted troops (partly because they were short-service volunteers who were repeatedly replaced) did not. There could be no more eloquent comment on this than the fact that as late as March 1902 a strong column under one of the most experienced commanders, Lord Methuen, was surprised and destroyed at Tweebosch by the commando (De La Rey's) it was pursuing.

Even before Lord Roberts handed over the South African command to Lord Kitchener in November 1900, after announcing that the war was 'practically over', it was clear that there would be no swift, clean military success. Dirtier methods were set on foot. The columns might not be able to locate or destroy the commandos, but they could strip away their logistic base by destroying their farms and crops. A methodical programme of 'devastation' was accordingly begun. At first this strengthened the guerrillas by stiffening moderate Boer hostility to the British. In the long term, however, it closed off vast swathes of land to commando operations. Despite their astonishing resilience, their capacity to bear hardships and privations, there were limits beyond which even burghers could not subsist.

The policy of farm-burning was inherited by Kitchener from Roberts, though its nature changed after the annexation of the two republics by Britain. Devastation had been unexceptionable as a war measure, but became increasingly dubious as a measure of internal security. Another, more novel, response to Boer mobility was developed under Kitchener's own auspices.

Out of two unavoidable policies, the depopulation of the devastated lands, and the defence of railway lines against sabotage, Kitchener wove a coherent strategy of concentration camps and blockhouse lines. This strategy was cruel and unimaginative in the view of many (including many soldiers), but it seemed that these qualities offered the only way forward.

The final machinery has always been directly associated with Kitchener himself, and some thought must be given to his outlook and methods. A natural centralizer, constitutionally incapable of delegating work, Kitchener ensured that the counter-guerrilla machinery was built in his own image. It was an odd image: his reputation as an organizer, a sort of latter-day Carnot, was belied by the confusion of his actions. 'K of K' was proverbially rendered 'K of Chaos' in South Africa. His mishandling of the assault on Cronje's laager at Paardeberg, when he was Roberts' chief of staff, set the tone for his loose control as Commander-in-Chief, as he dispatched flying columns to beat across the countryside in random, ineffectual patterns. (This he called 'hustling' the enemy.) Just as he had achieved little as Chief of Staff, so he failed to establish a chief of his own to coordinate operations. More seriously still, he never developed an intelligence service to secure the information needed to locate the commandos. Even the financial efficiency on which he had built his reputation in Egypt and the Sudan was flouted in South Africa: the prodigal expenditure of manpower and material (the *Times History* talked of the 'sickening waste of horseflesh' involved) not only militated against the building-up of expertise, but helped to keep the *bittereinders* in the field long after devastation should have paralysed them. By the end of the war most Boer survivors were clothed in variants of British uniform and armed with Lee-Metfords, in place of their old Mausers. Deneys Reitz provides at one point in his journal a graphic account of the refitting of a tiny, exhausted group of fighters at British expense.

> The English soldiers were notoriously careless with their ammunition. If a round or two dropped from their bandoliers they would never trouble to dismount, as they knew they could get more, and at their halting places one could always find cartridges lying spilt in the grass.[18]

By riding back along the line of march of a British column for a day or two, Reitz and his companions were able to pick up nearly a hundred rounds.

Kitchener's crucial contribution was not so much organizational skill as his ability to create an atmosphere of confidence and determination. He built up the image, as much as the reality, of a remorseless grinding-machine that would inexorably reduce the Boers to dust. Undoubtedly this told on the spirit of the Afrikaner population as a whole, even if the most active commando leaders remained unimpressed by the machine's efficiency. This image drew much of its substance from the concentration camp system, an administrative expedient in which Kitchener took little direct interest. Only gradually did the camps turn from *ad hoc* accommodation for the Boer families displaced by the devastation programme into central symbols of repressive will. Without showing any urge to visit a camp, Kitchener imperturbably fended off the charges of maladministration laid by increasing numbers of visitors. The statistics of disease and death, which became a major public scandal, left him unmoved. The psychological impact of the camps, which was their most important effect, appears to have been an accidental by-product of unpreparedness.

The blockhouse system also bore his personal (or impersonal) impress. A mere expedient to protect railway lines in the first instance, the blockhouse was progressively refined into a cheap and easily erected key to a gigantic network of barbed-wire fence lines. The need to make blockhouses proof against assault became easier to meet as Boer formations diminished in size, and more importantly in firepower, as artillery was gradually abandoned by the guerrilla commandos. The fence lines could never resist the passage of determined groups with wire-cutters at night, but they imposed a definite penalty on movement. Kitchener's object was to divide the entire zone of operations into areas which he first labelled 'paddocks'; his imagery soon changed to that of the grouse moor – the blockhouse lines became butts against which the quarry was 'driven' by lines of beaters. The resulting captures of Boers were 'bags'. The system promised to eliminate the elusiveness of the commandos, and the intelligence gap between them and their pursuers.

But even within these lines, 'drives' remained an uncertain quantity. The biggest mechanical difficulty was synchronization. Under skilled leadership, free of Kitchener's control, the complex coordination that was needed could be achieved. Even so, the 'bag' of commandos was always disappointing. Ian Hamilton, who had Kitchener's trust, succeeded in putting together a model drive in the western Transvaal in May 1902; 17,000 troops operating over six days bagged a few hundred bedraggled survivors.[19] Sir John French was given the freest hand of all, with responsibility for controlling Cape Colony, and his persistent action there at least kept the invading commandos on the move.[20]

In the end, the winding up of the war was a political rather than a military issue. Milner could not accept Kitchener's careless, haphazard methods – with brilliant perceptiveness he wrote to Brodrick in November 1900 that Kitchener, 'a man of great power, is stale. Worse than that, he is *in a hurry*. Now the essence of the business in its present form is that it must be done gradually.' Milner had in fact grasped the essence of guerrilla warfare: 'it is no earthly use dashing about when there is nothing to get at the end of the dash'; what was needed was 'gradual subjugation, district by district, leaving small entrenched garrisons . . . and mounted police to patrol between these posts.'[21] Kitchener was unsympathetic. He was indeed in a hurry to take up command of the army in India, and complained that the Cape Government did not want to end the war.[22] Milner sabotaged the first round of peace talks at Middelburg in February 1901 because he wanted unconditional surrender, conquest rather than compromise. Yet all the military operations of the next twelve months failed to drive the Boers into significantly greater concessions. The Vereeniging peace laid the basis of future Afrikaner ascendancy in the eventual Union of South Africa, and sealed the fate of Milner's dream of a model Imperial state.

Milner could rightly lay some of the blame on Kitchener's ineptitude. The lesson of the South African war was the extraordinary difficulty of adapting regular armies to cope with 'intelligent' guerrillas (the adjective used to distinguish white irregular fighters from primitive native warriors). Great efforts, mental as much as physical, were needed, and very few soldiers were interested in making such adaptations. It is possible that a more rapid refinement of counter-guerrilla techniques might have given Milner the victory he wanted, but in all internal wars simple conceptions of victory are dubious. Milner's vision of a new British super-colony was unreal as long as 'pacification' within acceptable political limits remained insufficient to subdue Boer resistance.

3 South Africa II: 'When is a war not a war?'

In June 1901 the Liberal leader Henry Campbell-Bannerman posed and answered the question 'When is a war not a war?' 'When it is carried on by methods of barbarism in South Africa'. With the unerring instinct of the professional politician 'CB' had fixed on a phrase that would gain instant celebrity. Its impact has scarcely been diminished by the experience of two world wars. But the spectacular ethical charge has perhaps overshadowed the legal issue that gave it root. Campbell-Bannerman prefaced his question with the remark, 'A phrase often used is that "war is war". But when one comes to ask about it, one is told that no war is going on – that it is not war.'[23] This was the crucial ambiguity of internal war.

In many subsequent counterinsurgency campaigns, soldiers have been heard to complain that all would be well if only the government would recognize the existence of a state of war, so that truly warlike measures could be applied. In the Boer War, by contrast, there was no obvious problem of this sort: the struggle began as a war of conquest, the army was on active service (which, amongst other things, eased its financial constraints), and even in Cape Colony military rule was largely unchallenged. The Secretary of State for War, in his polite efforts to moderate the severity of military rule, always accompanied his mild protests with the admission that 'of course war is war', thereby ensuring that they would be ignored.[24] The army thus had an ideal opportunity to demonstrate the efficacy of martial law.

Yet it was still unable to impose a military solution. Political restrictions hemmed it in. After the republics were annexed and turned into the 'new colonies', the Government was reluctant to admit that a state of war still existed. In Cape Colony the clash of views was sharpest over the treatment of the 'Cape rebels' – Afrikaners who openly joined 'their people' during the Boer invasions of the colony. The military attitude was predictably straightforward; the political line equally complicated. To soldiers they were virtual outlaws, traitors who could be shot out of hand. Brodrick confessed to Kitchener 'I fear you think our limitations too strict as to shooting rebels. I wish we could go further, but it is a dangerous business . . .'[25] Where did the danger lie? Was it in the excessive zeal of General French, who ordered his standing court martial to proceed against captured rebels 'with the utmost vigour', and compelled 'disloyal Dutch' to watch the public execution of rebels in Dordrecht and Middelburg?[26] This action created a political storm, and there seemed no doubt that it was unnecessarily tough. But it was not clear where the line could be drawn. Even Milner, enthusiast for beating the Boers into submission, showed the queasy instinct of the administrator when it came to the treatment of 'civilians'. 'It won't pay,' he suggested to French, 'to treat every Dutch speaking man as a rebel unless he proves the contrary.' The army's presumption of guilt rather than innocence might prove self-fulfilling. Milner clearly feared long-term political damage from military harshness, but who in practice was to decide which actions were necessary and which excessive? Political reservations might undercut every active policy – farm burning, concentration camps, martial law itself. As Kitchener protested, 'hampered in this way I do not know what I can or cannot do.'[27]

All that was certain was that there were some things he could not do. There were limits to what could be done to fellow-Europeans. The depth of Boer resistance might make this a total war for the *volk*, but it remained a 'white man's war' isolated within a black world.[28] The British were as conscious as their opponents of the dangers of this European civil war. However great their contempt for the personal habits of the Boer womenfolk, they were reluctant to humiliate them openly and undermine white prestige. The *Times History* assumed that 'nobody will deny that, in a war between two white races, destined in the future to live side by side in the midst of a vast coloured population, natives should be armed only in case of the last necessity'.[29] When, at one point, the military command in Natal authorized Zulu chiefs to repel any Boer incursion and to seize Boer stock when opportunity offered, the Prime Minister of Cape Colony protested

> Such action on the part of the natives will not only tend to provoke reprisals, but it will also tend to embitter the Boers . . . and the natives will become imbued with a spirit of lawlessness which will be likely to be permanent and far reaching in its demoralizing effects.[30]

It is instructive to compare the restraints on the British campaign to pacify the Boers with those on the Natal government's campaign against a small Zulu rebellion five years later.

In February 1906 a clash at Trewirgie, near Pietermaritzburg, between a police detachment and a section of the Funzi tribe who had refused to pay a new poll tax ended in the stabbing to death of the detachment commander and one of his men. Within twenty-four hours of this minor incident, martial law had been declared over the whole of Natal. Military operations commenced and continued in various forms until the end of July. Martial law was maintained in force until early September.

This was the drastic response of the Natal authorities to a sequence of passive and semi-active Zulu resistance that can only by some stretch of the imagination be labelled a rebellion, as it was at the time.[31] Indeed, it has been suggested that the crisis was deliberately provoked by the whites in order to give the natives a lesson and squash the 'spirit of lawlessness' and 'insolence' that had been noticed since the Boer War. The most judicious modern study of the disturbances finds no evidence of direct provocation, but it is clear that the authorities' ferocious reaction had the effect of driving passive resisters into the open, and magnifying the scale of the confrontation.[32]

Throughout the insurgency the key to the authorities' actions lay in martial law. As understood in Natal, at least, this simply made manifest the real foundation of white authority over the black population – that is, force. There were few if any restraints on the application of force under martial law. The basis for the declaration of martial law seems to have been the general expectation of rebellion: the incident at Trewirgie had been preceded by a spate of white-animal killings, and the imminence of another Zulu war under the leadership of Cetshwayo's successor, Dinuzulu, was widely credited (though in the event Dinuzulu never became involved). The justification for ruthless repression paralleled that claimed by Dyer in the Punjab in 1919 – to nip rebellion in the bud and to deter future resistance. The common law canon of immediate necessity was not met, and it would thus appear that the declaration of martial law was unjustifiable. This impression is reinforced by the conduct of the white militia forces employed to hunt down the few *impis* which assembled under the chiefs Bambata, Sigananda and Mehlokazulu.

No regular troops were deployed, but the Zululand Field Force under Colonel Duncan McKenzie and the Umvoti Field Force under Colonel George Leuchars seem to have done their best to imitate the operations of the regulars in Jamaica under Governor Eyre. One prominent planter in Mapumulo spoke angrily of

> irresponsible men who act as demi-gods and who, armed with a kind of self-imposed authority think it the correct thing to flog unoffending people . . . Pray let us have a level-headed man at the head of affairs . . . and put a stop to this nonsense of having every man in uniform requiring every native to conform to his idea of what salutation consists of.[33]

It is obvious with the benefit of hindsight that even after Bambata had assembled superficially formidable forces in the Nkandhla forest, they posed no military threat to the government. Straddling the epochs of primary resistance and modern insurgency as they did, they failed to find an effective guerrilla technique or indeed to show the elementary military skills which earlier Zulu forces had clearly possessed.[34] The first catastrophe of their campaign, the 'battle' of Mpukinyoni, was a tiny, tragic repetition of Ulundi. In the final destruction of Bambata at Mome Gorge the Zulu forces took no initiative and were surprised after failing even to post sentries.

McKenzie's military operations were a model of restless energy; he specialized in surprise night marches which required careful control and attention to secrecy.[35] But the lack of military expertise on the part of the insurgents allowed him the maximum freedom to plan sweeping convergent movements with detached columns. Even in difficult terrain like the Nkandhla forest, no Tweebosch could afflict him. McKenzie's outlook was the epitome of the hard line. He was 'a man who held in its utmost development the idea of governing the natives through fear', noted the colonial official Sir Matthew Nathan. His operations were frankly terrorist, and were justified by the conviction that only exemplary force could prevent a rising of a million natives, accompanied by 'the nameless barbarities which the savage mind alone can conceive', designed 'to drive the white man into the sea'.[36] The free hand that he and other column commanders were given shows that his views were in line with those of the Natal government.

The Colonial Office was less happy with them.[37] It was especially unhappy about the proclamation of martial law across the whole colony (a sign of 'exaggerated excitability', in Winston Churchill's view), the imposition of censorship ('pure folly'), the number of executions carried out under martial law, the maintenance of martial law long after the end of any open conflict (in defiance of strict colonial instructions issued after the Jamaica case), and the form of the Act of Indemnity passed by the Natal Legislative Assembly. One Colonial Office minute spoke of this Act as 'contrary to precedent, unsound and dangerous'. The Under Secretary characterized the whole response as 'preposterous'. But the Colonial Secretary decided not to interfere: when he had tried to halt the executions in March, the Natal Government had riposted by resigning *en masse*.[38]

The same posture of impotent hauteur was taken up by the Colonial Office over the court martial and deportation of a chief who had carefully sat on the fence throughout the insurgency, Tilonko. Churchill called this 'a hateful business'; but only when the colony rashly asked that Imperial war medals be struck for the campaign could the Under Secretary give vent to his spleen. He noted sarcastically that there had been

nearly a dozen casualties among these devoted men in the course of their prolonged operations and more than four or even five are dead on the field of honour. In the circumstances it is evident that special consideration should be shown to the survivors.

But in view of the 'distaste' which Natal had shown for 'outside interference of all kinds', he added with heavy irony, the most appropriate 'memento of their sacrifices and their triumphs' would be 'a copper medal bearing Bambata's head, to be struck at the expense of the Colony'.[39] (Bambata's corpse had been decapitated after the battle of Mome Gorge by McKenzie 'in the cause of humanity', to dispel the myth of his invulnerability.)[40]

4 Egypt and the Sudan

The Imperial Government's efforts to restrain colonial regimes, and to impose the 'British way' in alien conditions, can be seen as symptomatic of a tension within the British Empire. The impatience of aggressive settlers with the cautious *non possumus* of the Colonial Office, which was to be marked in Kenya, Rhodesia, and elsewhere, mirrored the process by which much of the Empire was originally acquired. The 'forward' thrust of local commercial interests dragged against the reluctance of those who would be called on to foot the military bill. A related tension was very visible in Egypt. Britain's reluctance to become involved in Egypt is legendary. Only the determination to thwart Napoleon Bonaparte's oriental dream had brought British forces there at the end of the eighteenth century. French cultural interest in Egypt found no echo in Britain. The Suez canal, another French vision, was taken over by Britain only when its strategic implications became belatedly obvious. Thenceforth Suez determined Britain's stance in Egypt. The main object was to maintain political and financial stability, and to prevent internal disorders: Britain's overriding priorities were thus conceived in law-and-order terms.[41]

The British military occupation of Egypt in 1882 occurred under a Liberal administration notoriously hostile to imperial adventures. Gladstone procrastinated but, faced with a nationalist rising, he finally acted. General Wolseley's swingeing victory at Tel-el-Kebir demonstrated Britain's interventionist reflex: any threat to the security of the canal was henceforth met with overwhelming military force. This reflex was triggered again in 1919, and for the last time, disastrously, in 1956. In between the political circumstances had changed radically, largely as a result of the insurgency of 1919–23.

The political circumstances of Egypt at the beginning of the twentieth century were unique. Technically, Britain was no more than *primus inter pares* of the foreign powers whose rights of interference were secured by the 'Capitulations'. In practice, British hegemony was recognized. The British High Commissioner, Lord Cromer, was indisputably the ruler of Egypt, even though the fiction of Egyptian ranks and titles (Sirdar, Pasha, Bey) was maintained for British administrative personnel. Yet because British rule remained indirect and limited, it bore unevenly on Egyptian life. Cromer pursued a policy of economic modernization – predominantly through irrigation engineering – but only in order to achieve political stability. Social change, the natural concomitant of modernization, was resisted for fear of political disturbance. Britain ruled through the traditional landed elite; the growing middle class was kept on the economic and political margins, while the condition of the *fellahin*, the peasantry, actually worsened.[42]

The ambiguity of the British presence was suddenly resolved in 1914. Britain's long cosseting of the Ottoman empire was rewarded with Young Turk belligerency on the side of the Central Powers; Britain denounced Ottoman suzerainty over Egypt and declared a protectorate. Along with the protectorate came an open-ended declaration of martial law over the whole country for the duration of the war. This rather desperate resort was a consequence of Britain's earlier reluctance to build up a civil administrative structure – its inability, in short, to decide either to govern or to leave Egypt alone. The political damage caused by martial law, and the unexpected duration of the war, was worsened by an avoidable breach of faith. Britain tried to sugar the pill of 'protectorate status' by pledging that Egypt would not have to bear the burden of its defence against Turkey. This promise was dishonoured as *fellahin* were recruited into auxiliary forces to meet the exigencies of war.

By 1919 discontent was not confined to the nationalist intelligentsia. The authorities, however, took a characteristically dismissive view of the *Wafd* movement, with its demands for an end to martial law and press censorship (neither of which could be justified after the end of the war). The Foreign Secretary, Balfour, told the High Commissioner in November 1918 'the state has not yet been reached at which self-government is possible. His Majesty's Government have no intention of abandoning their responsibilities for order and good government in Egypt and for protecting the rights and interests of both the native and the foreign populations of the country'. (As so often, what the imperial power saw as 'responsibility' was seen by others as self-interest.) The High Commissioner, Sir Reginald Wingate, was less insensitive, but was out of favour politically: influential Foreign Office officials thought him too soft on Egyptian nationalists.[43]

While he was absent in London for consultations early in 1919, his deputy reported that the *Wafd* agitation 'is dying out, or is at any rate quiescent in the country at large'.[44] In spite of this he proceeded to arrest and deport the leading 'agitators', headed by Saad Zaghlul. This preventive action closely paralleled that taken at the same time in the Punjab. As in Amritsar also, remarkably few – indeed no – security precautions were taken to deal with possible repercussions of the arrests. The authorities were clearly taken by surprise when an upsurge of violence and disorder resulted. A student strike spread to the professions of Cairo on 11 March; riots in the delta towns of Tanta, Damanhur, Zagazig and Mansura had to be met by gunfire; and by 15 March disturbances had spread to Upper Egypt. The first Briton was killed in a delta town on 14 March, and on the 18th eight were killed and mutilated on a train between Luxor and Cairo. At Minieh the railway station was attacked by Bedouin from the desert and 'other rabble armed with guns and knives, in a mob estimated as 4000 strong'. The attack was driven off with heavy casualties by 150 men of the 46th Punjabis.

Was this a rebellion? One observer's view was that it 'almost amounted to a general rising'.[45] In its totality it was certainly a formidable challenge to British rule, though it was clearly mixed in motive, and typical of agrarian revolts in that political awareness was confined to urban areas. For the peasantry the target was not British rule but government as such (carried on by Egyptian officials). This disjunction between urban and rural movements enabled the British to portray the crisis as the result of an extremist conspiracy, and to underestimate the extent of opposition. Yet the persistence of sporadic violence, including terrorism and assassination, for four years after 1919 showed the determination of the nationalist leadership to take control of Egyptian public awareness.[46]

The British response, as has been indicated, was to deploy overwhelming force to suppress the outbreak. The circumstances were unusually propitious for such action. Martial law was already in existence, and substantial military forces – albeit in process of demobilization – were on hand in Egypt. The man on the spot, Allenby's deputy from Beirut, Lieutenant General Bulfin, acted with unhesitating and ruthless energy. Because of Wingate's fortuitous absence in London there was no civilian figure with the weight to counterbalance the military commander, who thus had unusual freedom of action.

The result was a short and sharp military campaign. Bulfin's journey to Cairo from Beirut was punctuated by a series of violent incidents which no doubt, as Sir Charles Gwynn put it, gave him 'an appreciation of the violent temper of the people'. He set about reassembling units which had become separated from their horses and equipment in the first phase of demobilization, and formed strong columns to regain control of the railway lines from Cairo to Alexandria, Port Said, and the south. A force was sent by river to relieve the beleaguered Europeans at Aswan. Once the communications were secure, Bulfin was able to form no less than eighteen flying columns to comb out the rural districts, working outwards from the railway lines. In the towns of Lower Egypt the military role was mainly defensive, providing assistance to the police. In the countryside the operational method was to send out detachments to 'show the flag', interview village omdahs, and hold summary courts. Arrests were, in theory, to be made only by the police. 'The troops were to live as far as possible on the country and their passage was marked by the re-establishment of civil authority.'[47]

The sheer strength of the forces used seems to have sufficed to cow most resistance, and it is not clear whether the degree of violence involved was unreasonable. An impression of extreme severity was certainly generated; as one staff officer observed, 'Of course we went through the country with fire and sword.'

Air bombing was used against crowds on one or two occasions. But allegations of military brutality, though widespread, seem to be weakly substantiated.[48] Gwynn claims that although the delay which the rising imposed on demobilization might well have created ill will towards the population, the troops remained in good temper. Collective punishments were evidently used in places, sometimes rough and ready. But there were few reprisals.[49]

The impact of the suppression of the 1919 rising on Egyptian public opinion did not match the official evaluation. Though open resistance was crushed within a month, sporadic violence continued. It may be doubted whether such dispersed resistance could have influenced British policy, which in this case was unusually clear in its objective. The intention to preserve the protectorate by force if necessary, and to crush the nationalist movement, was signalled by the appointment of Allenby as High Commissioner, and only Allenby's unexpected espousal of Egyptian autonomy produced the volte-face of 1922, when independence was restored.

The uncompromising British action in 1919 was possible because an ambiguous power relationship had been temporarily clarified by the 'exigencies of war'. In Egypt as elsewhere (not least the United Kingdom itself) these wrought remarkable changes in the British way. But forceful action was routinely more acceptable in the control of overseas territories, and especially of peoples prone to outbreaks of 'fanaticism'. Confronted with a fanatical mob, the British felt that the normal rules were automatically suspended. Fanaticism was impervious to reason, and if reasonableness could not work, force was justified. Order had to be restored, and the structure of that order had to correspond with British preconceptions. Anarchy, however self-regulating, was no good. The gulf between British political culture and native cultures was always visible to some degree, but it was nowhere more marked than in Egypt's southern appendage, the Sudan.

If the political status of Egypt was ambiguous, that of the Sudan was doubly so. After Kitchener's conquest of the Mahdist state in 1898, power was exercised through an Anglo-Egyptian 'Condominium'. The Governor-General of the Sudan, whether Kitchener, Wingate, or Stack (who was to be assassinated in

1924), was indubitably British, but as Sirdar of the Egyptian Army he maintained the polite fiction of Egyptian participation. The British could not bring themselves to antagonize Egyptian feeling by denying Egypt's historic claim to the Sudan (which was the basis on which Britain had conquered it, to control the Nile waters). But, believing that Egyptian misrule had been the cause of the Mahdist movement – a belief inherited from General Gordon – they could not avoid taking 'responsibility' for government.

Mahdism was the obsessional bogey of the British administration of the Sudan. The official view of this fundamentalist Islamic revolution was deeply contradictory. Whilst recognizing and deploring the religious conviction that drove the dervishes to the mass slaughter of Omdurman, British administrators followed Gordon in trying to play down the religious significance of the Mahdist movement, and suggesting that it was primarily a revolt against Egyptian oppression (which included, incidentally, Gordon's own efforts as Sirdar to suppress the slave trade run by Arabs out of the southern Sudan). Yet the implication of this, that it was a nationalist movement, was also resisted. Britain's view of its role in the Sudan was a textbook example of paternalism: the Sudanese were a backward people who could be brought towards development by firm but fair control.

The bloody annihilation of the dervish army at Omdurman did not annihilate Mahdism itself. A sequence of small risings followed, inspired by the unnervingly accurate prophecy of the seventeenth-century sheikh Farahwad Taktuk, that 'at the end of time the English will come to you, whose soldiers are called police, they will measure the earth even to the blades of sedge grass. There will be no deliverance except through the coming of Jesus' (*nabi 'isa*).[50] None of these was on a very threatening scale, but the threat of Mahdism was persistently exaggerated, and by the time of the First World War a prepossession with internal security had become ingrained in the British official outlook.[51] This prepossession tended to obscure a further complication in the governance of this vast territory, the enormous difference between the Moslem north and the pagan south. In practice, for all the fears of the administrators (which derived in part from the dramatic personal experiences of Gordon's erst-

194

while lieutenant Slatin), resistance in the north could always be dealt with by well tried methods. In the last great open rebellion, in Darfur, the rebels were slaughtered *en masse* with dum-dum bullets in 1916 as they hurled themselves at the government troops' *zariba*.[52] And however repugnant to British values the Mahdist state had been, it had certainly been recognizably a state. The northern Sudan could be governed.

The southern Sudan was another world. The society of the Nilotic peoples, the Shilluk, the Dinka, most of all the Nuer, was as impenetrable as the *Sudd* swamp itself, the awesome mass of tangled vegetation that blocked the Nile and formed the fastnesses where the Nuer held out against civilization. Harold MacMichael, Civil Secretary of the Sudan, visited the area in 1927 and described it to the Governor as 'the most dismal portion of the Sudan – a Serbonian bog into which has drifted or has been pushed all the lowest racial elements surviving north of the Equator, and a great deal of equally decayed vegetation'.[53] Here the British were confronted by fanaticism of the obscurest kind, the power of magicians (*kujurs* or prophets) who seemed the only authority in a naturally anarchic community.

The confrontation was a long-drawn-out one, mainly because of the financial weakness of the Sudan Government. Such funds as were available were consumed in the north; the creation of an administrative infrastructure in the south was postponed. Military punitive expeditions to suppress cattle raiding were almost prohibitively expensive, and practically ineffective. Their only means of acting was to seize cattle as a form of punitive taxation. 'Administration by *razzia*' was the Nuer experience of civilization for over twenty years.[54]

All this was changed by technology at the end of the First World War. Military aviation dramatically lengthened the arm of the law, and the southern Sudan became a testbed for the effect of air action on undeveloped peoples. As in India, however, the RAF did not have things altogether its own way. In 1919 it spearheaded a military campaign against the so-called 'Mad Mullah' in Somaliland, and believed that this had conclusively demonstrated the effectiveness of air action in the control of tribal territories. The whole doctrine of air control, as developed in the Middle East, was based on the Somaliland experience.[55] The army remained unconvinced, and the civil authorities continued to worry whether 'civilization' could be established by bombing. But in dealing with the Nuer there seemed to be little alternative. Once the Dinka had submitted to British protection, continuing Nuer cattle-raids on them became a breach of order and a challenge to the Government's credibility.

The intangibility of the Nuer fighters created enormous difficulties. The main counterinsurgency campaign took the form of two 'patrols' (S8 and S9) in 1927–8. The central objective was the pyramid of the *kujur* Ngungdeng, now the power centre of his son Guek. According to the Governor-General, Guek had 'become definitely hostile to Government' since mid-1927, and there was 'danger of unrest spreading'. Guek had terrorized his locality, and there seemed 'no chance' of his surrendering 'or reducing his following by peaceful methods'.[56] The British view was well put in the comfortable prediction of *Punch* –

> I fear that Messrs Pok and Gwek
> Will shortly get it in the neck,
> And that an overwhelming shock
> Is due to Messrs Gwek and Pok.

The RAF was confident of its ability to hit and destroy Guek's pyramid, and also of 'the moral effect of the mere presence of aeroplanes on these primitive peoples'. In both respects, however, the RAF sorties were somewhat disappointing. The pyramid was merely damaged, and the uncowed Nuer shot back at the attacking aircraft, wounding a pilot in the thigh.[57]

The most overwhelming shock to the RAF, however, was the termination of air sorties on political instructions after only two days. The same thing was happening as on the North-West Frontier; it happened again in March 1929 when air attacks on Nuer cattle were stopped, leaving the Nuer secure in the belief that their magic had driven the aircraft off. Whereas, the Air Staff never ceased to stress, the crucial function of air action against uncivilized tribes 'is to create in their mind the belief that they are confronted with a weapon against which they cannot retaliate'.[58]

As on the North-West Frontier, a fierce contest went on between the advocates of air and land power. The latter argued that air action was both inhumane and ineffective. The civil authorities, Maffey in Khartoum and Lloyd in Cairo, tended to follow the traditional line that only the opening-up of roads could advance 'true' pacification and civilization.[59] The airmen were frankly contemptuous of the roadbuilding impulse, in Sudan as much as Waziristan.

> It is imposible to share Lord Lloyd's opinion that the solution is to be found in the improvement, at great expense, of ground communications which are of no value other than from a military point of view in order to increase slightly the mobility of inherently slow moving forces who will yet be unable to compete on equal terms with the amphibious inhabitants of the swamps. Even when your road is made your web-footed Nuer is not going to be so obliging as to remain on the road to be shot by troops.[60]

Doggedly refusing to appreciate the idea that pacification involved economic development (in which communications were of primary value), they maintained that if only the civil authorities could grasp the 'control without occupation' concept they would realize its advantages. To Lloyd's objection that it was 'an axiom of Sudan warfare' that only the elimination of individual magicians could guarantee the ending of disturbances, and that air action lacked the precision to achieve this, they replied, 'no magic survives a good bombing'.

In the event it took a conventional battle, in which Guek lost his divinity and his life leading his small army behind a white bull, and carrying the brass pipe of his father Ngungdeng, to lay the basis of pacification. The final campaign was somewhat euphemistically labelled 'Nuer Settlement' rather than 'patrol'. It demonstrated the priorities which appeared in campaigns elsewhere: the resettlement of the population in new villages, and 'the building up of a native administration on the foundations of tribal custom and organization'. This presented special problems with the Nuer, who had no recognizable chiefs, but the British were prepared to go 'to the point of inventing an organization' where tribes had 'lost their own'. As the Governor of Upper Nile Province put it, 'until the Chiefs can be sure of securing obedience for a legitimate order, the "Settlement" cannot be said to have been attained.'[61] The

degree of force needed to secure this obedience was still dis-
concertingly high: this tough nut would yield only to a sledgehammer, so it seemed. Maffey told MacMichael in the midst of
the campaign that he was 'surprised at the extent of military
activity. It is a "war" and I had the impression that it was going
to be something else.'[62] To Campbell-Bannerman's question
'When is a war not a war?' in this context, the answer might
have been, 'When it is a settlement'.

5 The Mau Mau Emergency

The mental gulf between Europeans and Africans visible in the
Sudan took its most spectacular form in Kenya in the 1950s. Its
main line was the disruption of the finely-balanced customary
society of the Gikuyu (or Kikuyu), the biggest and most developed tribe, through the impact of British settlement and administration. The process was luminously analysed by the anthro-
pologist L.S.B. Leakey, who identified the erosion of traditional
education, marriage contracts, and the religious underpinning
of Gikuyu society as factors of instability within the tribe.[63]
Most important of all was the fact that the Gikuyu landholding
system, uniquely in Africa, contained a concept of private
property as well as of inalienable family rights.

The British failure to understand the Gikuyu system, evi-
denced in the official belief that the lands alienated from the
Gikuyu had been quite legally purchased by the white settlers –
and hence that the land issue was a bogus agitation got up by
political extremists – was accompanied by failure to achieve a
decisive military 'pacification' at the time the colony was established. The Gikuyu never formally submitted to British rule. It
seems that the sporadic resistance culminating in the secret
society organization known as Mau Mau was in effect a continuous, if amorphous, insurgency.[64] At the same time, Leakey's
contention that the Mau Mau organization, far from being a
'throwback' (as most settlers alleged) to earlier Gikuyu savagery,
was a novel phenomenon, seems incontrovertible.

The essential change, in Leakey's view, occurred in the form
of the oath-taking that held the societies together. Traditional
Gikuyu oaths had to be administered in daylight and in public;
Mau Mau oaths were administered secretly at night, and usually

under duress. (The oathing first came to the authorities' attention via Christian or older Gikuyu who did not accept the binding nature of the new oaths.) The oathbound societies were undoubtedly terrorist in one important sense. The accompaniment of the increasingly bloodthirsty 'killing' oath and the *batuni* oath by the ritual torture and slaughter of animals and birds, and occasionally the killing and mutilation of humans, was intended to enforce their authority through fear.[65] The extent to which they formed a revolutionary guerrilla movement is more doubtful, since the British counterinsurgency campaign got under way while they were still at a formative stage, and before they were able to mount any substantial assault on the government. Their most striking military success was the overpowering of the police post at Naivasha, an operation with more than a touch of the Irgun's efficiency about it, which raises the question why it was not repeated elsewhere. The answer may lie in the structure of Mau Mau. The societies reached a total strength of over 12,000, but their main working units remained the 'platoons' (*batuni*). The more grandiose British military labels (generals, armies, battalions) which they used – and for which they were much mocked by the authorities – seem to have been conscious parody rather than functional description. Only at Lari was a really large force (some 1000) assembled from different districts.

Though some Mau Mau organizers were physical-force nationalists, the primary motivation of Mau Mau was the destruction or expulsion of the settlers and the recovery of the lost land. For many Mau Mau leaders these aims were more important than formal political independence. The authorities were, however, unable to exploit the division by offering land reform. Although the Colonial Office had abandoned its original endorsement (through Governor Eliot) of white supremacy, and now aimed at securing a multi-racial constitution, this was as far as Britain could go.

Nonetheless, when the newly arrived Governor of Kenya, Sir Evelyn Baring, toured the colony in late September 1952, there were good reasons for his rapid decision to declare a state of emergency. Mau Mau, whatever it was, had started a panic; it could only be seen as a challenge to government and public security, and one which the civil authorities manifestly could not cope with. The political line taken was consistent. While it suited the authorities to play up publicly the primitive, 'mindless' savagery and criminality of Mau Mau, and to portray it as a Gikuyu civil war (atavists versus modernizers) rather than an assault on British rule – these qualities being ferociously illustrated in the most destructive single event of the war, the massacre of eighty 'loyal' Gikuyu at Lari – in private they invariably recognized their opponents as 'rebels'. In fact Baring told the Colonial Secretary, 'we are facing a planned revolutionary movement . . . there is a plan, a rather ragged and a rather African one, but nonetheless formidable for that.'[66] But the apparent criminality of Mau Mau, both in Western 'civilized' terms and (if Leakey was right) in terms of Gikuyu tradition, ruled out the possibility of compromise, and validated the most severe military repression.

Martial law as such was never declared. The reason usually given was that the disturbances were confined to a relatively small part of the colony, and that administrative practice was to impose martial law, if at all, throughout a colony. There was no legal basis for this – legally the reverse was the case – and martial law could perfectly well have operated within the disturbed area without prejudice to the rest of Kenya. In practice, certain zones designated 'Prohibited Areas' (Mount Kenya and the Aberdares) were put on an open war footing: bombing was permitted and the use of weapons was unrestricted. (These were 'free fire zones' in later terminology.) The rest of the disturbed area, totalling about one-sixteenth of the colony as a whole, but forming its most vital region, included the 'white highlands', Nairobi itself, and the Kikuyu Reserves. These were designated Special Areas, where a range of restrictions were enforced. It seems clear that the main reason for not declaring martial law was political, and it is interesting that the pressure in favour of martial law came largely from the Labour Party in Britain. Conservatives tended to back the settlers in resisting direct military control and favouring 'decentralization' – that is, putting the campaign in the hands of the local white population. The Commander-in-Chief wanted martial law in order to get control of the police, especially the reserve force (the local settlers). The Governor, carefully balancing political interests, denied him this power.[67]

Still, the development of the Emergency Committee system, similar to that in Malaya, gradually produced effective coordination at the operational level. The Emergency Regulations were far-reaching, and though there was persistent criticism of Baring as 'most indecisive', an 'easy wicket Governor' incapable of supplying the aura of leadership needed to maintain morale, there was no suggestion that military measures as such were restricted or hampered by civil interference. Detention without trial was used on a large scale, from the first mass arrest of suspects (including Jomo Kenyatta) in Operation 'Jock Scott' onwards. The death penalty was progressively introduced for sabotage, illegal possession of arms and explosives, administering certain oaths, and aiding illegal groups. 'Mau Mau' was banned, though the best efforts of the Crown lawyers never succeeded in demonstrating that such an organization actually existed. It was the oathing system rather than a formal organization that formed the target of the counterinsurgency campaign.

Under the umbrella of civil control, the issue of operational command was tackled in two stages. First, the inability of the existing military headquarters at Nairobi (a sub-command of Middle East Land Forces at Cairo) to tackle the complex problem of the secret societies led to the appointment of Major General Hinde as Personal Staff Officer to the Governor. This liaison post was soon given the more explicit title 'Director of Operations', the first of many conscious parallels with Malaya. But Hinde's vague remit produced modest results. When the C-in-C Middle East visited the colony in May 1953 he found inadequate coordination of operations, and recommended that Hinde be replaced. Since his removal would 'cause some consternation', the C-in-C felt that his replacement should be 'not "just another major general".'[68] He suggested a lieutenant-general; the War Office went one better. Nairobi became an independent command (GHQ East Africa) under a full General, Sir George ('Bobbie') Erskine. Hinde stayed on as Director of Operations.

Erskine's weight and forcefulness made an impact (perhaps a slightly theatrical one) in a situation which was, by common consent, deteriorating. Erskine described some areas as virtual 'Mau Mau republics', and recognized in October 1953 that Mau Mau was 'far wider spread and deeper rooted than was thought possible even six months ago'.[69] Oathing had spread to the Embu and Meru tribes, and there were fears – certainly greatly exaggerated – of a general collapse. The police force was exiguous, only 563 regulars in the whole Central Province at the beginning of 1952, supplemented by some 900 Kenya Police Reserve. These totals were increased to 2775 and 7741 by the end of 1954, but in the interim the army formed the front line.[70] Erskine's first and probably most persistent problem was to fend off demands for the dispersion of all available forces. 'Everyone wants personal protection,' he wrote shortly after his arrival, 'and I found an Elected European Member who had demanded and been given a platoon . . .' – at which rate every soldier would rapidly have been swallowed up in protecting the legislative assembly alone. He was determined to concentrate substantial strength for offensive action, at the 'calculated risk', as he often stressed in his reports, of further deterioration in some areas.

That he was able to do this was largely due to the limited striking power of Mau Mau. Military forces, however small, were seldom attacked; and more importantly, the vulnerable railway line on which the whole colonial economy depended was never seriously sabotaged. Had Erskine faced a more ambitious or capable guerrilla organization it is unlikely that he would have been able to avoid dispersing much of his force in a defensive role. The concentration of force was in any case only a shibboleth unless effective ways of using force in an offensive role could be found. In Kenya, as elsewhere, this was the kernel of the problem. The very weakness of Mau Mau at the political level reflected its low-level resilience. GHQ Middle East recognized at the outset that 'a spasmodic murder campaign can be kept going by a small handful of terrorists provided that the native population is sufficiently frightened'. Quick results were unlikely; yet time was important: 'all Africa is watching Kenya'.[71]

The pressure from the European settlers, and to some extent from the 'loyal' Gikuyu as well, was for rough measures, to overwhelm the Mau Mau terror with unstinted violence. The operations of the white part-time Kenya Police Reserve provided plenty of examples of such roughness. Even the regular police operated on the margins of legality. When Colonel Young was brought from Malaya to take charge of the Kenya police, he tried to implement the same policy of following the 'British bobby' model; but here he failed. His resignation was a considerable scandal. If Mau Mau brutality had been conceived as provocation, in the fashion of modern terrorism, it would have been highly successful. But the element of Gikuyu civil war was reflected in the steady recruitment to the Kikuyu Guard (eventually 20,000 strong), and the often violent anti-Mau Mau activity of these local militias. Both were symptoms of a real civil war, of the primal terror inspired by Mau Mau, and the 'pathological atmosphere' felt by many in Kenya at this time.

Erskine loathed such symptoms (as he did the settlers), and did his best to keep the whole campaign in step with military ideals of restraint and self-discipline. Almost his first act on arrival in Kenya was to issue a General Order requiring that 'every officer in the Police and the Army should stamp at once on any conduct which he would be ashamed to see used against his own people'.[72] Military reprisals remained infrequent, though this owed something to the fact that troops seldom suffered casualties. The problem, indeed, was that the contacts between troops and rebels were too infrequent to give loyalists much confidence that the counterinsurgency campaign was making headway. Throughout the war, the continuous patrolling of the uplands (Mount Kenya and the Aberdares), arduous though it was for the troops involved, could achieve little more than keeping the insurgents 'on the run' and inflicting (it was hoped) cumulative demoralization. The main value of these intensive operations seems, in fact, to have lain in the training of the troops themselves. A similar judgment may be made on the air bombardment of the Prohibited Areas. Erskine reposed almost as much faith in this as did the RAF itself ('pilots were convinced they had hit target and had seen area strewn with dead . . .')[73] But early optimism, based on reports that 'everyone was frightened of the forest' after the bombings, wore off as the fighting dragged on, and it became clear that the only definite result was the danger to patrolling troops from big game maddened by terror or injury.

Rather as in Malaya, patrolling worked on a 'hit or miss' basis, and the same was true of the few larger sweeps carried out. The biggest of these, Operation 'Hammer One', which was mounted as late as January 1955, was certainly not cost effective. The single big cordon-and-search operation, 'Anvil' (the metaphor, if intentional, may be significant), may have been more worthwhile. Early in 1954 Erskine decided to give priority to the 'cleaning-up' of Nairobi, and concentrated a large proportion of his force for this. Although he had recognized that 'Mau Mau direction from any central point does not exist', he thought Nairobi was crucial. 'So long as it remains the main supply centre . . . it will NOT be possible finally to destroy the gangs.' He had a further hope: 'the elimination of the Mau Mau organization in Nairobi would have far reaching effects on the terrorists – quite apart from its value as a supply base. It might, in fact, herald the end of serious resistance.'[74]

What was meant by 'cleaning up'? Erskine held that 'if Nairobi is to be cleaned up, the most drastic action is necessary; palliatives or half measures cannot achieve lasting results'. He offered two alternative procedures, (a) the detention of all adult male Gikuyu in the city and the return of all women and children to the Reserves; or (b) a comprehensive screening to arrest those involved in the Mau Mau organization. Recognizing that course (a) would cause economic dislocation (which was probably a considerable understatement) as well as political problems, he still pressed for its adoption in preference to the 'less courageous and effective' course (b). He called for the construction of a huge internment camp with a minimum capacity of 100,000. What he did not say was that the less 'courageous' course was likely to be less effective because of the need for accurate information on which to base the screening process.

Perhaps inevitably, Baring opted for (b). The operation carried out in April-May 1954 was nonetheless a major demonstration of governmental power, using five regular battalions and part of the Kenya Regiment to cordon and search the city sector by sector, arresting some 17,000 Gikuyu. In the opinion of some experts it was 'a turning point in the Emergency', because it was perceived as a defeat for Mau Mau, and was followed by an acceleration in the flow of information to the security forces.[75] But such moral achievements are hard to measure, and, as in Malaya, the step from a 'turning point' to the elimination of the hard core of activists harbouring deep in the forests was a long one. The problem of getting to grips with the *batuni* could not be solved by random patrolling, sweeps, or 'hustling' flying-column operations of the sort initially favoured by Erskine –

> The operations of this Column are quick and depend for results on speed and surprise. We surround a market or search a village and the next day we move twenty miles. Nobody is quite sure where we shall appear next.[76]

As always the solution lay in the spheres of intelligence and public opinion. Nobody doubted that only a shift of Gikuyu support from the rebels could produce a restoration of normality. An imposed military pacification would at best be transient. The particular difficulty in Kenya was that, in contrast with Malaya, the alienation of the disaffected Gikuyu was seen to be psychological as well as economic in nature. Oathing had generated 'new men'. Resettlement of the sort used in Malaya could only work if it was accompanied by a genuine repudiation of the oaths.

Much intellectual energy (including Dr Leakey's) was devoted to the question of the oath's significance. The general consensus was that oathing triggered an irrational fanaticism, an altered mental state which was impervious to reasoned argument. Only the cathartic 'confession' of the secret oath could begin a reverse process of 'rehabilitation'. To this end an elaborate series of internment camps were established, the so-called 'pipeline' through which Mau Mau suspects were filtered back into society. The filters were the loyalist Gikuyu, whose leaders determined the extent to which any individual could be accepted as rehabilitated. Suspects were graded from 'black' (irreconcilable) through 'grey' to 'white' – a revealing colour-spectrum – and the hardcore irreconcilables were gradually concentrated in remote high-security camps such as Hola. There a final effort was made to break down resistance by a system of 'dilution', in which they were put into groups of cooperators on the theory (the 'Cowan plan') that a single act of cooperation would have the same effect as confession in beginning the rehabilitation process.[77]

Cooperators, the vast majority of suspects, poured steadily

back into the Reserves, to be placed in new villages under the eye of military and KG defensive posts. 'Villageization' coupled with an elaborate system of controls and identity checks kept the likelihood of recontamination to a minimum. What the counterinsurgency machinery did was to create the conditions in which Gikuyu could repudiate – for whatever reasons – Mau Mau control. This process produced the most significant military development, the employment of surrendered fighters. Until this happened, the intelligence system in general was unable to cope with the insurgency.[78] The transformation was achieved after mid-1953, when Captain Frank Kitson was appointed as one of two District Military Intelligence Officers. His initial task was to integrate the work of the military Field Intelligence Assistants, drawn largely from the Kenya Regiment, with that of the police Special Branch. Using surrendered Mau Mau fighters he went on to pioneer the most revolutionary of all methods of securing operational information, which he called the 'pseudo-gang'. Disguised Europeans, and later, as trust in them increased, ex-insurgents as well, operated in the forests as Mau Mau, tracing movements and establishing contacts with *batuni* still at large.[79]

The success of this hazardous mimetic technique was to establish a durable paradigm of counterinsurgency action. It clearly owed something to the near absence of a central command and communication system within the insurgent movement, and could not, for example, be repeated in Malaya. At least as important were the new techniques of intimidatory (but nominally nonviolent) interrogation evolved by Kitson and others, and the sheer enthusiasm and hard work put into the business of 'developing' background information into contact information.[80]

By 1955 the combination of inflexible political aim and sophisticated security procedures had reduced the Mau Mau challenge to a shadow. Yet the formal Emergency was prolonged until 1960, and the end of the struggle was not the restoration of settler supremacy but the granting of self-government. The rejection of political compromise, and the reliance on force, failed in the long run. If Kitson was a child of his time, so too were Harold Macmillan and Iain Macleod. To those who had sniffed the wind of change, colonial wars, however skilfully waged, were more of a primitive throwback than Mau Mau itself. The new political priority was a race to decolonize. Kenyatta, whom the settlers believed to be the instigator of Mau Mau terrorism, became another in the line of criminals finally recognized as statesmen.

An equally dramatic, though less public, metamorphosis occurred with the detainees. Detention became an increasing political embarrassment to the Westminster government, and pressure to empty the camps meant that rehabilitation was progressively accelerated until it became a bare formality. The acceleration came too late to prevent a major scandal blowing up over the treatment of 'black' detainees at Hola Camp, eleven of whom died through the forcible implementation of the 'Cowan plan'. The disaster was due to an attempt to apply an impossible distinction, between 'compelling' and 'over-whelming' force – the former permissible, the latter not – in handling the hardcore detainees, and was to have echoes in the interrogation procedures used subsequently in Aden and Northern Ireland. Yet when, at last, the irreconcilables were bundled out of the camp and back into society, still bound by their Mau Mau oaths, it might be said that a revolution in British perceptions was complete.

Notes to Chapter v: Africa

1. D. Killingray, 'Law and Order in British Colonial Africa', paper given at Institute of Commonwealth Studies, University of London, 22 Jan. 1985, p.1.
2. UNESCO, *General History of Africa. VII: Africa under Colonial Domination 1880–1935*, ed. A.A. Boahen, London 1985.
3. T.O. Ranger, 'Connexions between "primary resistance" movements and modern mass nationalism in East and Central Africa', *Journal of African History* IX, 1968.
4. See the critical *Report of the Nyasaland Commission of Inquiry*, 1959 Cmnd 814.
5. As laid out in book 6, chapter 26 of Clausewitz' *On War*.
6. T. Pakenham, *The Boer War*, London 1979, pp.473–4, 520–1.
7. *The Times History of the War in South Africa*, Vol.v, p.545.
8. C. Townshend, 'Martial law: legal and administrative problems of civil emergency in Britain and the Empire, 1800–1940', *Historical Journal* 25, 1982, p.182.
9. W.K. Hancock, *Smuts*, Vol.I, Cambridge 1962. D. Reitz, *Commando, a Boer Journal of the Boer War*, London 1929.
10. Hely-Hutchinson to Chamberlain, 2 July, 3 Oct. 1901. Ibid., p.134.
11. Maj.Gen. Wynne to Governor Cape Colony, 17 Sep. 1901. WO 32 8128.
12. Kitchener to Brodrick, 8 Sep. 1901. Sir G. Arthur, *Life of Lord Kitchener*, Vol.II, London 1920, p.31.
13. Kitchener to Brodrick, 20 Sep. 1901. Kitchener papers, PRO 30/57 22.
14. AG, Cape Town, memo. on 'Administration of Martial Law', 27 Aug. 1901. DO 119 589. Hely-Hutchinson to Chamberlain, 10 Sep. 1901. WO 32 8124.
15. Deputy Administrator to GOC and Administrator, ORC, 8 Dec. 1901. DO 119 589. Lord Basil Blackwood to Marchioness of Dufferin and Ava, 30 Nov. 1899. Blackwood papers, PRO Northern Ireland, D.1231/M/6/63.
16. Brodrick to Kitchener, 12 Apr. 1902. Kitchener papers, PRO 30/57 22.
17. *Times History*, Vol.v, pp.265–8.
18. Reitz, *Commando*, pp.187–8.
19. H. Bailes, 'Military Aspects of the War', in P. Warwick (ed.), *The South African War*, London 1980, pp.100–1.
20. R. Holmes, *The Little Field-Marshall: Sir John French*, London 1981, pp.112–6, is slightly reticent on the exact detail of French's operations during this phase. There is a more detailed, if less critical account in Vol.VII of L. Creswicke, *South Africa and the Transvaal*

War, London nd, which includes many interesting contemporary
illustrations.
21. Pakenham, *Boer War*, p.469. Cf. Milner to Chamberlain,
1 Nov. 1901. J. Amery, *Life of Joseph Chamberlain*, Vol.IV, London
1951, p.45.
22. Kitchener to Brodrick, 26 July 1901. Kitchener papers,
PRO 30/57 22.
23. J. Wilson, *CB. A Life of Sir Henry Campbell-Bannerman*, London
1973, p.349.
24. Pakenham, *Boer War*, pp.494–5.
25. Brodrick to Kitchener, 6 July 1901. Kitchener papers,
PRO 30/57 22.
26. French's diary, 8 June 1901. Holmes, *French*, pp.113–4.
27. Kitchener to Brodrick, 26 July 1901. PRO 30/57 22. In fact a
Martial Law Board was later established to adjudicate complaints.
28. D. Denoon, 'Participation in the Boer War: People's War,
People's Non-war, or Non-people's War?', in B.A. Ogot (ed.), *War
and Society in Africa*, London 1972. P. Warwick, 'Black People and
the War', in *South African War*.
29. *Times History*, Vol.v., p.250.
30. PM to GOC and Administrator, Natal, 28 and 30 Mar.1901.
DO 119 590.
31. Cf. W. Bosman, *The Natal Rebellion of 1906*, London 1907.
J. Stuart, *History of the Zulu Rebellion of 1906 in Natal*, London 1913.
32. S. Marks, *Reluctant Rebellion: the 1906–1908 Disturbances in
Natal*, Oxford 1970, and 'The Zulu Disturbances in Natal' in
R.I. Rotberg and A.A. Mazrui (eds.), *Protest and Power in Black
Africa*, Oxford 1970.
33. Cf. Marks, 'Zulu Disturbances', pp.252–3.
34. On the impenetrable nature of Bambata's thinking, see Marks,
Reluctant Rebellion, p.208.
35. Bosman, *Natal Rebellion*, pp.99–100.
36. Ibid., Preface, p.VI. Sir Matthew Nathan, q. Marks, *Reluctant
Rebellion*, p.189.
37. The rift is followed in R. Hyam, *Elgin and Churchill at the Colonial
Office 1905–1908*, London 1968, pp.239–62.
38. Churchill's minute, 12 Feb.1906. CO 323/522/5096. CO Minute,
Aug. 1906. CO 179/238/33117. Marks, *Reluctant Rebellion*, p.237.
39. Churchill's minute, Governor of Natal to Sec.of State for Colonies,
14 Sep. 1906. CO 179/237/36793.
40. D. McKenzie's Introduction, Bosman, *Natal Rebellion*, p.XIV.
41. R.O. Collins and R.L. Tignor, *Egypt and the Sudan*, Englewood
Cliffs 1967, p.87.

42. P.J. Vatikiotis, *A Modern History of Egypt*, London 1969, pp. 239–42.

43. E. Kedourie, 'Sa'd Zaghlul and The British', *The Chatham House Version and Other Middle Eastern Studies*, London, 1970, provides a clinical analysis of British policy throughout the crisis.

44. Milne Cheetham to Curzon, 24 Feb. 1919. Lord Lloyd, *Egypt Since Cromer*, vol.I, London 1933, p.290.

45. Sir C. Gwynn, *Imperial Policing*, London 1934, pp.69–71; E.W. Polson Newman, *Great Britain in Egypt*, London 1928, p.220.

46. Vatikiotis, *Egypt*, pp.258–9.

47. Gwynn, *Imperial Policing*, p.73.

48. M. Travers Symons, *Britain and Egypt: the Rise of Egyptian Nationalism*, London 1925, pp.84–7.

49. Gwynn, *Imperial Policing*, pp.76, 80–1.

50. H.A. Ibrahim, 'Mahdist Risings against the Condominium Government in the Sudan, 1900–1927', *International Journal of African Historical Studies* 12, 1979.

51. Collins and Tignor, *Egypt and the Sudan*, p.119. Cf. R.O. Collins and R. Herzog, 'Early British Administration in the Southern Sudan', *Journal of African History* 1961.

52. Notes on Sir J. Maffey's CID paper 904.B, Slessor papers, AC 75/28/26.

53. MacMichael to Maffey, 29 May 1927. R.O. Collins, *Shadows in the Grass. Britain in the Southern Sudan, 1918–1956*, New Haven 1983, p.122.

54. Collins, *Shadows in the Grass*, pp.114–5.

55. D. Killingray, '"A Swift Agent of Government": Air Power in British Colonial Africa, 1916–1939', *Journal of African History* 25, 1984. C. Townshend, 'Civilization and Frightfulness: Air Control in the Middle East', in C. Wrigley (ed.), *Warfare, Diplomacy and Politics*, London 1986.

56. Maffey (Governor-Gen., Sudan) to Lloyd (High Commissioner, Egypt), 11 Dec. 1927. FO 141/519/19215.

57. Collins, *Shadows in the Grass*, p.129.

58. Air Ministry to Foreign Office, 13 June 1928. FO 141/519/19215.

59. Lord Lloyd, speech in House of Lords, 9 April 1930.

60. J. Slessor, Notes on Sir John Maffey's CID paper 904.B, Slessor papers, AC 75/28/26.

61. C.A. Willis, (Governor, Upper Nile Prov.), Report on 'Nuer Settlement', 28 June 1929. FO 141/519/19215.

62. Maffey to MacMichael, 25 Feb. 1929, MacMichael papers, MEC.

63. L.S.B. Leakey, *Mau Mau and the Kikuyu*, London 1952.

64. C.G. Rosberg and J. Nottingham, *The Myth of 'Mau Mau';*

Nationalism in Kenya, Stanford 1966.

65. *Historical Survey of the Origins and growth of Mau Mau* by
F.D. Corfield, 1960, Cmnd 1030, ch.VI, 'The Evolution of the Oath'.
Corfield noted that a further function of oathing was to break
individuals' social ties and enforce dependence on the societies.

66. Governor, Kenya, to Sec.of State for Colonies, 9 Oct. 1952.
CO 822 444.

67. In fact Erskine carried around a letter empowering him to act as
Military Governor if necessary, as had Macready in Belfast in 1914.
A. Clayton, *Counter-Insurgency in Kenya 1952–60: A Study of
Military Operations against Mau Mau*, Nairobi 1976, p.8.

68. GOC East Africa to VCIGS, 30 Apr. 1953. WO 216 851. C-in-C
MÉLF, Report on Visit to Kenya, 11–16 May 1953. WO 216 852.

69. GOC-in-C E.Africa to CIGS, 3 Oct. 1953. App.'A' to Brief for
Sec.of State for Colonies. WO 216 861.

70. Cmnd 1030, ch.XII, p.240.

71. GHQ MELF to War Office, 5 Nov. 1952. WO 216 811.

72. Gen.Orders, 23 June 1953. Clayton, *Counter-Insurgency in Kenya*,
pp.38–9.

73. C-in-C East Africa to CIGS, 14 June 1953, App.'A'. WO 216 853.

74. Appreciation on Future Military Policy in Kenya, 1954.
WO 216 863.

75. J. Paget, *Counter-Insurgency Campaigning*, London 1967,
pp.98–9.

76. C-in-C East Africa to CIGS, 7 July 1953. WO 216 855.

77. *Documents Relating to the Deaths of Eleven Mau Mau Detainees at
Hola Camp in Kenya*, 1959 Cmnd 778.

78. Cmnd 1030, ch.III.

79. F. Kitson, *Gangs and Counter-Gangs*, London 1960.

80. F. Kitson, *Low Intensity Operations*, London 1971, esp. ch.6.

Notes on Further Reading

The best general history of the Boer War, T. Pakenham, *The Boer War* (Weidenfeld & Nicolson, London 1979), deals quite well with the guerrilla phase, though such indefinite warfare is formidably difficult to convey in conventional narrative. The most complete account is likely to remain *The Times History of the War in South Africa*, of which Volume v (edited by Erskine Childers, London 1907) is devoted to the guerrilla war. There are several good modern perspectives in P. Warwick (ed.), *The South African War* (Longmans, Harlow 1980). The memoirs of the bitterest of the 'bitter-enders', C. de Wet, *Three Years War* (Constable, London 1902), are important but unyielding. Those of Deneys Reitz, *Commando: A Boer Journal of the Boer War* (Faber & Faber, London 1929), are in another league as a human document, one of the best accounts of warfare ever written.

On the Zulu insurgency, S. Marks, *Reluctant Rebellion* (Oxford University Press, 1970), is a display of near faultless scholarship, shaped by a highly modern awareness of structural issues. The same awareness, if not always the same lucidity, marks the large-scale UNESCO *General History of Africa* (Vols. VII and VIII, London 1985). B.A. Ogot (ed.), *War and Society in Africa* (Frank Cass, London 1972), is an interesting range of approaches. M. Gluckman, *Order and Rebellion in Tropical Africa* (Cohen & West, London 1963, 1971), does not quite deliver all its title promises. For the north, P.J. Vatikiotis, *A Modern History of Egypt* (London 1969), is amongst the best of several good general histories. J. Darwin, *Britain, Egypt and the Middle East* (Macmillan, London 1981), provides a close scrutiny of imperial policy between 1918 and 1922. On the Sudan, the sequence of big books by R.O. Collins, of which the latest, *Shadows in the Grass* (Yale University Press, New Haven, Conn. 1983), is most relevant to this study, is marked by impressive industry but marred at times by a shaky grasp of the British system.

There is a major reappraisal of Mau Mau in C. Rosberg and J. Nottingham, *The Myth of 'Mau Mau': Nationalism in Kenya* (Stanford University Press 1966), but their repudiation of every aspect of F.D. Corfield's *Historical Survey of the Origins and Growth of Mau Mau* (HMSO, London 1960) is not uniformly convincing. For a readable journalist's account which is not as uncritical of settlers and adminis-tration as is sometimes implied, see F. Majdalany, *State of Emergency* (Houghton Mifflin, Boston 1963). Two important memoirs should be mentioned, one from either side: by the enlightened settler leader M. Blundell, *So Rough a Wind* (Weidenfeld & Nicolson, London 1964), and by J. Kariuki, *Mau Mau Detainee* (Oxford University Press, London 1963). Frank Kitson's personal account, *Gangs and Counter-*

Gangs (Barrie & Rockliff, London 1960), which graphically etches the career of the lone officer in the exotic unknown, bears comparison with the work of T.E. Lawrence, not least for its skill in story-telling.

Index

Mahdism, 194
Maji Maji wars, 171
Malaya, 35, 155–65, 201, 202
Malayan Communist Party
 · (MCP), 155, 159, 162, 163
Malayan Races Liberation Army
 (MRLA), 155, 163–4
Mappillas (Moplahs), 140–4
martial law, 20–2, 26, 48, 52,
 53–4, 61, 64–5, 70, 72, 87, 90,
 91, 101, 107, 116, 137–9, 141–2,
 158, 172, 176, 186, 190, 200;
 'statutory martial law', 56;
 'controlled areas', 118
Mau Mau, 198–207
Maxwell, Gen. Sir John, 54
Meinertzhagen, Col. R., 91, 98
Midnapore, 148
military aid to the civil power
 (MACP), 20, 31, 49, 70, 107
military operations, and counter-
 insurgency, 30–3;
 Operations: Optimist, 63,
 Demetrius, 71, Motorman, 71,
 Agatha, 116, Elephant/Hippo-
 potamus, 117, Hammer, 163,
 Jock Scott, 201, Hammer One,
 203, Anvil, 204; food denial
 operations, 164, 180–2
Milner, Sir Alfred (HC South
 Africa), 177, 183, 185
mobility, 31–2, 64
Montgomery, Maj. Gen. (Field
 Marshal Viscount) B.L. (GOC
 8th Div.), 108, 112; (CIGS),
 115–16
Moplah Outrages Acts, 140

Nablus, 104, 106
Nairobi, 200, 201, 204
Napier, Gen. Sir Charles, 20
Natal, 172, 186–9
New Violence Party, 145, 146

Northern Ireland, 22, 68–72, 88,
 207
Northern Ireland (Emergency
 Provisions) Act, 69
North-West Frontier Province,
 79, 94, 145, 149–55
'Nuer Settlement', 196–8
Nyasaland, 171–72

O'Dwyer, Sir Michael (Govr.
 Punjab), 134, 137, 139
Orange Free State (Orange River
 Colony), 172, 180

Paget, Julian, 9
Palestine, 22, 33, 35, 79, 81,
 82–92, 99–120, 158, 164; British
 Mandate in, 81, 88, 113, 120;
 Occupied Enemy Territory
 Administration (OETA) in,
 85–9; immigration into, 88,
 106, 109
Pathans, 150–1
peace, 13, 15, 34, 56–7;
 'peacekeeping', 16
Peake, Col. F.F., 93
Pearse, Patrick, 146
Peel Commission, 107–8
Peshawar, 101, 154–5
Plumer, Field Marshal Viscount
 (HC Palestine), 90, 100, 103
police, and counterinsurgency,
 23–6; intelligence and special
 branch, 28–9, 161–2;
 gendarmeries and 'third forces',
 25, 91–2, 103, 110; Civil
 Constabulary Reserve (UK), 4;
 Kenya, 200–3; Malaya, 160–2;
 Malappuram Special Police
 (MSP), 143, 145; Palestine, 88,
 91, 103, 105; Royal Irish
 Constabulary (RIC), 24, 47–8,
 51, 56, 57–60; Auxiliary